Praise for the novels of Maisey Yates

"[A] sure-fire .... d."
— .... *Burn Co...*
.... starred rev...

"This .... ave readers
believ .... ove."
— ....ekly on *Down Home Cowboy*

"Yates's new Gold Valley series begins with
a sassy, romantic and sexy story about two
characters whose chemistry is off the charts."
—*RT Book Reviews* on *Smooth-Talking Cowboy*
(Top Pick)

"Multidimensional and genuine characters are the
highlight of this alluring novel, and sensual love
scenes complete it. Yates's fans...will savor this
delectable story."
—*Publishers Weekly* on *Unbroken Cowboy*
(starred review)

"Fast-paced and intensely emotional.... This is
one of the most heartfelt installments in this
series, and Yates's fans will love it."
—*Publishers Weekly* on *Cowboy to the Core*
(starred review)

"Yates's outstanding eighth Gold Valley
contemporary...will delight newcomers and
fans alike.... This charming and very sensual
contemporary is a must for fans of passion."
—*Publishers Weekly* on
Cowboy Christmas Redemption (starred review)

Also by Maisey Yates

Secrets from a Happy Marriage

Gold Valley

Smooth-Talking Cowboy
Untamed Cowboy
Good Time Cowboy
A Tall, Dark Cowboy Christmas
Unbroken Cowboy
Cowboy to the Core
Lone Wolf Cowboy
Cowboy Christmas Redemption
The Bad Boy of Redemption Ranch
The Hero of Hope Springs

Copper Ridge

Part Time Cowboy
Brokedown Cowboy
Bad News Cowboy
The Cowboy Way
One Night Charmer
Tough Luck Hero
Last Chance Rebel
Slow Burn Cowboy
Down Home Cowboy
Wild Ride Cowboy
Christmastime Cowboy

For more books by Maisey Yates,
visit www.maiseyyates.com.

MAISEY YATES

The Last
Christmas Cowboy

HQN

HQN

ISBN-13: 978-1-335-01404-7

The Last Christmas Cowboy

Copyright © 2020 by Maisey Yates

Recycling programs
for this product may
not exist in your area.

This edition published by arrangement with Harlequin Books S.A.

For questions and comments about the quality of this book,
please contact us at CustomerService@Harlequin.com.

HQN
22 Adelaide St. West, 40th Floor
Toronto, Ontario M5H 4E3, Canada
www.Harlequin.com

Printed in Lithuania

MIX
Paper from
responsible sources
FSC® C021394

To Jane Austen, cowboys and Christmas.
Which seemed like a logical combination to me.

The Last
Christmas Cowboy

CHAPTER ONE

Rose Daniels was happy with her life. She had the best job in the entire world, working on Hope Springs Ranch, spending her days outdoors riding horses and wrangling cattle. She loved it. The idea of having an office job made her want to crawl out of her skin, and the thought of sitting still was even less appealing than that.

Sure, her primary coworker was hardheaded and a bit of a pain, but Logan was also like a brother to her, a good friend and a decent enough horseman.

Her brother, Ryder, was the boss, and he could be a whole challenge, but ultimately, he was the one who had raised her after the death of their parents, and she loved him with all of her heart. Working on the ranch allowed her to be close to her family, another bonus of the whole situation.

And over the last couple of years, she had watched her sister Pansy find the love of her life, followed by her brother, Ryder, with his best friend Sammy.

It had her thinking a lot, though, about her sister Iris.

Rose was the youngest of the Daniels children, and after the death of their parents, it was Iris who had taken on the maternal role for Rose.

She'd always been there for Rose, for the whole family. Cooking, cleaning, offering support. She'd combed Rose's hair for school, helped choose her clothes. Had walked Rose through buying her first bra and all the other ills of puberty.

And Iris was still living at the ranch, cooking for all of them, caring for them all.

Rose had to wonder if it was why Iris didn't seem to care at all for herself. If it was why Iris was alone.

Rose didn't like to see Iris alone. She had been so young and helpless when her parents had died. She hadn't been able to take care of anyone. They'd all cared for her. She wasn't a child anymore, though. That early feeling of helplessness had formed her. Shaped her. And now…now she wanted to fix things. It was who she was. It was the way she'd found a place on the family ranch. The way she'd made herself matter. Whether it was a calf with an ankle injury or a person with a wound in their heart, Rose wanted to see that it was put to rights.

And now she was considering Iris. Who, were they in Regency times, would be considered a spinster. Not even just close to being on the shelf. Not even simply past her initial first blush.

Granted, it was not the Regency period, and it wasn't really fair to judge anything by those standards. But Iris was a traditional sort of woman, and Rose imagined that her sister must want to be in love and married.

"Rose, get your head out of the clouds and your feet back in the mud. We've got work to do."

She glanced over at Logan, who was standing there looking taciturn, his tan cowboy hat pulled down low over his eyes. He was wearing a matching work jacket and gloves, and seeing him appropriately dressed made her skin prickle with goose bumps, more aware of the chill in the air than she'd been a moment before. She'd run out with nothing but a T-shirt and a denim button-up that she left open.

She was adapting slowly to the change in weather, resenting it. She preferred to be outside in the sunshine. And she liked the crisp, clear fall weather, that often saw her removing outer layers as the day wore on. But they were beginning to turn the corner into outright winter weather here in mid-November, and she was not prepared.

"I'm just thinking," she said.

"That's what concerns me," he said, a smile tipping his mouth upward. "When you think, *things* seem to happen. And somebody has to clean up the mess."

"Nobody asked you to do it," she said. "Anyway, I seem to recall a time, though it was several years ago, when you got to thinking that jumping your bike off that rise down by the north pasture was a good idea, and you ran into the barbed wire fence, and I cleaned up that mess."

"I was a teenager."

"Yes, and I was seven. I still remember it."

Something flickered in his blue eyes, but he didn't say anything more. Instead, he turned back to the fence that he was repairing, and she picked up a wire cutter and joined him on the line.

"I want to help Iris find someone," she mused.

"Rose..."

"Hear me out. She's alone. It's going to be Christmas. I hate the thought of that."

"She's always alone. Seems to me at this point it's a choice. And you should respect it."

Rose shook her head. "Nobody wants to be alone."

"*You* are also alone," he pointed out.

"I'm twenty-three," she said. "I have no designs on being anything but alone for quite some time. This is not about me. I want nothing more than to see the people I love most settled and happy."

"Iris is happy," he said.

"What if she isn't?"

"Then she will do something to fix it. Or she won't. But either way, it's none of your business."

She made an exasperated sound. "It's not about whether or not it's my business. And anyway, that's not true. We are family. In a way that few other people ever will be. We... We had to raise each other."

"Pretty sure Ryder did most of that."

"I know," she said.

She had been six years old when her parents had died. She barely remembered them now. She remembered not understanding. For a very long time. She had grieved when she'd been given the news, because she had known that dead was terrible. But forever was something that she hadn't been able to wrap her mind around. And there was a point where it felt like they would surely come back. They had to.

But of course she had started to realize that the way her brother's mouth was set, always turning down, meant something bad. That he didn't go away to college like he had planned to.

When she was seven she had asked Logan, while she was bandaging his hands up. She'd been feeling proud because she knew where the first aid kit was. Knew how to help with his cuts. And she hadn't been scared of the blood.

She'd felt helpful and she'd felt strong, like she mattered.

"When are they coming back?"

He had just looked at her with those blue eyes, and she had seen fear in them. Fear that hadn't been there after he'd cut himself up. It was the fear that got to her.

He hadn't spoken for a moment.

"They aren't," he'd said finally.

"How come? They love us."

"Of course they do, Rosie," he'd said.

Logan was the only person who had ever called her that. She'd thought it was for little kids and had been annoyed by it until that moment in the barn, when she'd been bandaging his arm and he'd used that low, husky voice that had made her feel soothed in spite of the sharp, dark hurts inside her heart.

"Then why are they staying away?"

"They didn't choose to. But dying is forever."

"Forever is a long time," she'd said.

"I know, that's the thing. It's forever."

She hadn't cried. Even then she had known there was no point in crying. Because forever was forever, whether she cried or not. She understood it then.

And Logan had been there for it. Like he was there for everything. Dishing out advice and giving support. The problem was, he still did it, like she was seven years old.

"I wasn't actually asking your opinion," she said archly.

"That's fine. You don't need to ask for it to get it."

"You're *so* annoying," she said.

"And you insist on talking to me."

"We are fixing a fence. If we didn't talk it would be boring."

"Then don't complain when I make it interesting by giving you my opinions."

"You are a man who thinks a bit highly of himself," she said. But she wasn't actually mad at him. She could never really be mad at Logan. Not after everything.

"I think highly of myself because no one else will."

He winked, and she had to suppress a silly grin that tried to spread over her face, and when she didn't allow it to, her cheeks prickled slightly.

It was strange.

She chose to ignore it.

"Who do you think would make a good match for Iris?"

"Don't look at me like that," he said.

"What?"

"Not me."

"Don't be silly. Of course not you. You're basically our brother. But there must be somebody else. Somebody who is calm and steady. Not a cowboy. Not for Iris. Iris needs somebody who likes to be indoors. Likes to read. She likes to talk about books and TV. And she loves to bake. She likes yarn."

"So," Logan said slowly, "you should get her a cat."

"I know," she carried on as if he hadn't spoken of cats. "Elliott Johns. He would be perfect."

Logan's eyebrows lowered, and went flat. "The water filtration guy?"

"Yes. I mean, he knows everybody in town because of his job. And he must have a good reputation or people wouldn't keep using him. So, somebody with a job like that is pretty safe, I would think. Plus, he's sort of soft-spoken and good at making conversation."

"I thought you wanted to get Iris some excitement."

"I do. But the right kind of excitement. The kind that suits her."

"Would you ever in a million years have thought that Pansy's kind of excitement would be a cowboy ex-convict?"

"Pansy is an anomaly. And she doesn't count."

"Okay. Well, good to know that you just get to decide who you think you know."

"Pull the stick out of your rear, Logan."

"Look, matchmaker, you meddle in people's lives on your own time. It's fence-fixing time."

"Fine. But tonight when we go to the bar, I'm going to put feelers out."

"God save us all from your feelers," he said.

"I'll be successful. You can bet."

LOGAN ALREADY NEEDED another drink, and they'd only been at the Gold Valley Saloon for twenty minutes.

This time of a year was a bitch anyway. His slow slide into seasonal grinchhood began in November and continued all through December. He didn't do Christmas. Not at all.

Not since his mother had died.

So he was already prone to irritation as it was. And Rose was being particularly Rose.

There was no stopping Rose Daniels when she was on a tear and Logan knew that better than anybody. She was a frenetic lightning storm wrapped in skin. And she drove him crazy.

In all the ways that could apply.

Much to his endless chagrin.

He had known pretty little Rose Daniels since she was a child.

His mother had been best friends with her parents, and after they'd died he had moved in with the family and essentially become part of it.

But there was something about Rose. She got under his skin, and made it itch. And that itch had transformed into something wholly inappropriate after she had gone from girl to woman, which had happened seemingly overnight. She had gone to bed, seventeen and a pain in his ass. And woken up eighteen—still a pain in his ass—and recognizably far too pretty for his own good.

No. Rose wasn't like a sister to him. But the feelings he had for her were deep, special, forged in fire.

He had known that long before he had ever found her beautiful. He would be her protector. When she was seven years old, looking at him with eyes that were far too serious and asking when their parents were going to come back, because death was a concept that was simply too big for her to grasp, he had vowed it then. And he kept it now.

But sometimes the kid needed protection from her damn self.

He had turned protecting her from *him* into an art form.

It was her harebrained schemes that he couldn't quite manage.

The woman had a habit of grating on him. And tonight, she was going to test every single one of his nerves, he had a feeling. More than a feeling.

He could think of nothing that Iris would like less than to have her younger sister trying to find her a pity date. Because whether Rose realized that was what she was doing, she was. He recognized it. Well, because he saw what Rose recognized in Iris. He did. She spent most of her nights at home baking and knitting. When she did go out, it was with the whole family.

At this point, it wasn't like he did a whole lot else.

Not since his libido had transformed into something spiky and untrustworthy. Yeah. Sometimes he went out of town and found a woman. But he didn't like hooking up here.

Iris hadn't come out with them tonight, and from the looks of things, Ryder and Sammy were going to have to call it an early evening. Which would leave them with West and Pansy. He was fine with that, he liked the man that Pansy was engaged to. They were going to have a Christmas wedding, which was likely half of what had Rose so amped up about romance, and seeing her sister happy.

He got Rose a bottle of her favorite beer, and went back to the table. He had snuck her beer a time or two starting when she was about nineteen. Ryder would be angry if he knew. He had been a stickler for minding the rules. But Logan had figured it was a rite of passage. And since all Rose really wanted to do was have a beer out on the back porch, he had never seen the harm in it. As a result, he had a pretty good idea of what she enjoyed.

"He's here," Rose whispered.

"Who?" He sat down at the table next to her and passed her the beer.

"Elliott."

"Rose, what did I say?"

"When have I ever listened to you?"

"Well, you should listen to me. You should listen to me now."

"What are you saying exactly?" she asked, her tone far too sweet.

"To leave well enough alone."

"What are you two whispering about down there?" Pansy asked.

Rose's older sister was looking at them keenly.

"Nothing," Logan said.

"Logan doesn't approve of me," Rose said.

"Well," Pansy said, "I should think that would be a goal of yours."

"Yes. I don't really care about whether or not I am meeting with anyone's approval. It has to be said."

That wasn't strictly true, and he knew it. Rose wasn't really a rebel, so much as she was…exuberant. She acted before she thought, and spoke even sooner than she acted.

"I'm exhausted," Sammy said. "Even though I really do want to stay and hear about what all Logan disapproves of."

Sammy was five months pregnant, and Logan knew that her desire to be in the middle of the fray often lost out over her current level of energy. He was happy for Ryder, that his friend was able to get over some of the trauma of his past and begin to make a new life for himself. A new family. It had been completely obvious to him that Ryder had been in love with Sammy for the last decade and a half. His friend had denied it, but Logan had known.

And, it had turned out he was right.

That made him feel slightly uncomfortable, given that he was currently judging Rose for trying to get involved in people's love life. But he had not gotten involved in Ryder's. Not without his asking for input.

Anyway, in some ways he felt extra connected to Sammy. The two of them were the odd ones out. They weren't genetically related to the Daniels clan, but had found themselves a part of Hope Springs Ranch, bonded together by the tragedies of life. For Logan, it had been the loss of his mother. For Sammy, the fact that her parents had been absolutely terrible. Her mother was still alive, but she wasn't part of Sammy's life.

For all the good they'd done raising her, she might as well have lost them.

"See you tomorrow," Logan said.

"Bye," Rose said.

"We'll hang out for a while," Pansy said.

Though, he could tell by the way West was looking at his fiancée he was hoping to make it an early night, for pretty obvious reasons.

Logan's stomach tightened up. Because that would mean being alone with Rose. And he didn't like that. Not one bit. He'd already played with fire when it came to late nights and a little bit of beer with her. And she had no idea how close she'd come to being burned.

No. He'd never burn her. He wouldn't. Never once had

he thought seriously about acting on any of the feelings that he'd experienced for her over the last couple of years. But he'd been in situations where they had been closer to the surface than he wanted them.

And he wasn't about to put himself back there again.

"I'm going to make a move," Rose said, as Ryder and Sammy filed out of the saloon.

"What the hell are you talking about?"

And that was when the irrepressible brunette scampered across the saloon and approached Elliott Johns.

He gritted his teeth and watched in horror as she began to talk to him, and Logan could see interest lighting up the other man's face.

He was also absolutely certain that Rose was over there being an ambassador for Iris, and only for that reason.

Elliott clearly thought otherwise.

Oh, Rose. You don't know what you're playing at.

About thirty seconds later, they were crossing the bar, and she had brought him back to the table. "Logan, will you get another beer? Elliott is going to join us for the evening."

CHAPTER TWO

ROSE FOUND ELLIOTT to be perfectly pleasant. He was friendly and polite. His hands were very clean. Rose thought this notable because often she was around men whose hands were not clean. Not that they didn't wash their hands. But there was a sort of ingrained dirt in the hands of a cowboy. It got down underneath their nails so deep the nail would probably have to come off in order to get the grunge. She understood.

She was a cowgirl. It wasn't like her hands were much cleaner.

Anyway. She noticed clean fingernails.

Rose imagined that her sister Iris would, too. Iris was not a cowgirl.

Iris was the soft, steady maternal figure in her life. She'd had Sammy too, who had moved in with them the same year their parents had died, and become friends with Ryder. A free-spirited earth-mother type. She infused the house with fun. Iris brought dependability. Made sure Rose's hair was brushed for school, that her clothes had been neat and washed.

She'd mended holes in socks and kept the first aid kit stocked.

Sometimes she gave her sister a little bit of a hard time for being quite so staid and sensible. She was practical all the way down to her shoes. It was part of Iris's charm. And for as long as Rose could remember Iris had been the soft touch in her life.

After the loss of their parents, between Iris and Sammy they had all been very well cared for, for a ragtag group of orphans.

Rose had been too young to give back.

She had been reliant on Ryder and Logan to keep the ranch going, to keep income coming in. Colt and Jake helped with that later, often sending money back from the rodeo. She had been dependent on Sammy and Iris to cook for her.

And of course Pansy had been… Well, she'd been younger too, but she had been Rose's older sister. Someone she had looked up to. Pansy had taught her to take their hardships and make purpose out of it.

Rose wasn't sure what she'd done for anyone. At least beyond being a little bit of a burden. Not that she blamed herself. Not really. She had been six years old when her parents had died.

But she could make up for it now. She worked Hope Springs Ranch along with Ryder and Logan, with the occasional help of their cousins Jake and Colt.

She was invested in the happiness of her family. Makeshift and otherwise.

Granted, she had been wrong about Logan and Sammy. She grimaced, remembering that just five short months ago she had been advocating for the two of them to get together. But it had honestly never occurred to her that Sammy would hook up with Rose's older brother. The two of them had been best friends for so long that Rose had figured they saw each other as brother and sister.

They clearly did not.

Still, she had a feeling about this. She had a feeling about

Elliott. Elliott and his clean hands, and his very nice manners. After she had invited him to come sit down at the table he had offered to buy her the next beer that she had.

"So," she said, "tell me more about water filtration systems."

She could feel West and Pansy looking at her with great skepticism, and she could feel Logan next to her. He was vibrating with some kind of repressed energy that she couldn't name.

"Well," he said, "the things they're doing with whole house filtration systems now are very interesting."

It was not interesting.

But he was very competent and knowledgeable about the subject, and on some level she supposed she had to respect that. Even though she was citing football statistics in her head, and thinking about... Literally anything but what he was saying. Like picking dirt out of a horse's hooves. Cleaning out her own fingernails. The current market price of hay...

"I noticed that the new bakery closed," Pansy said.

"What?" Rose asked, running over Elliott's water filtration monologue.

"Yeah," she said, sounding tragic. "I really enjoyed it."

"Me, too," Rose said. In her opinion, there was no such thing as a dessert that was too sweet, and everything there had been akin to a sugar bomb. She had loved it. "Of course, Iris made much better baked goods." She thought it was a great opportunity to introduce the topic of her sister. "You know who Iris is, right?" she asked Elliott.

"Yes," he responded.

"She makes amazing food."

"The problem with businesses around here is that they try to open up and they don't have any consistent hours. Because one person is always running the place," Pansy said. Changing the subject back to the bakery, which Rose found annoying because she'd just figured out how to get talking about Iris. "I can't count on a place that is randomly closed on a Monday or Tuesday, and then a Thursday next week."

"Well, when it comes to business startups, you really need to be committed to losing money for the first five years. But that was one of the bonuses of becoming an independent contractor for Clearwater."

And Elliott was off again, talking about water. She understood that water was important. Honestly, one of the more important things in life. Certainly more important than cupcakes. But when it came right down to it, she would rather talk about cupcakes. But Iris… Iris would probably appreciate it. Iris was practical. Elliott was practical.

Boring though it was to listen to him talk about water, she felt bolstered by it. And more and more convinced that she was on the right track when it came to him and her sister.

"Well," Pansy said, "we have to go. You know, Emmett is at home."

Emmett was West's younger brother, and Pansy and West were his guardians. Though, the kid was sixteen, not six. Still, she had a feeling that they were making up excuses so they could leave.

"Okay," she said. "See you tomorrow."

"Tomorrow?" West asked.

"You know, because we are all meeting here tomorrow," Rose said, suddenly struck with inspiration.

Pansy cast her some side-eye. "I'll talk to you tomorrow morning," she said.

Logan shifted beside her, and she felt that shift in the air. He was that kind of guy. Big and solid and exactly the kind of partner that you wanted working out on the ranch. Logan could lift his own weight and then some. And at the same time, he never made her feel like she might not be doing her share just because she was a woman, and smaller than him.

Now, he had other ways of making her feel small and silly. And she had a feeling he was gearing up for one.

She looked over at him. His face was set in stone. And he didn't look like he was planning to say anything at all. That was almost worse somehow.

"We're meeting tomorrow," she said, deciding not to give any space to Logan at all. He could keep his disapproving shifts to himself. "The group of us. You should come," she said to Elliott. "Give me your phone number, that way I can get in touch if anything changes. But we should all be here around eight."

"Okay," he said, looking happy about that.

"Yeah. We'll all be here. Ryder, his wife, Sammy. Our other sister, Iris. Maybe she can bring some of her baked goods."

"Great," he said.

She took her phone out, and he gave her his number, which she programmed into it easily. "Excellent. Well, we better get going. You know. Ranch work. Very early rising."

"Yeah, me, too," he said. "Water filtration systems won't install themselves."

"No," Rose said, forcing a smile. "I don't imagine they will. And my cows won't... Well, they won't castrate themselves. Bastards. No thumbs."

Somehow she could feel a groan come from Logan without him actually making any noises. She didn't know how he managed that. Total silent disapproval that somehow rumbled within her.

Elliott, for his part, laughed. A little bit too hard, Rose thought.

"See you tomorrow," she said.

She stood and swept out of the saloon, Logan on her heels.

"What the hell was that?" he asked, once they were headed toward the truck.

"A setup," she said.

"He thinks *you* like him."

The idea was so ridiculous Rose dismissed it immediately.

"He doesn't," she said. "I'm too young for him."

Logan stopped walking. She could feel him staring at the side of her face.

"What?"

"How old do you think he is?"

"I don't know. Thirty-two?"

Logan huffed. "I'm thirty-three."

"Yeah," she said. "Anyway. He's going to meet Iris. He's going to *love* Iris."

"Do *you hate* Iris?"

"No," Rose said emphatically. "I love Iris and I want her to be happy. He's practical. He owns his own business."

"I think he's a subcontractor."

"He's still a business owner," she insisted. "And it's doing something stable and profitable. It's exactly the kind of stability that Iris would admire."

"He talked about water filtration for twenty-five minutes."

"And we could talk about cows for longer than that."

"Yeah, but cows are interesting."

"My point," she said, "is that we all find different things

interesting. It isn't that he's uninteresting, it's just that we are uneducated about the topic."

"I'm educated now," he said. "About a thousand times more educated than I ever wanted to be. And I think you're making a mistake."

"I'm not. We're going to go out tomorrow night and Iris is going to meet him, and everything is going to be great."

"Why do you feel like you need to do this?"

"It's not that I need to. It's just that… Think about it, Logan. There's all these things in the world, all these people. And life is fragile. It's precious. What if people miss out on their chance to make these connections because they're busy working? Or just because… Someone needed to intervene."

"And you think that someone has to be you?"

"If Iris ends up alone it might be because of me," she said, the words bursting from her before she could stop them. Logan's blue eyes went far too sharp, and she didn't like it. It made her feel strange and exposed and it pushed her to keep on talking. "Iris has taken care of me all of her life basically. She didn't go to school dances, she didn't date. She was home cooking for us. For me. I was a kid the longest. I was the one who… She's the last single one."

"Except for you," he pointed out.

"It's not the same."

"How isn't it the same?"

"I mean… Logan, I'm twenty-three. I'm not remotely ready to settle down or anything like that. I love my life."

"Maybe Iris loves her life."

That made her pause. She thought of her sweet sister, who only ever showed how funny and bright she was in a room surrounded by her family. Who liked to bake and knit and spend her evenings at home. And she just couldn't get past the fact that she wondered if Iris had made the best of the box she'd been pushed into. Maybe it would have been who she was...eventually. But not as a young woman.

Maybe if she hadn't had to raise Rose she would have dated.

Maybe she'd be settled at home knitting with a husband and children of her own and not...in a house that was, well, it was different now. Ryder and Sammy were married and it was Sammy's house too now.

They'd be having a baby soon.

Even Ryder, who had devoted all that he was to taking care of them after their parents' deaths, had found someone. Was moving on.

Iris remained.

And how could Rose ever...how could she ever move on if Iris didn't? Knowing she might be the cause of her sister's current situation?

"And so much of what she does is because she had to settle into that role too soon. She's basically a spinster aunt and she's only thirty-one."

"Please say this to Iris, because I have a feeling it would go over really well."

"I *have* said it to Iris," Rose said. Okay, not in those terms. She didn't want to hurt her sister's feelings.

Logan shook his head and jerked his truck door open, and Rose climbed into the passenger seat beside him. "I'm telling you," he said. "This is not a great idea."

"I'm sorry, Logan, if this were a matter of cows, I might listen to you, but this is a matter of people."

"And you think you have superior experience with people than me?"

"I think that you deliberately don't have a lot of experience with people. You ranch, you drink, you sleep."

"I do other things," he said, his tone exceedingly dry.

"What things?"

He was driving, so he didn't look at her, but again, she could feel what he was thinking. She didn't know how he managed that. To make his feelings so clear to her that she could feel them inside her own chest sometimes.

She shifted uncomfortably, because she had a feeling that he was thinking of… Well, things she didn't want to think about concerning Logan. He was her friend. Her co-worker. She didn't need to go thinking of him as a…as a man. Doing things men did.

"Never mind," she muttered.

"Well, don't ask if you don't want to have a conversation."

"I'll bet you that they hit it off," she continued, happy to step away from the more disconcerting part of the conversation.

"Fine," he said. "You're on."

"If I win… If I win I get to set you up."

"Not a damn chance."

"So you're afraid that I'll win."

He said nothing.

"You are," she said. "You're afraid that I'll win."

"Fine," he said. "If you successfully hook the two of them up, you have my permission to seek out someone for me."

She felt immediately flat. Because the fact that he agreed likely did mean that he didn't believe that she was right about this. But she did. She didn't need for his vote of confidence to be sincere.

"It's a deal. You'll see."

"Oh, I imagine I'll see plenty."

And with that, Rose decided she was done with him.

Done having the conversation. Sometimes there was no one more infuriating in her life than Logan Heath.

But he was her closest coworker. And in many ways, had grown into being one of her best friends. Except, an older, grumpy, superior best friend, who could be a serious pain in the ass sometimes.

So really, another brother.

She was going to succeed with Iris. And then she would set Logan up, too. She wouldn't let him put a damper on her plans. On that she was determined.

CHAPTER THREE

"WHAT'S THIS I hear about going out to the bar tonight?"

Logan let out an exasperated snort as he was approached by his friend the next day. He stopped moving in the middle of scooping up a shovel of stall shavings. "Your sister is cooking up one of her harebrained schemes."

He didn't have to specify which sister.

Ryder knew without needing to be told.

And Logan could see a train wreck coming from a mile away. But Rose wasn't going to be convinced. She wasn't going to be convinced until she forced everybody into an awkward situation. She had done that with himself and Sammy, and thankfully the two of them were self-actualized enough—and not into each other enough—that it hadn't bothered him at all.

Logan had known that it was Ryder who was in love with Sammy. And he had been reasonably confident that Sammy was into Ryder, and had absolutely no designs on Logan at all. It had been confirmed when Sammy had gotten pregnant, and the father was Ryder. Now the two of them were married, which was basically how Logan had always thought it should be.

And frankly, confirmed that he had a slightly better eye for these things than Rose.

In Rose's defense, she was young.

As she had pointed out, thirty-two was *too old* for her.

At twenty-three, she was determinedly going around trying to write checks she didn't have the experience to cash.

He tried not to remember the way he had felt when she'd said that. Thirty-two being *old*.

It had been like a barb under his skin. Made him feel like exactly what he had been concerned he might be for the past couple of years. Nothing more than a dirty old man.

Hell, it was just wrong to notice that his best friend's little sister was hot as hell. But it was more than hot. It was a chemistry thing.

Which he also had experience enough to know.

It seemed to be one-sided, which was a gift in and of itself. Because Rose was like a determined little terrier, and when she got her teeth sunk into an idea she went full bore with it. And the last thing he needed in the whole world was for Rose to decide to sink her teeth into him.

He gritted his teeth against the kick of arousal he experienced at the thought.

In front of her damn brother.

"What is she up to?" Ryder asked.

"She thinks that she's going to set Iris up."

Ryder frowned. "What, with a man?"

"Yep."

Ryder let out a howl. "No shit."

"Seriously," he said.

"Well. I have a feeling that's not going to go very well for her."

"Nope."

"Are you going to go?"

"Yes," Logan said without hesitation.

"Why? I think you should let her make her mistake."

And he realized that no matter how silly he thought it was, he couldn't let her go off and do this on her own. Be cause the fact of the matter was, Elliott was going to believe that Rose was interested in him. She was officially biting off more than she could chew, and he actually wasn't willing to leave her to that.

It wasn't because he couldn't stand the idea of another man touching her.

No way in hell.

He was protective.

"Hey, I'm just not willing to miss the show," he lied.

"Better you than me. Sammy's energy is at a premium, and I think I would rather be at home with her than out watching Rose be a heap of trouble."

"Hell," Logan said. "If Iris decides not to go out we'll all be better off."

"You could warn her," Ryder said.

"I could," Logan responded. "Of course, then *Rose* would kill me. Anyway, you're right. Rose needs to learn her lesson."

He was going to be there, granted. But the fact of the matter was Rose did need to learn. She was up in people's business far too often. And he could see that this was headed for absolute disaster.

It might be necessary for her to take a fall. But he was damn well going to be there when she did.

Because that was what he did. He protected her. He'd done it all her life. But then his feelings had begun to shift, begun to change.

And after that shift there had been moments. Late nights on the porch drinking beer. Times when they'd be out working and their bodies would brush against each other, and he was close enough to press his lips to her neck if he just angled his head.

It had forced him to make a choice. Between changing what they were, and staying her protector as he'd always been. When working with her had started to become a strain. When he had begun to notice the softness of her body when he would press up against her while they wrangled a calf, or noticed the scent of her when the breeze kicked up when they were out in the field together.

He'd recommitted himself. To keeping her safe.

Even if it meant keeping her safe from him.

Because this place was his home.

Because Ryder Daniels had supported him through the worst thing in his life, while grieving his own losses.

He remembered the night they'd found out their parents had died. Clear as if it were yesterday and not nearly eighteen years ago. They'd all been staying in the main house on Hope Springs, caring for each other while their parents went on that trip. They hadn't known they'd end up like that always.

Ryder had been stoic. Ryder had been the only one over eighteen. The one who'd had to sign paperwork and deal with Child Services. The one who'd had to wrangle insurance and plan funerals.

The only thing Logan had been able to do for him was let him break.

He could remember that night well. It had been six months after they'd died. He'd found Ryder out in the barn, by a big old box of beer bottles. He was halfway through his fourth beer and tipsy and angry.

Ryder's dad and uncle had kept a whole supply of beer outside in the colder months, and Ryder had stumbled upon it and figured…why the hell not drink it.

"No one's here to stop me," he'd said, kicking one bottle over. "Have a beer, Logan. I'm your guardian. I say you can."

And Logan had. Then he'd had two. Then three.

And by the end they were both drunk and broken. It was the only emotion he'd ever seen Ryder show. The only time he'd faltered. And he'd cracked apart.

"I'm not supposed to be here," he'd mumbled, sitting on the ground with his knees pulled up to his chest. "I was supposed to be a thousand miles from here. In college. Playing football. I wasn't supposed to be everyone's dad."

"Sorry," Logan had slurred. "But I don't know where I'd be if you weren't here. I wouldn't have anyone. My mom was all I had."

"You have us," Ryder had said. And it was like he'd found that strength again, that he'd been leaning on all those months, that had cracked just for a little while. "What-if doesn't matter. You have us."

He knew what this had cost Ryder. And he...he could never take for granted what Ryder had sacrificed for them.

He wasn't a part of the Daniels family. He was the out-lier in a way that not even Sammy was.

Because no matter what, no matter how much time passed, he would always bear some of the weight of guilt for what had happened.

And touching Rose would be the greatest sin he could ever commit.

Ryder's youngest sister. The sister he had always trusted him with.

Even worse, Rose trusted him.

Plus, Rose didn't look at him like that at all.

If Rose even realized he was a man he'd be shocked.

So he protected her. It was what he did. Because if he was actively protecting her, if he was standing guard, then he couldn't... Well, then, he couldn't do anything that both of them would regret.

"So, you're not coming to the bar tonight?"

"I'd rather die."

"Fine. I'll give you a full report."

"I knew I could count on you," Ryder said, clapping him on the back.

And that was the thing. Ryder knew that he could count on him.

And that meant he had to keep on doing exactly what he had been.

"Always."

He meant it.

"I'M REALLY GLAD that you agreed to come out tonight," Rose said cheerily, parking her truck on the curb and getting out, her sister Iris following behind her.

Iris's version of dressing up wasn't particularly eye-catching. Not that Rose could judge really. Her version of dressing up was to put on a belt with rhinestones and a clean T-shirt.

But Iris wasn't… She didn't work outside and her clothes tended to be dowdy. Rose might not fix up, but she didn't downplay her beauty. It seemed sometimes like Iris did. Tonight her brown hair was pulled up in a ponytail, and she was wearing a demure sweater with a high collar and snowflakes knitted into it.

Logan was meeting them there, at least. Ryder and Sammy had bailed. So had West and Pansy.

It occurred to her, though, that it was a little bit strange. In general. Because with her trying to set Iris up with Elliott, it created sort of a pairing-off situation.

She wished that Jake or Colt were around. Her cousins could have helped defuse that feeling. Although, it might be a good thing. After all, there was no temptation for her and Logan to actually think they were being paired off, so if Elliott thought that was the case, all the better. It would give him the idea of what was happening a lot quicker.

He was already there when they arrived. He was wearing a collared shirt. It was plaid, but she had to give him points for trying. She looked over at Iris, and then back at Elliott. "I'm so glad you're here," Rose said. "This is Iris," she said. "Iris, do you know Elliott?"

"I'm sure that we've met," Iris said, casting Rose a glance.

"Well, here's a formal meeting. I met Elliott last night, and I invited him to join us for drinks tonight."

"Great," Iris said.

Her sister sounded hesitant, but Rose knew that it was just taking her a while to get warmed up. Because Iris wasn't used to going out. And meeting with people that weren't family anyway.

The door opened, and Logan walked in. He was wearing a black T-shirt that molded tightly to his hard body, honed by hours of manual labor outside, and a black cowboy hat. She couldn't help but think that he looked better in a T-shirt than poor Elliott did in plaid.

An odd feeling settled over her skin. A strange sense of…pride or something. As if her being linked to him in some way made it special that he was good-looking. But she knew that women liked Logan. And she got to work with him every day. It did make her feel a little bit smug and proud.

He was special to her.

She had just gotten them settled at a table when Logan approached them, and she grabbed hold of his arm. "Let's go get beers," she said. "Iris, Elliott does water filtration systems. He can tell you all about it."

Then they began to walk quickly over to the bar. "That was mean, Rose."

"It was not mean. He likes to talk about his business. And Iris will see that he is eligible."

"He's boring as hell."

"Now who's mean?"

"Let me ask you this—why are you so intent on setting your sister up with him and not you? If you really thought he was such a great guy, wouldn't you want to go out with him?"

"Because I don't want to be set up with anyone." There was something in her eyes that went beyond resistance. It was almost fear.

"But you think the rest of us should all line up to employ your matchmaking services?"

"I'm not at the age where I need intervention yet."

He huffed a laugh. "Oh, okay. So we're supposed to accept this pity dating service from the young and fresh-faced?"

"It's not a pity dating service. But everybody... Everybody took care of me, Logan," she said, vibrating with frustration, irritated by the fact that he had managed to use his words and implacable demeanor to scrape down a layer inside of her and reach parts of her heart that she didn't particularly want to feel herself, much less perform for anyone else.

"Now, I want to make sure that everyone is taken care of. I want Iris to be happy. Don't you think... It took Ryder so long to figure out that he loved Sammy. Pansy never dated anybody until she met West. I already told you I worry... I just wonder if Iris poured so much into taking care of me, into mothering me, that she's never had a chance to go out and be with anyone. I don't think she's ever been on a date."

"Neither have you," he pointed out, his words a missile hitting their target directly. As they often were.

"Well, maybe I will. After this. After I make sure everyone is taken care of."

He shook his head. "You know, that's not what everybody needs to be happy."

"No one wants to be alone."

"Iris isn't alone," he said. "You're not alone, I'm not alone."

"You know what I mean."

"But you just said you don't want to be matched up with anyone."

"Right now," she said.

"Okay. So you think that maybe Iris hasn't ever been with anyone because she was so busy taking care of you. And you haven't taken care of anyone. So why is it that you're by yourself?"

She blinked. "I don't have time for it."

"You don't have the time for it? Here we are, out having a beer. You could be having a beer with Elliott just as easily as Iris is."

They both looked back at the table where they had left the other two behind. Iris looked like she wanted to pull her eyelashes out, so great was her discomfort. Elliott didn't seem to notice.

Iris would be fine if she wasn't so wound up about the whole thing.

"Well, there doesn't seem to be much *easy* about that," he said dryly.

"She just needs time to warm up."

"Why are you meddling?"

"I already told you," she responded. "I want to make

sure that everyone is taken care of. That's it. I want to give back something of what I got."

"Next time make her a cake."

"She's better at baking than I am. She's better at… everything than I am. The only thing I've ever done for Iris is give her a potential streak of premature gray hair and teach her enduring patience. Nothing has made this clearer to me than watching…watching my other siblings do new things, have new lives, while she hasn't. She had to raise me, and don't think I'm not aware of that. You, too," she said.

He drew back. "I didn't raise you."

"You know. But you are always there. You and Iris and Pansy and Ryder. Colt and Jake helped out, too. You were all there for me. And I was the baby. I couldn't contribute anything."

"Nobody would have asked you to."

"I know that," she said. "I know. But still."

Laz Jenkins, the owner of the bar, sidled up to where they were standing. "Anything I can get you?"

"Yes. Four beers," she said. "Whatever you have on tap that is good."

Laz nodded in the affirmative and pulled four beers, setting them out on the counter. "On your tab?"

"Yes," she said.

"Come on," she said, picking up two of the beers.

"Maybe we should walk slow."

"Why?"

"Because I'm not in a particular hurry to get back to that."

"Come on. We need to help Iris feel at ease."

"I don't think anything is going to do that."

By the time they got up to the table Logan had plastered

a smile on his face. He was obviously ready to at least pretend to be well-behaved, and for that she was grateful. Because knowing Logan it could have gone either way.

"We were just talking about…water filtration," Iris said.

"Well," Elliott added, "Iris was also generously sharing her sourdough recipe with me."

"Oh, yes," Rose said, feeling animated now. "Iris makes absolutely the best sourdough bread. She's been making it for me since I was a kid. She got the recipe from our mother."

Iris nodded, forcing a smile. "Yes. I did."

"Iris can send it to you!" Rose said. "It's really a great recipe."

She realized he might not bake, but he did seem enthused about the subject so that was potentially a good sign.

"That would be terrific," Elliott responded.

They found a rhythm in the conversation, and while it was true that Elliott could never be called a sparkling conversationalist, he was serviceable enough. And in fact, this time around they got a chance to see a little bit of his humor. Iris began to warm up, bringing her own sly humor to the conversation, which Rose always enjoyed. Iris wasn't flashy or animated with her humor, but she was clever. Rose had always thought that about her sister. That she was a diamond in the rough for anyone who wanted to actually get to know her.

She wasn't obvious. She was understated, and so often understated tended to get overlooked.

Which really was what had drawn her to Elliott for her sister in the first place.

She had seen him around for years, and he seemed very nice.

He didn't attract the kind of attention that Logan did. Or even the way her brother, Ryder, did.

But they were tall and obvious in a chiseled sort of way, both of them very clearly cowboys. Then there were her cousins Colt and Jake. Rodeo cowboys who didn't just emanate that sort of rugged charm, but who also seemed to carry a layer of danger with them. Women made fools of themselves for them.

But Iris was steady, and she wasn't going to like someone like that. No, she was well suited to somebody who was like her. Someone put together. Someone who could manage their life.

Rose knew it.

So Logan and even Iris could doubt her all they wanted, but she did know what she was doing.

She did.

"Who feels like dancing?"

Rose thought it was a little bit of a funny question coming from Elliott, since she wouldn't have thought that he was much of a dancer, but if he wanted to get Iris into closer proximity, then that was great as far as Rose was concerned.

"Me," she said cheerfully. "Come on," she repeated, goading Logan and Iris.

She knew that Logan was more than capable of dancing when there was a woman on the dance floor he was interested in getting his hands on.

She'd seen it a couple of times. She had never particularly liked it. It was just one of those things that seemed beneath him. Like he was too… She didn't know. Something. To behave like other men did and to be motivated by…that stuff. But that was all kind of childish thinking, and she realized that.

There was a part of her that still hero-worshipped him.

Because he had been such a large, defining figure in her life for so long.

Because of the way he had cared for her. Because of the way he had talked to her straight about grief and life and big, hard things that a kid shouldn't have been explaining to another kid. But they'd had no choice.

They'd had each other.

So yeah, she always felt a twinge of discomfort when she saw the way that women responded to Logan, and the way that he responded to them.

It was uncomfortable. And stranger, it made her feel like she was standing outside a window, looking in at something.

But the real point was that he did dance, and she knew it. So he could suck it up and do it now. With a long-suffering glance, he got out of his chair, and they all went to the dance floor, where a high-tempo country song was playing. Rose stuck near Iris as her sister reluctantly began to move.

"You heard the man," she said, pointing at the jukebox. "You're supposed to shake it, country girl."

The music was too loud for this to be possible, but Rose could swear she heard her sister sniff. "I don't *shake it*."

Rose laughed, and proceeded to dance, throwing her hands up in the air and shimmying to compensate for her sister's lack of it.

Elliott, for his part, seemed to enjoy himself immensely, and the smile that lit up his face highlighted that he was a cute guy. When the song changed and the music slowed, she found herself standing across from Elliott, and then awkwardly drawn in for a dance.

She saw that Logan had taken hold of Iris, partnering her so that there was no lag, which meant that she was going to have to redirect and quickly and stop looking at Elliott like he had slapped her with a fish. She smiled.

"Thank you for inviting me out," he said. His eyes darted over Rose's shoulder, in Iris's direction, and she took that as a very good sign.

"Of course," she responded. "I'm really glad you came."

She danced impatiently with him for a good half of the song, and then saw her opportunity. Neither he nor Iris were particularly bold, and she just had a feeling that they were going to need a little bit of boosting.

"Partner swap," she said, separating off and pulling at Iris's shoulders before giving her a gentle push toward Elliott, and positioning herself in front of Logan. When Logan settled his large hands on her hips, an echo of something very strange shot through her body.

Surprise. That was all it was. It was very weird because she had just been dancing with a man, but she became suddenly so conscious of the fact that his hold was firmer than she had anticipated, his hands larger. That same energy that he radiated when he did things like disapprove of her felt amplified now.

His body was also especially warm, which she found strange and foreign and utterly surprising. She looked up at him, his electric blue gaze connecting with hers like a lightning strike.

"Be careful," he said, his words hushed.

"What?"

"He likes you."

"He was looking at Iris while we were dancing."

"Yeah, because I might have given him a mean look."

Rose blinked. "Well, they're dancing. Anyway, I think I would know if a man liked me."

Logan's face turned to granite, his features hardening, his jaw going tight. "I don't think you would."

"I do," she shot back.

"You have to be careful, kid," he said. "You're playing with people, and that could easily bite you in your little ass." Something about his words made goose bumps raise up on her arms.

"I will assure you that my ass will remain *unbit*."

"You can't guarantee that."

"I can," she whispered. "Everything is going to be fine."

He shifted his hand then, a little bit higher on her waist, and she suddenly became very conscious of his thumb. She didn't know why his thumb. Except that she could feel it. His thumb specifically. Resting precariously high on her midsection. She and Logan came into physical contact fairly often when they did manual labor, but it was imprecise. They would bump up against each other sometimes. Sometimes he would wrap his arms around her while bracing her so that they could wrangle a stubborn calf.

But this was pointed. Targeted.

This had an echo.

She had never felt a touch that had an echo.

The song ended, and he let go of her, the withdrawal abrupt. She felt slightly dizzy, like she had been in an insulated box, and suddenly she was back out in the open, all the sounds amplified, the air feeling colder. It was like her senses had been reduced for a moment, narrowed down entirely to Logan and their dance.

She hadn't been entirely aware of it until it had ended.

She also felt unaccountably sheepish. Like somehow he had taught her a lesson even though she refused to agree with him.

She had no idea what the lesson was.

But she was done dancing.

She made her way back to the table and grabbed her beer, pulling it to the edge and taking a long sip. Elliott, Iris and Logan stayed out on the dance floor for a while longer. Then Elliott and Iris returned, and Logan stayed.

Rose watched as he found a blonde with exposed skin that looked as soft as a calf's ear. Rose wasn't often jealous of other women. Her body was serviceable, after all. It allowed her to do the chores that she needed to get done.

But women like that made her very aware of the fact that her hands were rough. That she did hard labor and it had a hard effect on her appearance.

Rose's hair was dry from the sun. Even though she used sunblock she was often a bit wind chapped and sunburned. She had calluses on her palms and she didn't think she had ever radiated the kind of dewy smoothness that Logan's current dance partner did.

"I better call it a night," Elliott said. "But maybe I can give you my number and you can send me that recipe." Elliott addressed Iris for that last part.

"Of course," Iris said.

The two of them traded numbers, and Rose bit back a sound of triumph.

She was right. And it was going to work. Logan, with all of his dour skepticism, was wrong. He was going to lose the bet, and she was going to be able to set him up, too.

She looked back at the dance floor. He was doing a decent job of setting himself up, she supposed.

She still didn't like it.

That was hookup stuff. And that had nothing to do with real companionship.

She could remember still the way that Logan had looked when she had bandaged his hand all those years ago. That sadness on his face. And the way he tried to cover it up. So that he could care for her.

He needed somebody who could shoulder the kind of burden that he carried. Who could deal with the kind of grief they'd been through. It was tough to find someone who could.

They had lost so much, all of them.

Logan needed somebody who would be able to understand that.

And what about you? What do you need?

She deflected that question. She didn't want to think about it. She didn't need to think about it. She had been honest when she had said to Logan that she wasn't in a space where she felt like she needed anyone at all. And she didn't think it was a double standard.

She was twenty-three. She didn't need to worry about it, not yet.

And anyway, there was something about thinking about it that reminded her too much of the yawning void she had felt after her parents had died.

She wasn't alone anyway. She had all of them in such a deep, profound way.

When Elliott left, she turned to Iris. "See?" she practically chirped. "I was right. He's nice."

"I guess," Iris said.

"What?"

Iris shook her head. "It's nothing. You're right. He's nice. And… perfectly sensible."

"That's a good thing," Rose said, suddenly feeling the first twinge of uncertainty over the whole thing. Because it had gone well, but Iris didn't seem overjoyed or giddy or anything like that, and the fact that Rose seemed more excited about it than her sister didn't seem quite right. "Isn't it?"

"Of course it is," Iris said. "I mean, we all know how difficult life can be, right? Making sensible choices when it comes to the men that you date is arguably the most important thing somebody who's been through the kind of experiences we have can do."

"Of course, our sister is marrying an ex-convict at Christmas."

"Our sister the police chief," Iris said, shaking her head.

Rose found her gaze wandering back over to Logan and his mystery lady.

"Yeah, I would rather not see that," Iris said, her lip curling. "Too much like watching a family member hook up."

Rose pondered that. And she decided that must be the truth. It must be why it felt like there was a rock in her stomach. "Yeah," she said. *"Yeah."* Affirming it. That was what it was. Definitely like if she were watching one of her cousins, or even worse, Ryder, trying to get it on with a random girl.

She had walked in on Ryder and Sammy making out before anyone had known they were together, and she had felt decently emotionally scarred by that. Since Sammy felt like a sister and all. It had felt like a violation of everything she believed to be true about their dynamic, and the family dynamic. So she imagined that had to do with the discomfort that she was experiencing at the moment.

"Why can't *we* do that?" Rose asked.

"Because I don't like blondes," Iris said dryly.

"You know what I mean. Why did they get to do that? Why don't we?"

"You don't want to," Iris said sagely.

"Maybe I do," Rose said. Privately, the idea of approaching some random guy and dancing with him made her want to jump out of her skin, but she wasn't going to admit that now. Not since she had made it an issue.

She just... She'd never met someone who made her want to do that. Had never seen someone on the other side of the crowded bar and felt enticed to cross the room to talk to them.

"Well, go right ahead," Iris said. "I would support you."

She had to wonder if what Iris had said earlier was true of her too, as she sat so resolutely rooted to her chair. If there was something inside of her that made her feel a lot more...cautious about all of it. To her, love felt like a precious commodity. Not something vast and infinite, but a shiny gem you might run out of. She had been so young when her parents had died. So much of what she was had been shaped around that tragedy. And around all the things and experiences she hadn't had since.

Logan had been sixteen. So while she knew he had been profoundly affected by losing his mother, he had also been a good bit of who he was by the time it had happened.

Rose hadn't even begun to become who she might be.

She wondered if she still hadn't.

For a moment she wondered what would happen if she did walk up to one of the men on that dance floor. Wrapped her arm around his neck and smiled. If she led with a bold joke, which she had no problem doing with men she knew. Of course, she didn't do it to be flirtatious with them. But what if she did?

Except... Suddenly in her mind she had a clear picture of replacing that blonde in Logan's arms.

She squeezed her eyes shut.

"Okay," she said. "I don't really want to. And you can call Elliott. You're right. He's nice."

"I think *you're* the one who said that," Iris said. "So you're just saying that you're right."

Rose shrugged. "Life doesn't hand us wins, Iris, you have to seize the ones that you're owed."

"I'm not saying that you have a win," Iris said. "But given that I haven't actually…gone out with anybody in…"

Rose bit her lip.

Iris narrowed her eyes. "You're not going to say something about how I never go out?"

Rose shrugged mutely.

"You're just trying to behave so that I don't defy you for the sake of it."

"I don't have it in me to behave. Not for any reason at all."

The blonde touched Logan's face. Rose turned away. "I'm ready to go."

Iris looked at her skeptically. "Are you okay?"

"I'm great. I'm really glad that you hit it off with Elliott."

"*Hitting it off* might be overstating it. But I am willing to give him my sourdough recipe. Which isn't nothing."

"Good. Well, I'm glad of that."

They slipped out of the bar, after settling her tab with Laz, and wandered down the street. They paused briefly in front of the now vacant bakery storefront. "Wouldn't it be something to own a piece of this?" Iris looked longingly at the building. "To have a place right here on Main Street."

"You want to own a bakery?"

Iris laughed. "Not seriously. I'm not that much of a dreamer."

"No," Rose said wistfully. "I don't suppose you are. I don't suppose I am, either."

Iris laughed. "You are a dreamer, Rose. That's why you meddle in people's business. But I like that about you. I quit having those kinds of dreams a long time ago. But I've found a version of reality that I like quite a bit." She squeezed her sister's arm. Iris smiled. "It's a good thing, too. Because nobody can keep a business going in this building, and I have no reason to believe I would be able to do any better. So it's a very good thing that I'm just too practical to ever take something like that on. Plus I don't have the money."

Rose didn't feel glad of any of that. Rose just felt sad. Sad and sorry that life had taken her sister's ability to dream away from her.

But it made her more determined to do the dreaming for her. And it made her feel even more certain of her decision to try and get Iris and Elliott together.

"It's not that nice anyway," she said, looking at the beautiful redbrick building and lying horribly about its aesthetic appeal.

"Yeah. I get to bake bread and cake for you." Iris nudged Rose's shoulder with her own, and the two of them began to walk toward the truck. "I know you might not believe it, Rose, but taking care of you makes me happy."

For some reason, it just made Rose want to cry.

CHAPTER FOUR

LOGAN WAS THANKFUL that by midday his chores had not put him in proximity to Rose. Damn that girl.

He was still fuming over last night. She was being dense as hell. And she didn't seem to think so. In fact, the little hellion was dead set on arguing with him, sure as shooting that she knew when a man was attracted to her.

She didn't. And if she had any damned clue what had been going through *his* mind…

He'd had half a mind to teach her a real lesson. Right out there on the dance floor in front of God, Iris and everybody.

He hadn't. He wouldn't. And until he got that through his thick head, it was best he didn't see her.

He was out in the far north pasture, having just driven the cows from one field to the next. The ride had done him good, though not enough good.

He maneuvered his horse around and looked behind him, at the broad expanse of green rolling to the base of imposing mountains, covered in jagged pines with sharp peaks rising up above the treetops.

He had spent the first sixteen years of his life on a modest street just off the main drag of Gold Valley. His mom was best friends with Linda Daniels, and he had spent hours here on the ranch. Ryder had taught him to ride a horse.

Still, he couldn't help but wonder what might have happened in his life if he hadn't ended up living on Hope

Springs Ranch. He hadn't exactly planned on growing up to become a cowboy. Mostly because he didn't know that was an option. He wouldn't have been able to figure out the steps a kid took to get from the life he'd been born into to a life on a range. Sure, he knew that Ryder's dad did it. But Ryder's father had also been the chief of police in Gold Valley, in addition to being a rancher, and his uncle had worked odd jobs at other ranches to make ends meet.

Ryder had managed to turn the place into a profitable full-time operation, and some of that was the willingness of Logan and Rose to work for free for a while. But now they were all doing decently well, and it was one of those things that Logan couldn't help but...

One of the weird-ass things in his life that was difficult to sort out.

He missed his mom. Every damn day. She had been his only parent. The only one he never needed. Didn't matter who the hell his biological father was. He didn't care.

Jane Heath had been all the influence and love he had needed. She had given him everything.

And losing her had been a blow he hadn't thought he could live through. The guilt that went along with it was a gift in some ways. Because he'd had to keep going since she couldn't.

His heart had to keep beating for her, because he owed it to her. And there was no amount of time he could put in that would ever make it right.

And this time of year...when the weather got cold and people got merry, it just reminded him of every step that had gone into creating that tragedy.

Of presents that had turned into curses.

Losing her had shaped him. Was the reason he was sitting here now on a horse.

Her loss had made him the man he was and he supposed that was the very best tribute he could offer. Even if it did make everything he did, everything he was, chafe like a son of a gun sometimes.

Tragedy felt so wound up in the good things in his life that he didn't know how to separate it.

"There you are."

He turned and saw Rose riding up on her paint, her cowgirl hat pulled down low on her head, her ponytail flying in the wind. She was wearing a battered old ranch jacket that was unzipped, revealing a scoop-neck top underneath. And with every motion the horse made, he could see a hint of soft, pale flesh.

Damn.

He blamed last night. He blamed holding her in his arms.

And even more, he blamed the look of confusion on her face when he had shifted his hand over her waist.

He had recognized what was happening. That there was a spark underneath that touch. That if he kept going, created the right friction, a spark could become a flame. But she didn't recognize it.

A blessing.

Still, it didn't do anything to ease the fire banked in his gut. Great for her that she didn't know what the hell it could become. Great for them both.

"I figured you'd know where I would be," he said.

"Well, I need your help," she said. "I was moving hay and something in the damn tractor blew. I've got it taken apart, but I'm having trouble identifying the problem."

"If you can't fix it, I doubt I'm going to be able to figure it out. We're probably going to have to call Dan Swift out."

"Yeah, probably. Still, if you could go have a look before we do that."

"Sure."

"Have you eaten?"

He hesitated. "No."

"I brought food. Because I figured that was probably the case if you are out here driving cattle. You know, you shouldn't do that by yourself."

"It was a pretty short move."

"Still. If one of them decides to break off..."

"I know what I'm doing," he said, testier than he intended to.

"I didn't say you didn't," she said, dismounting her horse and reaching into one of the saddlebags in the back. She produced sandwiches. And bags of chips. And soda. And then he found he couldn't be as irritated with her as he wanted to be.

"You going to tie her up?" He indicated her mare.

"No. I'm going to let her graze for a minute."

He shrugged his shoulders and dismounted, leaving his gelding to do the same. Rose plopped down, right there in the field, a testament to how comfortable she was with the place. Not worried about cows or cow pies.

This ranch would have always been Rose's reality. But he wondered... He did wonder if she would have decided to work here if she'd still had her parents.

She liked to help people. Maybe she'd have gone to school. Gotten into medicine or teaching. He could see her excelling in either field. She was tireless, relentless and good down to her soul.

She took all that and poured it into the ranch, but where else could she have channeled that?

And he didn't need to know the answer to that. There was no point pushing for that kind of discussion. Not now.

Not when he should be shoving his sandwich down as quickly as possible and getting back to work.

"So," Rose said around a mouthful of sandwich. "Did you get lucky?"

Heat crept up the back of his neck like fire burning along a line of gunpowder. "Excuse me?"

"With the blonde," she said, still chewing. "You were very friendly with her."

"Are you asking me if I had sex?" He asked the question baldly, making deliberate eye contact with her. And was gratified when she looked away.

"I guess so." She sounded a little bit shamed, but also stubborn. And he could tell that she was in no kind of mood to back down.

That was the problem with Rose. The problem and the beauty of her all at the same time.

Her name was well suited to her.

He had often thought the other two girls had been saddled with albatrosses when it came to their names. Iris had basically been born the old maiden aunt. Pansy had a name that was so opposed to who she was as a person, a tough-talking police chief. The name added a layer of difficulty to her life. Combined with the fact that she was petite and a woman, she tended to have trouble getting taken seriously in her chosen profession anyway.

Rose, on the other hand...

She was beautiful. Even sitting there with her knees up, her forearms resting on them as she ate her sandwich. Wearing practical jeans and that top that was offering him tempting views of skin he shouldn't be thinking about.

The wind whipped up then, blowing strands of light brown hair over her face. Beautiful just like her namesake.

Her lips were a pale pink that reminded him of the flower, too. And looked soft as velvet.

But she had thorns.

Often, he gave thanks for those thorns. Because they were what made Rose resilient enough to get through the hard times that life had dumped onto her.

But right now, they were kind of a pain in his ass. It was that part of her that didn't back down. And right now, he kind of wanted her to back down.

He could lie to her. He could tell her that he had. It would destroy any camaraderie in the moment, and he wasn't sure why he was so certain of that. But something told him she would be upset if he had.

But he hadn't.

He hadn't wanted that woman. Not with the memory of Rose in his arms so close to the surface. He'd thought it might be convenient if he could.

But at that point he'd realized that if he was trying to put an effort toward wanting a woman it was a lost cause. He'd just kept on dancing with her to keep some distance between himself and the object of his torture.

He managed to deal with Rose just fine in general. Every so often things whipped up to the surface. Typically when physical contact was involved.

But he'd been coping pretty well for the last couple of years.

He'd struggled for a while with the initial, skin-crawling disgust of finding himself attracted to his best friend's younger sister. A woman he'd known since she was a child. And now, it wasn't about that.

The thing was, he'd been working with Rose since she was sixteen. And he'd watched her change. There was no doubt in his mind that she was a woman. Tough and capable, with a clear-eyed view of the world.

In many ways.

It was the way she didn't see the world at all that concerned him.

She had lost both of her parents. She had dealt with bringing calves into the world, and burying them when they didn't make it. She'd cut herself on barbed wire, dislocated a shoulder hefting bales of hay and he'd watched her walk off a particularly nasty *literal* kick in the butt from a spooked horse.

He'd also damn near crawled out of his skin when she had lowered the waistband of her denim and shown him the deep purple circle left on one plump cheek the next day.

She hadn't thought anything of it.

He'd thought an awful lot of it.

And it was the fact she hadn't hesitated to show him that shamed him down to his soul. Because she felt like he was family, clearly.

He did not.

He also couldn't bring himself to lie to her, even if the better part of valor would've been to lie. Disappoint her. Make her angry. Make her contend with the fact that it made her angry.

"No," he said.

"You could have," she pointed out.

Well, there she was being observant.

"I could have," he agreed.

"Why didn't you?"

"I don't just have sex whenever I feel like it," he said, continuing to speak in bold, frank terms, because he wondered at what point she might get uncomfortable and back down.

"Why not?"

It was a genuine question. She looked confused.

"For a lot of reasons."

"I mean, I thought you did. Iris and I were talking about it last night."

This conversation was just getting weirder.

"You and Iris were…talking about it."

"How it doesn't really seem fair that you and Jake and Ryder and Colt can just kind of hook up willy-nilly and for some reason we can't."

"Did anyone say you can't?"

"I guess not."

He was ready to change the subject.

"Do you do it because you're lonely?"

"What the hell?"

"I'm genuinely curious."

"I do it because it feels good," he said.

"Okay. So why don't you do it sometimes?"

He wanted out of this conversation, and quick. Rose was fascinated because she had no experience, and maybe if she knew…maybe if she knew the truth she'd shut the hell up.

"Sometimes it makes you more lonely, Rose. There you have it. That's the truth of it. When you're a dumb, dense guy and all the blood rushes down below your belt you can forget. For a while. Then you finish. And you just feel… emptier than when you started."

Now he wished he would've just asked her if she'd always wanted to be a cowgirl. It would've been a hell of a lot more innocuous than this. He'd wanted to make her uncomfortable, but he was the one who felt exposed.

"Then why do you do it?"

"Because sometimes it's worth it. To feel good for a minute."

"Maybe I should try it."

He bit back the immediate denial. He didn't know what the hell she was playing at. And because he wasn't sure, it was best that he just kept his opinions to himself.

"Nothing to say?" She put the last piece of her sandwich in her mouth and tore open her bag of chips.

"Do you require my opinion?"

"No. But you usually give it anyway."

"All right, fine," he said, her bright determination finally taking hold of him right where he didn't want. Because the idea of her going out and… "Here's my opinion."

She rubbed her hands together in mock glee. "Oh, goody. I can't imagine what I would have done without it."

"You don't know what the hell you want. You think sex and you think romance."

She sniffed. "I do not."

"Well, you know what you don't think? About the reality of it. About the fact you're going to have to decide that some guy in that bar is good enough to put his hands on you. That he can touch you, see you naked. Take you back to his place or his truck or whatever. You aren't thinking about the fact you're talking about someone being inside you, Rose." He let their eyes meet, and he held them. "Skin to skin. But more. Inside."

He didn't know how the hell he managed to look at her because his stomach was burning. His whole damn body was burning.

Her face had turned a deep shade of red, and she clenched her hands into fists. "Sex isn't a fantasy, Rose, it's physical. Hands and mouths and teeth."

"Teeth?"

He ground his own together. "You're not ready if that shocks you."

She picked at crumbs in the bottom of her chip bag. He was sure that he must have terrified her a little bit. God knew he'd tested himself to the limit with that speech because he was tempted to answer all the questions he'd seen raised in her eyes.

"I'm sorry that you're lonely," she said.

He huffed and took a bite of his sandwich. "Everyone is lonely sometimes. It's just part of life."

Not one he wanted to talk about. And he sure as hell didn't want her pity. This wasn't supposed to be about him.

"I know," she said. "I don't want you to be lonely. I don't want Iris to be lonely."

"It's not your responsibility."

"You took responsibility for me," she insisted.

"Why are you so worked up about that right now?"

"I told you. I was kind of just realizing…how much time passed. How much time you all invested in me."

"Because Iris is the last remaining single? Well. Other than me. And other than you."

"You know I caught Ryder and Sammy kissing," she said.

It wasn't what he'd expected her to say. But then, he had no idea what to expect out of this conversation at all.

"They kiss all the time."

"No. I mean before anybody knew they hooked up."

"I'll stop you there. Because I knew they hooked up the night they did it."

"How?" She looked slightly infuriated by that.

"I happened to be sitting out on the porch when Sammy came out doing her walk of shame." Yeah, he'd been sitting out on the porch in the dark and the cold, on a clear July night, staring at the stars and asking why the hell he had the bad fortune to have a fixation on Rose's body. There had been no answers forthcoming.

Instead, Sammy had come stumbling out the door, looking rattled, her hair a wild tangle that spoke volumes about what she had just been up to.

And given that he had suspected for a long time that his friend was in love with her, it hadn't taken an emotional genius to figure it out.

"Oh," Rose said, looking genuinely deflated. "I thought I was the first one to know."

"Sorry, kid." He emphasized that word. Anything to put distance between them. "I told you, I know about chemistry. I know about sex. Sorry if it bothers you that I might be a step ahead of you when it comes to this sort of thing."

"You're going to lose our bet," she said. "You're halfway to losing already."

She pitched forward and nudged him with her elbow, and he drew back. She looked up at him like he had said something mean. And he immediately regretted that reflex. The whole point of not touching Rose was to avoid hurting her.

"Yeah. Too bad I'm a sore loser." He decided to cover it up by making it seem like his concern was the bet.

"We never established what was going to happen if you win," she said.

"I thought you were so confident you didn't need to make allowances for the potential of me winning."

"To be totally fair, I have to. So. How about if I lose, then you teach me what you know about relationships," she said.

He nearly choked on the damn sandwich. "Relationships?"

"All right. Chemistry and stuff. The things that you seem to think that I don't understand."

His chest went tight, his airway constricting. And all

the blood in his body rushed down south of his belt. And just like he'd warned Rose, it was really hard to think when a man didn't have any blood in his brain. And currently, he was struggling. Struggling to form a coherent thought. Struggling to remember why it was a bad idea to pull her into his arms and teach her about chemistry here and now.

To explain to her exactly what it was she felt when he had touched her on the waist.

Because he had seen it.

She'd been confused. And she had looked at him like he was a stranger. She might not know why that was, but he did. In that moment, she had wanted him. Had wanted more of his hands on her body. More of his touch.

And he sure as hell had wanted to follow that line of inquiry that had flashed through her eyes.

Had wanted to answer all the questions he'd seen there. Questions he knew she didn't even realize she had.

But he wouldn't. He hadn't then, he wouldn't now.

"Sure," he said, his voice rough, knowing he wouldn't do anything of the kind, but also knowing he was not in a position to issue any denials at the moment, either. "Not saying you'll like the lesson. It'll involve you admitting you're wrong."

"If I lose," she said. "But if I don't lose I'm not wrong."

"But then who will tell you about *teeth*?"

Her cheeks went cherry again and he knew he'd overstepped. But this whole day was an overstep and it was her damn fault. He almost wanted her to win the bet.

It wasn't a good idea for him to explain anything to her.

Hell, eating a sandwich with her didn't feel safe.

Everything with her was thorny right about now. Just like the name.

"Then you have yourself a deal."

"Great."

But he didn't mean it. Nothing about this was great. But he lost control somewhere back there. Back where, he didn't know. Maybe he'd lost it longer ago than he realized. Maybe he hadn't been doing as good of a job pushing his attraction for her back as he'd imagined.

Because he had the feeling that his agreement now wasn't so much to placate her, but was allowing him to edge closer to dangerous territory.

Rose smiled at him. She had no idea what the hell was going on in his mind right now. Then it was for the best.

If he hadn't felt like a big enough bastard already, now it was even worse.

It was too bad she hadn't left him out here alone with the cows.

CHAPTER FIVE

BY THE TIME Rose came in for dinner, she was cold and sticky with sweat. It was one of the worst things about working outside in the winter. She could still manage to fire herself up into a clammy sweat, then she ended up shivering.

She could smell stew and fresh made bread, and she gave thanks for Iris and her amazing skills in the kitchen yet again.

Stomach growling, she took her hat off and threw it on the couch, and the three farm dogs rushed into the room. Their Australian shepherd jumped up onto the couch and immediately pounced on the hat.

"Hey," Rose scolded. "Don't do that."

Iris came into the room, making a shooing motion with her hands. The dogs ignored her. "I never wanted them to be in the house," she groused as they ran rings around the couch.

"Yeah, but there's nothing anyone can do about it. Because now they are in the house. And they think it's their house."

"I blame Sammy," Iris said darkly. "That little hippie is too permissive."

Of course, Iris loved Sammy as much as Rose did, and she knew she wasn't really mad at her. Well, maybe she was a little bit annoyed. But not seriously.

"Well, we let her in, too. So it's far too late to do anything about the dogs or Sammy and her permissiveness."

As if on cue, Sammy came down the stairs, her gait slightly unsteady, considering that she was currently six months pregnant. "I'm permissive of nothing right now," she said.

Ryder was close behind her. "She's not kidding," he said.

"*You* did this to me," she said, affecting a scowl. "I don't have to be permissive to you."

"I don't care. I like you stubborn," he said. "I liked you stubborn when we were just friends, why would I not like you stubborn when you were my wife?"

"True love," Sammy said, making her way into the kitchen. "I'm starving. This stew smells like true love to me."

"If Sammy ends up leaving me for a loaf of bread, no one be surprised," Ryder said.

Rose rubbed her nose, trying to get rid of some of the chill, then slipped her jacket off, leaving it haphazardly on one of the kitchen stools.

"Can you not?" Iris asked, picking it up and flinging it back at her.

Rose caught it. "I probably have to go back outside after dinner," she protested.

"It will take you two seconds to go hang it up."

Rose muttered as she went back into the living room to go hang her coat up on the peg. As soon as she touched the hook by the door, it opened.

And in walked Logan, looking as red-faced and cranky as she felt. "Fucking freezing out there," he muttered.

"No kidding."

They both quit moving, and suddenly, they were just

standing there staring at each other. Very close together. The warm air in the room seemed to expand between them.

And in that space it felt like their last conversation settled there and just stayed.

You aren't thinking about the fact you're talking about someone being inside you, Rose.

It's physical.

Hands.

Mouths.

Teeth.

"There's stew," she said, the statement falling out of her mouth and sounding exceedingly lame.

"Good," he said, his voice rough, probably from the cold winter air. "I'm starving."

"Me, too," she said.

Neither of them moved.

Rose realized that she was going to have to eventually.

But it felt like the air was made of molasses, and like the floor might be covered in a thick layer of muck—the kind that was mostly clay and sucked your boots down in deep, making it difficult to take a step. Something was holding her there.

And she had the oddest sensation of her stomach turning over inside her body when something flashed in Logan's blue eyes, and she had to ask herself if it was mud, molasses or that deep blue that reminded her of a summer sky holding her to the spot.

His eyes were familiar. Much like the beauty of the ranch around her, she woke up and saw those eyes every day.

She didn't think about them, consequently.

But she was considering them now. Deeply. As they considered her.

And she wondered.

What could he teach her?

What *would* he teach her?

"Dinner?" she squeaked.

"Yep," he said, his voice thick like the air, like the floor.

She swallowed and turned away from him, making her way toward the dining room. She could hear the heavy footfalls of his boots behind her. Pansy, West, and West's half brother Emmett had decided to join them for dinner. Which meant that it was a fairly full house. Rose liked it like this. It reminded her of being a kid. In spite of everything, it was a good memory for her. She had missed her parents terribly. But even then those years when the grief had been sharp and cutting, before it had dulled to an ache that just sort of sat there in her chest, before it had simply wrapped itself around her soul and become part of what she was, she hadn't felt alone.

She had missed her parents, but she had known that she wasn't an orphan. Not really.

Not in the way that those poor sad kids in that one movie were. Singing while they scrubbed the floors. She got to live in her house. She had her brother. Her sisters. Cousins.

Logan.

There had been a huge amount of security in that. Because something in her had felt confident that she would always have them. Yes, she had experienced loss. But this place was here. This house. These people.

It was the thing that sustained her. Preserved her.

Their chipped cups and plates, noisy get-togethers and animals running all around.

That sweet nostalgic mist was a lot more comforting than that moment back in the entryway when Logan's familiar eyes had become something else entirely.

"Arrest any bad guys?" Rose asked, sitting in the empty seat next to Pansy.

"No," she said. "I did have to tell off a deer that got into Mrs. Niedermayer's pond."

"I can't believe she has the nerve to call you and ask you to help her out, after she actively tried to keep you from getting your job," Rose said.

Barbara Niedermayer was a whole problem. A city councilperson with too much attitude, in her opinion. She knew that Barbara'd had it hard, with her son struggling with addiction issues and her husband leaving her a few years earlier, but that wasn't an excuse. She had tried to encourage Pansy to arrest West's younger brother, who had been causing a bit of trouble, granted, but the poor kid was all alone in the world. Rose had endless sympathy for that kind of thing. Considering she hadn't been alone because of the way her siblings had rallied around her.

West and Emmett hadn't been raised together, and they had a huge age difference, but of course once West had realized the situation that Emmett found himself in, he had taken the kid under his wing.

At the same time, Pansy had been starting a relationship with West and had been up for the job of chief of police. Barbara had been opposed to both lenience for Emmett, and Pansy getting that job.

Rose was still mad about it.

"Oh, you know Barbara," Pansy said. "I'm not supposed to take any of it personally. It was what she believed in, and she dug her heels in on it. But now things are different, and she is learning to adapt."

"If I were you, I would leave her garden and her pond to the deer."

"Yes, but it's better that Pansy is not as bloodthirsty as you are," Sammy pointed out. "Considering her position."

Rose shrugged. "I'm not bloodthirsty. I just believe in listening to people when they tell you who they are with their actions."

"You're suspicious," Iris said. "Naturally."

"I'm not, either."

She was a little. But parts of their childhood had been marked by visits from Child Protective Services, who had some natural concerns about Ryder handling the stress and grief of losing his parents and taking care of all the children. Even though they'd always been on the Danielses' side, Rose had always felt a little bit naturally suspicious. It was her deepest fear.

The loss of this safety net.

She had placed all of her trust in it. Even when she had discovered how harsh and cruel the world could be, losing her parents, her aunt and uncle, Logan's mother... They had been left with each other. And she had been sure on every level but the deepest one that that meant they would always be together.

But it was that core of her. That deepest part of her heart that feared losing this, too.

So yeah, she always had a little bit of suspicion when it came to stern-faced older women. Particularly ones that had power within the community.

Not fair, she knew. But it was that sense that they had power over her life that bothered her.

"Maybe a bit," she conceded. "But I just didn't like the way she took after Pansy. Or Emmett."

Emmett shrugged. "She's not so bad. I got to plant flowers for her a couple of times since then. At the community center, and at her house."

"We felt it was the right thing to do, considering he broke into her car," West said.

Emmett looked sheepish. "I did," he muttered.

"I still think she's a battle-ax," Rose said, reaching to the center of the table and taking a generous ladle of stew, pouring it into her bowl.

That was when she realized that all the bowls matched. "What's this?"

"I bought new bowls," Sammy said. "There's this woman that comes down to the market on Sundays and—"

"But what happened to the ones we always eat out of?"

"The chipped ones that don't match?" Sammy asked.

"Yeah, those," Rose said.

"They're in a box, in one of the barns. I thought you never know when we might need extra dishes, and I sincerely doubt anyone is going to want them."

"They're fine," Rose protested.

"I wanted matching dishes," Sammy said. "I live in the house now and…"

Rose tuned out the rest of Sammy's explanation, breaking off a piece of bread and biting into it angrily.

She didn't know why it bothered her. Unfamiliar bowls, and the familiar-unfamiliar blue of Logan's eyes. It was a weird, strange thing to get worked up about.

And if it wasn't for that moment in the entry with Logan she might not have.

Things were changing. That was the problem. Sammy and Ryder had found each other in a way that they hadn't before, and Sammy lived here now. It was her house. She was the…the matriarch. Except, it was Iris's kitchen, too. And Iris had never thought that the bowls needed to be changed out. Sammy hadn't seemed to think so until they were married and she was having a baby.

"What do you think of the new bowls?" she asked Iris, in spite of herself.

"I love them," Iris said. "I'm not attached to tableware that's falling apart."

Rose didn't know why she was.

And she didn't know why this was bothering her, considering that one of the things she was advocating for right now involved change. If Iris ended up with Elliott, things would change. She wanted Ryder and Sammy to be together—that was change. She was happy for West and Pansy, and that had brought about change, had brought new people into their lives.

She didn't know why something as stupid as bowls were bothering her.

Conversation shifted and changed around her—sometimes five or six times in ten minutes—and she just sat in silence. If anyone noticed that it was angry or uncharacteristic they didn't comment.

"Now, when I was shooing the deer out of her pond I did talk to Barbara about the upcoming Christmas parade."

"Don't tell me she's involved in that," Rose said.

"Yes," Pansy said patiently. "She is. It's my first Christmas as police chief, and this is one of the largest events that we hold in the town. I want it to be special. And I want to help in any way I can. Keeping it safe, keeping it organized… Just everything. And if my lovely family could find it in them to get involved, that would be great."

"Why do we have to get involved?" Ryder asked. "Doesn't what's his face Dodge always do a bunch of stuff for this?"

"Yes," Pansy said. "Wyatt Dodge does a hell of a lot every year for this. But I don't see why we can't contribute, as well."

The steel in her sister's tone made it very apparent that this was not a suggestion. Pansy was going to enforce the involvement of her family if it was the last thing she did.

"What is it you had in mind?" Rose asked.

"Well, I'm glad that you wondered. Because what I would like is for Sammy to do a jewelry-making demonstration—which is also going to be a great opportunity for you to sell your work—I would like Iris to bake some goodies, and the rest of you need to help with float assembly and other manual labor."

"I don't get a special job?" Rose asked.

She had gone from feeling mildly peevish to being outright annoyed.

"Do you want a special job?"

"Well, Iris and Sammy get special jobs. The girls get special jobs. Except for me."

"If it makes you feel any better my job is basically a manual labor one, too."

"It doesn't make me feel better."

"Do you want to help bake?" Iris asked.

"Spare me your pity bread," Rose said. "Fine. It's fine. I'll help with assembly and general lifting of things." She lifted up her arm and flexed, showing the evidence of all the hard work that she did around the ranch. "I guess that's what I get for spending all my time outside."

"Well, now," Logan said. "There's something to that. We could give a demonstration."

Rose's mouth dropped open. She couldn't believe Logan had volunteered to be part of this. Not at all. He didn't do Christmas. While the Danielses had never skipped a Christmas, Ryder doing his best to carry on normalcy even in the face of grief, Logan withdrew every year.

He didn't open gifts. He didn't exchange them. He didn't go to Christmas parades.

"Why?" she asked, the question sounding exceedingly dumb.

"Because you want to do something. So, I say we do something."

"What? Castrating pigs in traffic cones?" A lesser appreciated skill, she was sure.

"No, I was thinking maybe not castration. But what if we did a basic blacksmith demonstration?"

They weren't pros exactly, but they had basic ironworking skills and all the tools for it. Her cousin Jake was the one who did real accomplished blacksmithing stuff—it was what his dad had done on the side. But they had everything they needed for it at the ranch. "Do you think people would like that?"

"Sure," Logan said. "It'll be a cold day. We'll do stuff with fire and hot iron. Basic stuff. Let's make some horseshoes."

"Okay," Rose said.

"I think it's a great idea," Pansy said. "And no one has done it at the parade before. We can set you up far enough away from the booths that you won't light anything on fire, but close enough that people can meander down once they get cider and chili and all that."

"Great," Logan said.

"Now we just need to get all the other details finalized. Barbara wanted to have the parade at night this year. But I kindly pointed out the people might not want to stand out in weather that cold. Plus, we don't want it to be past the Girl Scouts' bedtime. So we're going to keep it separate from the tree lighting."

"Does she just change things for the sake of changing them?" Rose asked.

Again, she wasn't sure why this was bothering her so much. Except perhaps that it underlined the way things were moving and shifting in their family.

Moving on.

"I'm sure if you asked her that she would say no. Though sometimes it feels like it." Pansy sighed. "But you know, she does a lot for the community, and I'm grateful for her. I'm really not mad."

Rose was unmoved. "I'll be mad for you."

She took another piece of bread, and shot Iris a sly glance. "You made sourdough. Is that the same recipe you shared with Elliott?"

Ryder frowned. "You shared a recipe with Elliott?"

"She did," Rose said, giving her brother a furiously triumphant look.

"I did," Iris said, measured. "He's nice."

Again, her sister's tone sounded imbued with faint praise, but whatever. Iris was like that. She was cautious. Not one to show a great, outward display of… Well, much of anything. In Rose's opinion, her sister was one of the most delightful people in the world. But she did do her best to keep that information a secret that could only be given to a privileged few.

Iris was just reserved. It was how she was. It wasn't because she was snobby or anything like that. Iris had been forced to grow up far too early. Again, a sliver of guilt worked its way between Rose's ribs, and made it difficult to breathe.

Pansy was more even-tempered than Rose, but Pansy was stubborn and tough and couldn't have faded into the background if she'd made an effort. Rose had a bad habit of speaking and acting before she thought, and found that she rather enjoyed making the comment nobody else would. It seemed like a little bit of piss and vinegar ran in the family.

It made Rose wonder how much Iris had pushed down so that she could be the mature one. The one that took care of things.

"Color me shocked," Ryder said. "I figured you'd storm out of the bar and tell Rose where to shove it."

"I wouldn't do that," Iris said.

She wouldn't. That was the thing. Rose would. Pansy would. Ryder would. Iris wouldn't.

But surely Iris wouldn't let Rose run over her, either. They were sisters, and Iris could tell her whatever she needed to. Anyway, she didn't have to send the recipe to him.

"Elliott," Emmett said from his end of the table. "Is he the guy that does the water stuff? He came by the school a few weeks ago to install a new system. I dunno, something about expanding and needing more… I quit paying attention."

Emmett went to school on the Dalton ranch. The Daltons were West's family. His other set of half siblings. Apparently, Hank Dalton had bastard children littered around the country. West was one of them, and had only connected with his family a year or so earlier. But it had all worked out in the end, since his half brother Gabe had started a school for troubled youth, and his half brother from the other side, Emmett, was a little bit of a troubled youth.

"Yes," Rose confirmed. "That's him."

Emmett snorted. "Okay." West elbowed him. "Sorry," the kid said.

"Can we stop talking about it now?" Iris asked. "I would

much rather plan parade things. We only have a couple of weeks."

So they discussed parade business. And it wasn't until dinner was all finished and Rose had gone up to bed that she realized it was Logan who had jumped in and made sure she had something to do that she was excited about.

That made her think of his eyes again.

His eyes. And all the things he'd said to her earlier.

She didn't want to lose this bet.

Just considering losing the bet had her feeling...wrong.

She stripped off her clothes and walked into the bathroom that connected to her room, turning the shower on. She had never been half so grateful to wash the day off her body and she couldn't quite say why. Except that there was a general, strange electrical current running beneath her skin and she couldn't figure out the source.

So she did about the best thing she could think of. She didn't think about it at all. She scrubbed herself clean, got dressed and flung her tired, battered body into bed.

And if her dreams were full of blue, she chose not to remember them when she woke up.

CHAPTER SIX

NOT ONLY HAD he gotten himself roped into this whole parade thing, but thanks to the fact he hadn't been able to stop himself from jumping in to save Rose from disappointment, he also had to attend a planning meeting. He could think of nothing he would like less.

Well, at this point he could think of a few things.

It had been a hell of a week.

When he pulled into the parking lot of the community center, all he could think was that it was going to continue to be a hell of a week. He was allergic to stuff like this. Small-town politics and everything that went with them. People fighting to climb the social ladder of Gold Valley, which was a stepladder if he was being generous.

Add in Christmas and it was a potluck of hell.

And those people would collide with people like Pansy, who actually did things for the community for reasons other than their own self-aggrandizement, and all he would get was sad off-brand chocolate sandwich cookies and watered-down punch for the effort.

He pushed the door to the modest hall open and found all the folding chairs occupied already. He moved across the white-and-gray linoleum, standing toward the back.

The door opened not long after, and Rose scurried in. She looked around, and came to the same conclusion he did—that there was nowhere to sit—and then her eyes connected with his.

He was used to the tightening in his gut when she looked at him. He had to be.

But after the dance, the bet...

The idiot things he'd said to her about all she didn't know.

It was sharper now. Keener.

Which was all he needed considering it had been sharp enough before.

She waved at him, then tiptoed over to the table at the back, pouring two cups of punch while the woman that he didn't recognize continued to talk. She joined him against the back wall, handing him some punch.

He lifted it in mock salute, and she smiled.

They'd spent the whole day together, out in the field. There was just something about her out of context sometimes. Hell, there was something about her in context. He couldn't pretend otherwise.

Overall, the meeting was pretty boring, and didn't pertain to them. Then it was time for Barbara to take the floor.

"We have a few new submissions for space after the Christmas parade." She looked around the room, and it made him feel like he was in trouble. She reminded him of a particularly laser-focused teacher he'd once had who had always acted like he was up to no good.

In fairness, he had been.

But he wasn't now, neither was he a kid. The effect was still the same.

"Including," she continued, "a stall with baking activities, which gives me concerns regarding legality and the health department. A blacksmith demonstration, which could definitely be a fire hazard, and jewelry making."

All of that felt a bit pointed, and whatever Pansy had said about Barbara being fine with her being in her new position, he had to wonder if that was true.

"I feel like all of this needs to come under further review," she said. "We can't just go making changes to format simply because someone is in a new position and they are looking to leave their stamp on things."

He could feel Rose bristling beside him. "Don't do anything," he said, his voice low. "You know Pansy can handle herself."

"I will open the floor for discussion," Barbara said.

"I don't think there will be any more of a problem with my sister's booth than there would be with a general bake sale table," Pansy said, "if that helps with your concerns there."

"I have a food handlers' card."

That bit of information came from Iris, and while it wasn't a shock to anyone in the room, considering it wasn't a particularly huge revelation, it was definitely a surprise to him, and he could tell by the way that Rose's body jolted it was a surprise to her, too.

"Well," Barbara said, "that is something to consider. Though we are going to have to look into the cleanliness of the preparation. We need a station so that children can wash their hands."

"We can figure all of that out," Pansy said, keeping her voice even.

The way that Barbara moved on after that made Logan wonder if it actually wasn't personal. If the woman was just a stickler, and that there were no exceptions made at all. And every new idea was going to come under scrutiny, no matter who it came from.

"Now, the blacksmithing booth," she said. "I don't know

about that. It seems like a serious safety hazard, and we're definitely going to have to clear it with our insurance."

That was a fair enough point. He could tell by the tension in Rose's posture that she did not agree.

"As for the jewelry," she said, "we might have too much competition with the local shops, and we need to be very careful not to step on the toes of people who are grandfathered in to the booths."

"I don't mind," said Dana, the woman who owned Willow Creek, where most of the town's jewelry was sold. "I sell some of Sammy's designs in the store. And any demonstration that she does could only benefit me."

"It will be brought under advisement," Barbara said, clearly unmoved.

And that was when he felt Rose reach the end of her tether. "What I wonder," she said, "is if you keep shooting down other people's ideas so that no one will realize you don't have any."

Barbara's face went red. "Well," she sputtered. She was speechless, which was the first time anyone in the room had seen it.

A nervous giggle swept the crowd.

"I'm just saying. You know what they say. Those who can't do, plan or something like that?"

For the first time ever, Barbara Niedermayer didn't seem to have anything to say. And in fact, she said nothing else. She simply walked down from her position at the front of the room and took a seat.

An uncomfortable wave went through the room and Dana got up and started managing the meeting, speaking quickly and relaying the rest of the information as fast as possible. Logan looked over at Rose, who was leaning against the back wall, her arms crossed, her expression defiant.

As soon as the meeting was over and people began to disperse, he grabbed her arm and dragged her out the back door. "What the hell was that?"

"She's insufferable," Rose said. "I'm sick of her taking shots at my family. And Emmett is included in my family. I have a bad taste in my mouth from that already."

"She's one of those people," he said. "She means well, but she can't be flexible. She doesn't have friends, she doesn't have a family support system the way that you do."

She crossed her arms and looked up at him like he'd betrayed everything they were. "So I'm supposed to feel sorry for her?"

She was being…not as good as she could be. Or not as good as he gave her credit for anyway. To him, she was… bright and irrepressible but never mean. And Barbara might be difficult, but in the end she was a woman abandoned by a husband, whose son had abandoned her too, and Logan hated that.

It scraped against all his own feelings about his mother, and no, Barbara wasn't like his mother. Not even close. But his mom had been judged and she'd felt ostracized. And maybe Barbara was just…reacting to what she thought the town might give her back if she didn't lead with judgment of her own.

He knew what it looked like when women were left hurt and vulnerable. Victims of the choices men made, and scorned more than the ones that abandoned them ever would be.

He'd thought Rose would have the compassion to understand, too.

"Yes," he said. "You should. She doesn't have anyone.

You should give her some level of sympathy, a little bit of grace, dammit."

"Suddenly you're the expert on how to treat people?"

"At least in a room full of people, you should have the good sense to be kind to somebody who isn't working with as much as you are. Her husband is gone. He left her while their son spiraled into addiction. And you know that. So does everyone in that room. Doing things for the town is all she's got. Badly done, Rose."

He didn't know why it bothered him so much. Didn't know why everything about her was getting under his skin the way that it was now. But he couldn't stand to look at her. Not at this moment. So he turned and he walked away, leaving her there with no further explanation.

ROSE FELT WOUNDED. Scraped raw and even worse… Guilty. It wasn't fair. Barbara Niedermayer had deserved that. And what she had done wasn't that mean. She needed to be taken down a peg or two, and Rose had done it.

His face, his disapproval. It made her chest burn with humiliation.

Logan was often… Well, he was bossy like an older brother. He gave her a bad time. He told her she didn't know what she was doing or thinking, in that way an older sibling with a superiority complex might.

But this was different.

This wasn't him looking at her like a kid and claiming greater experience. He wasn't pretending to be long-suffering. He wasn't picking on her just to irritate her.

He'd looked at her like…like… It was disappointment and anger all in one and somehow it seemed to take down a wall between them.

On his side, he was the protector. On her side, the impetuous one that pushed and cajoled him and reluctantly made him smile.

That look… It had been something else and it burned her down in her soul.

She pushed it away because anger was easier.

How dare he? How dare he treat her like this? He wasn't perfect. He might think he was, all high-and-mighty and certain of attraction and *teeth*.

He didn't know everything. And he didn't get to tell her how to behave.

When she got into the car with Iris, she was still fuming. And of course, Logan had taken off immediately after scolding her like she was a child. He was such an absolute ass.

"Are you all right?" Iris asked.

"No," she muttered.

"I don't remember you ever losing your temper like that before," she said softly, the words a gentle introduction to the subject, but Rose could sense there was more emotion beneath her sister's words.

"I always lose my temper," Rose said. "I'm plainspoken. I say it like it is. The fact that anybody was surprised by that today is not my problem."

"You're often plainspoken, but you don't usually embarrass people."

She gritted her teeth. "Are you going to lecture me, too?"

"Who else lectured you?"

"Never mind," Rose said. She didn't want to talk about it. She didn't want to reflect on the impression his fingers had left on her arm, and the way his eyes had burned into her as he'd read her the riot act.

"Fine," Iris said. "Don't talk to me. Maybe you should talk to Logan."

Her head whipped around. "What?"

"Well, he's the one that you usually go to when you need to discuss something. And obviously something is going on with you."

"Nothing is going on with me. It's too bad Elliott wasn't at the meeting."

"Yes," Iris persisted. "Something *is* going on with you. I can tell because you don't want to talk about it. You so profoundly don't want to talk about it that you changed the subject to Elliott. I'm almost tempted to think that the real reason you're trying to set me up with him is because you need distracting from something that concerns you."

"I…" Rose sputtered. "I do not. Nothing is different with me. Nothing."

Silence settled in the car.

"Is that the problem?" Iris asked gently.

"No," Rose said. "Why would that be a problem?"

"It is for me sometimes. Nothing is different with me, either. And that's hard. I'm so happy for Ryder and Sammy, and I'm happy for Pansy and West. But I'm a little bit sad for me."

In the middle of her misery, Rose felt slightly validated. Because she'd just known Iris wasn't happy. She knew it. "We've all been one thing for so long," Rose said softly. "It shifting like this is weird. Good, but weird."

"Yeah," Iris agreed.

"Do you think…do you think if you hadn't had to take care of me your life would be different?" Rose asked, the question sticking in her throat.

"Our lives would have been different if that plane hadn't crashed," Iris said. "Us being there for each other wasn't the bad part. I was fourteen, and it felt like everything good in the whole world was gone when we lost Mom and Dad.

But there was you, Rose. You were good. Don't feel bad about me taking care of you. I don't."

Rose blinked back tears. She swallowed hard, but her throat felt tight, and she couldn't maneuver around the lump that had settled there.

"Just trust me," Rose said. "I'm fine."

"The problem, Rose," Iris said, "is that I'm not totally sure you would know if you weren't."

That dug underneath Rose's skin. And she decided to go ahead and be done with the conversation because there was really nowhere else for it to go.

When she tumbled out of the car, Iris started walking toward the house, but Rose didn't want to. She was too keyed up, and she needed to do something to clear her head.

"I'm going to the barn," she said.

Maybe she would go for a ride. Or maybe she would… clean a stall. Hope that it was a little bit dirty so that she had something to do.

She was not looking for Logan. She wanted to avoid Logan. He was actively being a jerk to her, and there was no reason for her to talk to him.

What her sister had said about how he was the person she talked to stuck in her craw, especially now.

ROSE GROWLED AROUND the barn for a while, raking dirt that didn't need to be raked and digging through shavings that were just fine.

She tried not to think of Logan.

She closed her eyes and took a deep breath, leaning against the shovel she was holding. The way he had looked at her. Those electric blue eyes.

Badly done.

She couldn't remember ever being scolded like that in her life.

She was twenty-three years old, and he was scolding her like she was a child. It was what he always did. In fact, it was what he had been doing for weeks now. Questioning everything she said, everything she did. Where did he get off?

Where did he get off being *right*?

The way he'd been lately…he'd been filled with lectures. And he had danced with her.

And he had disapproved of her in such a deep and horrible way tonight. Like he was above reproach. Like he was some beacon of kindness and goodness to the people of the community.

Not that he was a bad guy. He wasn't. He was nice, and he had always been nice to work with and be around. Until recently. It was hard now, and she didn't know why. She didn't know why lately talking to him was like walking through the woods, trying to work her way through a thicket full of thorns.

That brought her right back.

To sitting with him and eating sandwiches. To those eyes clashing with hers as he said it.

You're talking about someone being inside you, Rose.
Skin to skin.

The memory made her throat dry and her already pounding heart throb and she pushed all that toward anger.

He'd made everything strange and difficult. It was his fault. All of this was.

She prowled to the machine shed, and then started making her way down the line of outbuildings.

It wasn't that she was looking for him.

She was looking for something to do.

And Iris's suggestion kept on ringing in her ears.

That Rose talk to Logan. So she should talk to him about this, too.

"I don't need to. I don't need to. His opinion has been nothing but annoying. Nothing."

She saw his eyes again, not as they were when he was her friend, or even that moment when he'd come into the house the other night and everything had felt sideways.

But the way he'd looked at her today.

It had been different and she didn't know how or why, but it had been.

Some part of her needed to see him again.

To know.

She found herself pushing the door open to one of the barns they didn't commonly use, the barn that housed the blacksmithing supplies. Somehow, she had a feeling he would be there. Maybe related to the reason they had gone to the meeting in the first place.

It was hot in there, of course it was, because he had the forge fired up. The contrast between the air inside and outside was enough to take her breath away. At least, that's what she told herself it was.

Because there he was, standing at the anvil, hammering. And he wasn't wearing a shirt. Of course not. Because it was hot.

It was hot.

That kept playing in her head, over and over again.

So very hot.

He lifted his arm, and every muscle in his torso flexed and stretched before he brought the hammer down on the blazing metal that rested on the anvil. Sparks flew, a few of them hitting him right in his broad chest. But he didn't flinch.

His jaw was clenched, his expression intense.

He lifted the hammer again, and this time her eye was drawn to his biceps, his powerful shoulders. The way every part of his body seemed to move in service to this powerful explosion of strength.

They couldn't do a blacksmith demonstration at a Christmas parade. It was a family event. There would be children.

This was not appropriate.

It was…

Logan.

Her chest felt tight, her breath freezing. It hurt. It physically hurt. Her body, her lungs. Something about the way she had solidified there in her place, unable to move. Unable to breathe.

"I have a bone to pick with you," she said, the words rushing out of numb lips. She had no idea how she managed to say them. Especially because she had no breath.

"I'm sorry, what?" He turned, giving her a full, broad view of his chest. Smudged with soot and ash and dirt, and chest hair. Each and every muscle perfectly defined. He lifted the arm that was still holding the hammer, muscles straining as he wiped sweat from his forehead.

His eyes looked even brighter, surrounded by the dirt on his face, there in the dark.

She pushed past it. Pushed past the tangle in her chest, in her lungs, and went right at him.

"You heard me. You were… You were unfair, and you were mean to me. You keep treating me like a child. And it isn't fair. I'm not a child. And I'm not somebody that you can just lecture all the time. You don't think I know anything," she said, getting a good rant all built up in her chest. Oh, yes. She was ready to fight. She was ready to scream. Good and loud, too. "I have worked with you on this ranch for years. I know just as much as you do about any of the work we do here. What makes you think I don't know anything about life? I've caught calves and I've buried them. I lost my parents. I know what it feels like to lose things." She felt her tongue about to tip her right over the edge of decency. She'd been pushing it all day, starting with Barbara, and she was going further, worse now, and she did it anyway. "I know what it feels like to grieve. Twice what you did. Don't you dare treat me like I don't know my feelings."

Sparks burned in the blue, and his anger was like a palpable force. Good. She'd wanted it.

"Be careful, Rose," he said, his voice a growl.

She expected him to go on. To give her the fight she craved.

He didn't.

He turned back to the anvil.

"Don't you dismiss me," she said. "You don't have the right to dismiss me."

He didn't look back at her. She looked around, then she saw an empty soda can on the floor. She picked it up and hurled it at him. It hit him in the shoulder.

"What the *fuck*, Rose?"

"I said *don't dismiss me*," she said.

"You're acting like a child. You are quite literally throwing a tantrum here, while you tell me that you should be taken seriously. I think even you can appreciate how ridiculous that is."

"See? Even that. I'm the closest thing you have to a business partner, Logan. And suddenly you're acting like I'm a thousand years younger than you."

"You are. A decade younger than me, Rose. And the only reason you think you know everything is because you don't.

You profoundly don't. The difference between you and me is that I know all the things I don't know."

"That's a contradiction. You can't know what you don't know."

"You can. And I do."

"Just… I've had it with you," she said. "I'm right about Elliott and Iris. Barbara Niedermayer needed to be put in her place. She has no right to treat us this way just because she's resentful that Pansy has a position of power. And you know why she does it. The same reason that you're a jerk to me. Because I'm a woman. Because I'm young."

"I am not a jerk to you because you're young and a woman. I am a jerk to you because somebody has to be. Everybody else is a little bit overindulgent of you and your shenanigans. If I were Iris I would've told you where to shove it."

"Well, hopefully you'll get an opportunity to after all the stuff with Elliott works out, because then I'll get to set you up."

"You are not setting me up, little girl. Not happening."

"Why not? You don't seem to be able to set yourself up."

"Did you ever think maybe I'm making a choice."

"A choice to be alone?"

"A choice to be a better person than I damn well want to be."

The air crackled between them, hotter than the forge, louder than the pop of the sparks around them.

She closed the space between them, and with an open palm pressed her hand against his chest and shoved him back. Her skin felt scalded, and she ignored it. "I deserve your respect."

"You want me to start treating you like an equal? You want me to treat you like a woman?"

She took a step closer to him, something driving her that she couldn't name. Something dangerous churning in her gut. That she couldn't define it enraged her, because it fell into line with everything he had just said. That there was something out there, a great mystery that she wasn't privy to. Something that he knew, that she never would.

"You wouldn't know how. You still look at me and see a kid who needs her shoes tied. But I'm a woman who can put on her own damn cowgirl boots, and I don't need you to tell me how it is."

He took a step toward her, and another, those blue eyes never leaving hers. It was like that moment in the hallway had been a taste of this. The thunder in the distance. And now here it was, all around her. The storm.

She took a step back, then another, until her shoulder blades hit the rough wood wall of the barn. And still he was coming. Six foot plus of large, angry man, who could wield a mallet with no effort, who could pick a calf up off the ground and effortlessly heft a bale of hay.

And it didn't scare her, having all that strength right there, not even with him full of rage.

No, it was something else that twisted her insides now. Something else that made her stomach tight. And there was a big, panicked blank in her brain as she tried to figure out what it might be.

"You don't want that," he said. "Trust me, you don't.

"And do you know why you need somebody to tell you what's happening? It's not because you're stupid, Rose. It's because you don't want to see the damn world around you. And I can understand why. Because yeah, I do know the grief that you know. And more. I didn't lose both my parents, but my dad is a son of a bitch. Make no mistake about that. You think he's not in my life because I don't know who he is? I choose not to acknowledge that asshole. He's still walking around alive and my mother is dead. You want to talk about grief? That's grief. Oh, I know all about not wanting to see the world for what it is, but you take denial to a whole new level. You think that you can believe something into existence. That if you say Elliott doesn't want you and he wants your sister it will be true. But it's not."

He was talking. Saying so many things and she couldn't get them all straight. His father. But he was so close and she couldn't breathe.

"It..."

"You don't know what it means to have a man want you. And no, I don't mean him. He's got a little schoolboy crush on you because he doesn't know what it means to want a woman any more than you know what it means to want a man. But I know, Rose. I know."

His stare was hard and hot and she felt like it was pinning her right to that wall. "I'm so confident you're going to lose our bet, I could give you lesson one in chemistry right now."

She shivered, and he kept talking. "And if I were to teach you even half of what I know you would burn and bend like that metal I was just pounding. You wouldn't survive it. So strong, little girl, until you get heated up. You don't even know where that begins and ends."

He reached out then, and rough fingertips made contact with her cheek. She shivered as he traced a line down the side of her neck to her collarbone, where he dragged his thumb back and forth. Just like he had done on the dance floor.

That touch.

It wasn't just a touch.

There were layers to it. More to it than she had realized.

And she felt it. She didn't just feel it where he touched, but she felt it down deep. Felt it in her stomach. In her lungs, as she fought to drag in breath.

Felt it between her legs.

Logan's touch.

Chemistry.

She gasped, and she pulled away from him, putting as much distance between the two of them as possible.

"That's what I thought," he said. "Why don't you run along, and we can forget that this happened. You can go back to seeing life the way you want. But when you have to get reality checks, don't you get mad at me. Don't you get mad at me for telling you all the things that you refuse to see, Rose Daniels. Because you want it that way. You want to keep running. And sometimes I have to stop you from running off a cliff."

She did run. She ran like he was the very devil, chasing right after her. She ran like her life depended on it.

She started walking when she approached the house, when she got to the porch. She walked up the steps slowly, and pushed the door open.

Her whole family was in there. Dragging boxes out of the closet and unpacking Christmas decorations.

The one good thing about Christmas was that it would ward Logan off like it was garlic and he was a vampire. But right now she didn't feel like being in the middle of the circus, either.

She couldn't face this. Not now. Couldn't deal with cheer, Christmas or otherwise. Couldn't deal with her family, especially not *en masse*. Not while everything inside of her felt like it was bright with heat. Just like that horseshoe.

Just like he'd said.

Except, right about now she didn't feel like she was going to bend. She felt like she was going to break.

"Rose," Iris said. "We're getting Christmas decorations out."

"I was thinking tomorrow we could go up to Caleb Dalton's place and cut down our own Christmas tree." That suggestion came from Pansy.

"I... Sure," she said. She ducked her head, and moved through the room. "I just have to... Bathroom."

She ran upstairs as quickly as she could, her breath coming in harsh, uneven bursts. She flung the door open to the bathroom and looked at herself in the mirror.

Horror twisted her stomach.

There was a dark smudge on her cheek, a trail down her neck, to her collarbone.

She leaned in closer, drawing her shirt down, examining the path that his touch had taken. She started to breathe hard, and she felt dizzy.

She wasn't afraid of Logan. This wasn't fear. It couldn't be. He was the closest thing to...

Not a brother.

No. He wasn't.

He wasn't now, and he never could be.

He was...

She wasn't afraid. It wasn't fear that had her breath coming in the short, harsh gasps. It wasn't fear that made her heart race like this.

It certainly wasn't fear that made her pulse echo between her thighs.

Wasn't fear that had stopped her in the doorway and kept her staring at his muscles, either.

Logan Heath had turned her on.

It was like a flash bomb had gone off in her stomach,

decimating everything, and lighting it up at the same time. She had never been turned on by a man in practice. In theory, sure. Handsome men who graced movie screens and country artists who sang the sort of songs that spoke of dark nights and intimacy she didn't quite understand.

This was personal. It was real. He had been close enough to touch, and he had touched her. They had been sharing the same air. And his eyes... His eyes.

Why had no other men ever gotten to her? Now it seemed important to know, and she couldn't sort it out. Were there really no men around that seemed attractive to her or was it something to do with him?

The thought made her stomach pitch.

Nothing about him felt familiar right now.

Nothing about herself felt familiar.

She had to forget that happened. She had to. He'd been proving a point. Teaching her a lesson, and he'd said so. He'd been trying to scare her, like he'd been trying to do the other day when they'd been having sandwiches and he'd said all those things about intimacy. It hadn't been... to make her feel *this*.

No. Not for this. It couldn't have been.

She turned on the sink, ran cold water over her wrists. Then she looked at the smudge on her cheek, and took her wet fingers, scrubbing at it. Then at her neck. Her collarbone. Until it was gone. The evidence of all that had happened.

Except even as she left the bathroom, no longer bearing evidence of his touch she felt like it was still there, sunk down deep beneath her skin.

Like it still burned.

She did her best to smile. Her best to join her family in looking at Christmas decorations.

Go right back to ignoring the world.

Except she couldn't.

Because the things she ignored, she had been unaware of. The thing she ignored, she really hadn't known about.

She hadn't known what she hadn't known.

And now, because of his hands, because of that thumb, she did.

And she didn't see how she was ever going to be okay again.

CHAPTER SEVEN

THAT HAD BEEN a mistake. A huge damn mistake. He had never intended for it to go that far. He had never intended to put himself in that kind of position. Not ever. Not with her.

He'd always seen her as someone to be protected, and then something about yesterday...

She'd made a mistake.

And somehow that made her more touchable. Made it seem like she was more in his reach instead of up in the stars, protected by virtue of the fact she was Rose. A sort of otherworldly being to him.

And no, he didn't think she was a kid. He knew she was a woman.

He damn well knew it.

But he had put her on a pedestal. Put her out of reach.

Now that she'd fallen to earth with him...

He'd touched her. He'd touched her and she'd been as soft as he'd let himself fantasize she might be.

There wasn't an amount of physical labor to burn that out of him. He had continued to pound iron, but it had just reminded him of her. Of what he'd promised. Of how the heat between them would light her up. Ignite her. Ignite them both.

Hell, getting close to her like that, touching her the way that he had...

It had been damn near *innocent*. Compared to the way

he had touched women in the past. She had been fully clothed. He had put his hand on her cheek, on her neck, on her collarbone.

And he burned. All the way down. He was burned all the way to his soul. Little Rose Daniels was going to be the death of him. She had already become the death of everything potentially good or honorable inside of him.

Hell, if Ryder had any idea what he had wanted to do in that moment...

What he'd wanted to do in the moment was bad enough. Because he was supposed to protect her. He *felt* protective of her. Like she'd said, they knew the same grief. And he had known her since she was a child grappling with it. But the problem was, he wasn't confused about the fact that she was a woman. Because he did see her as a business partner. Because they worked together day in and day out. Because he had watched her grow from a child into an adolescent, into a smart-ass teenager, into a strong woman. Because he didn't doubt for one moment that she had the kind of maturity and passion to burn them both to the ground.

But she was avoiding it.

That he was right about. There was a reason she was fixating on doing things for Iris. On worrying about his loneliness.

Determinedly not seeing that Elliott so clearly had a crush on her, and redirecting it all toward Iris.

She didn't want to see any of this. Didn't want to know any of it. Him forcing it on her was...

She was denying it all for a reason, and hell if he knew what it was. He wasn't the person to try and figure it out, either. He was his own whole mess.

He gritted his teeth, making sure everything in the forge

was well handled before pushing the door open and greeting the cold air like an old friend.

"Well," came an all-too-familiar voice from behind him, "you look…angry."

He turned and saw Sammy standing there, her pregnant belly round, her eyes far too knowing. It was easy to see, even in the darkness.

"What the hell are you doing here?"

"We are doing Christmas decorating. So I came to see if you were committed to your yearly avoidance. And to see how you were because I know you hate this time of year."

"Just working."

"Okay. You seem pissed."

"Christmas," he growled. "And I'm roped into this whole parade thing and I'd rather not deal with it. You know that."

"Right." Sammy let out a slow breath. "And it has nothing to do with why Rose came running into the house looking like the hounds of hell were on her heels. And why she had soot on her face."

He gritted his teeth and looked square at his friend. "Are you accusing me of something?"

"Just a suspicion. One that's been growing for a while."

"I haven't touched her," he said, the lie tasting like grit on his tongue. "I mean, not like you're implying."

"But there's something there."

"It doesn't matter, Sammy. She's a kid."

"I don't think you mean that, Logan. Because while all of us sometimes fall into treating her like the baby around here, you never do."

"You know what I mean."

"You mean that you think you're not right for her. And that my husband would kick your ass."

"That," he confirmed.

"I can't keep secrets from him," Sammy said, her voice soft, a little regretful. Because he knew if Sammy would keep a secret for anyone, it would probably be him. But never from Ryder.

"There's not a secret to tell," he said. "I swear that."

A look of understanding dawned on her face. "That's why you were sitting out on the porch that night. When I left Ryder's bedroom."

"I told you, I was thinking about everything I shouldn't do." He took a sharp breath, the air cutting his lungs. "And I know what the hell I can't do. Don't worry."

She didn't say anything for a moment. She looked up at the stars, like she was trying to choose the right words. "Good," she said finally. "I love you, Logan. I really do. Like a brother. And I want you to be happy. I want Rose to be happy."

"You don't think I'll make her happy." He shook his head. "Neither do I. If I did..."

"It's different for us. It's different for us because we're not really part of them."

"I know that. I mean, you are now." She looked away. "Don't. I mean, don't feel bad about that. I'm not insulting you, or trying to be mean. Look, I'm not the kind of guy who falls in love. I'm around her a lot. I feel some things. But I'm man enough to know what it is. And I'm man enough not to act on lust. She and I had a little fight. It got a bit out of hand. But hell, you know Rose, she can take care of herself." He tried to laugh. "She threw a soda can at me."

"I do know she can take care of herself."

"You don't need to come out here and play mama bear."

She sighed heavily. "The problem is I feel like a mama bear to both of you."

"You don't have to. And I know what I am. I know what I can do, and what I shouldn't do."

Sammy was silent for a long moment. "Yeah, I knew all those things about myself, too. And now here I am."

He couldn't tell if Sammy was arguing for or against. And he had a feeling she didn't know, either. Because they'd gone over all this when she and Ryder's relationship had changed from friendship to more. The drawbacks. The risks. And in the end for her it had worked. So he could see why she felt torn now. Afraid him and Rose crossing a line would destroy all they'd built, also afraid she was telling him to turn away from love.

But that was all fine and good for her and Ryder.

Not him.

He was different. He was scarred.

Broken.

Rose wouldn't heal that. He'd just break her, too.

"Not everything ends the way it did for you two," he said.

"It could for you. If you wanted it to."

"With someone who's not Rose, though, right?"

"She's so young, and it isn't that I don't think you're great."

"You can't say anything to me that I haven't said to myself," he said. "Did you think I wanted to wake up one day attracted to Ryder's sister? I didn't. I agree with every reason you have that it's not going to happen with her."

"I know. But that doesn't mean it can't happen with someone."

"You're confusing a few things. The fact that I think she's hot doesn't mean I want anything else. That's the issue."

She looked at him skeptically.

"Don't do that," he said. "Don't psychoanalyze me. I don't need your hippie-dippy feelings bullshit."

"Fine," she said. "But Logan, there is someone out there for you. I know it."

He knew that she believed it. She believed that because she was able to heal from the wounds of her past, because Ryder had been able to heal from the wounds in his, that it meant they all could. Him, too.

But she didn't know. Not really. She didn't understand.

He had the kind of guilt that dogged a man like a demon straight out of hell. The kind of stuff that you didn't want to bother a partner with. The kind of stuff you didn't heal from.

He didn't want to see Ryder and Sammy slaves to the pain that they'd gone through. And he knew that Sammy thought it was the same with him.

The same kind of pain.

It wasn't. It couldn't be.

His mom had been the most important person in his life. She'd chosen to have him, to raise him. To make him the center of her world, and he'd made her the center of his right back. All he'd ever wanted was to protect her.

He didn't give a damn about his biological father. And he'd ignored his existence. The existence of his half brothers. Half sister. No matter what changed. No matter how close they got. He refused to acknowledge the connection because of the pain the man had caused his mom.

And Logan…

All he'd wanted was to give back to her.

He'd saved and saved for the best Christmas present he could think of.

The memory made his stomach turn sour.

No. There was no place for moving on. Not for him.

"Thanks for checking in. I'm just going to go back up to the cabin."

"All right," she said. "You can't avoid Christmas forever."

"I damn well can."

"No," Sammy said gravely. "You can't. I'm fruitful, and round with the life that I'm creating, which has made me gloriously filled with nesting instincts. I want nothing more than to bedeck every hall with a bow of holly. And you will not escape, Logan Heath."

"Watch me," he said, turning away from her.

But even in the middle of all his irritation, in the middle of this insanity with Rose, he felt remarkably grateful for Sammy.

She was the one person who came close to knowing how he felt about anything.

And yeah, she was perilously close to some home truths that lived inside of him, and perilously close to a man who would cheerfully snap him in half if he found out the kinds of things he thought about his sister, but still, all things considered it was good that he'd talked to Sammy.

It put it in perspective.

Because even Sammy thought he was bad for Rose.

Sammy was a romantic. She was an optimist. And she certainly saw better in him than he did.

If she couldn't even see a way for the two of them to have something, then the possibility didn't exist.

It wasn't just a road to nowhere. It wasn't a road at all.

And hell, he busted on through some brush tonight. Forged a path where there shouldn't have been one, forced to recognize something that he shouldn't have. But it didn't matter.

He would get it together. And he would deal with himself.

It was going to have to start with not caring quite so damn much about the whole situation with Elliott and Iris and Rose.

It was a mistake she was going to have to make.

And he didn't need to be there when she fell. Didn't need to be the one to pick her up.

In fact, he desperately needed to not be that man. She didn't want him to be. That should be enough. It had to be.

ROSE WAS STILL feeling peevish the next day. She was up early the next morning, as was her routine, but Iris was up much earlier than usual, and that irritated Rose, who wanted to sit in silence and marinate in her feelings.

"Elliott heard about your performance at the town meeting," Iris said prosaically.

"And how do you know that?" Rose asked, suddenly much more interested in the interaction.

"He texted me," Iris said.

Iris looked a little bit pleased and that made Rose feel good. Though that it was about her and her moral failings, as they all seemed to see it, didn't make her feel good.

"Well, I'm a little bit sorry that it's town gossip. But that's it."

"Rose, I thought you'd at least feel a little bad about it."

"No," Rose said, stubborn. "I am not the one who should feel bad."

"She's sad, Rose. You can't find any pity for her?"

Badly done, Rose.

And that was when inconvenient memories of the night before crashed into her brain, along with the vision of very angry blue eyes.

What would Iris think if she knew about that?

That he had backed her up against the wall. That he had…touched her.

He touched your face. With his thumb. You're the one that has turned his thumb into some kind of symbolic object.

She cleared her throat. "Anyway. I just want coffee. Not a lecture."

"You're unrepentant," Iris said.

"Well, so is she. About everything." She thought back to Logan's words. To what he had said about her being less fortunate in some ways than Rose was. Was that true?

With some of her anger mown down, it was easier to see his words more clearly. That annoyed her. Because she was…well, she was annoyed at him and she didn't want to see his point.

She'd been able to admit that he was…well, that he was right about some things last night. But that feeling hadn't come with any real clarity or introspection. But here it was.

She tended to think that no one was a whole lot less fortunate than the group of them. They had lost their parents, after all.

But she was loved. For the first time she wondered if anybody actually loved Barbara.

"What?" Iris asked.

"Nothing," she said. "It's just that… Now I'm thinking that Logan might be right." His name tasted funny on her tongue. What had been familiar only yesterday now seemed foreign.

"Well," Iris said, "that's something."

"Why are you so worried about it?"

She huffed. "Well, as a singular object of pity in a small town, maybe I feel badly for her."

"You are *not* Barbara."

"Sure."

"And anyway, Elliott is crazy about you."

Iris's lips twitched slightly. "I'm not sure that I would go so far as to interpret a few texts as *crazy* about me."

"You need to have more confidence in yourself," Rose said.

But her mind was halfway occupied on all the things Logan had said to her last night. It made her wonder if she had slightly too much confidence in herself.

"I don't know what I should have," Iris said. "I've never... This is the closest I've ever come to dating someone, okay?" Her sister's cheeks were pink. "And it doesn't feel how I thought it would and I'm trying to process it all so...so. Anyway, eat your breakfast."

Rose obliged, because she was starving. She would have normally felt a little bit more satisfied over Iris's admission that she felt something for Elliott, but she was consumed by unease over her present situation.

That made her feel guilty.

This was all supposed to be about Iris and somehow things were spinning and twisting inside of her and making her...

She pushed her thoughts away and she collected a couple of old mugs and took the old blue-and-white metal kettle out of the pantry, pouring coffee from the carafe into it. Then she went to the living room, took her coat and hat off the peg by the door, stepped into her boots and slipped outside. It was freezing.

Early in the morning, the sun had yet to rise, and the chill in the air spoke of frost and impending snow. She supposed given that they were into December now that was normal, but the first bite of freeze in winter always took her a little bit off guard.

Changing seasons brought with them a wave of nostalgia, and she fought to keep her mind in the present as she raised her shoulders up to her ears and trudged toward the barn.

But mornings like this lived strong in memory. Weather did, for Rose. That experience of her boot hitting the porch, and the first taste of a new season's air on her tongue could peel back the years, one by one. And this morning was no different.

She could remember a few years ago when she had come out on a morning like this and had gone to the barn, helping Logan with a cow in distress.

A few years before that, when she had just decided that working on the ranch was going to be her vocation, and she had struck out, bright-eyed and eager, completely inured to the cold, her excitement providing a layer of warmth.

The time she'd been fifteen, and she'd come out early before school to chatter at Logan while he mucked out stalls, and he'd flung a shovelful of dry shavings at her, and she'd retaliated. Which had sent her off to school with debris in her hair, but it had been so funny she hadn't cared.

She stopped, and she knew it wasn't the cold air that had suddenly taken her breath away.

She remembered walking down those steps, holding two metal camping mugs in her small hand. Her mom beside her with a kettle full of stove-top coffee.

"It's cold out this morning." Rose could remember clearly looking up at her mom, seeing her smile. Her dark hair had been loose, blowing in the early-morning breeze. *"They're going to need their coffee."*

"Good thing we're here to bring it to them."

Her fingers tightened around the kettle and mugs she was carrying now.

She had so few memories like that. And she tried not to

let them surface. Because when they did the grief sliced so sharp and hard she couldn't breathe.

The barn door slid open, the sound loud and grating in the silence of the winter dawn. And there was Logan, standing backlit by the light inside, a warm glow around his muscular frame.

"You all right?"

"Yeah," she said, blinking hard.

Except out here there were memories that she didn't want, and in there was him. Neither one seemed particularly safe right at the moment.

"This time of year," he said, his voice rough.

She nodded, unwilling to say anything or show emotion that might make him...do something.

She didn't know what he might do. Yesterday he had transformed himself into a particularly scary stranger. Certainly not the guy who had laughed and flung shavings at her when she had been fifteen.

And she didn't know which Logan she was going to get this morning.

Then he smiled. "Good. Let's go. We have to move the cows from one side of the ranch to the other. We gotta get them up from the creek down to the lower pasture."

"It's freezing," she muttered.

"I know. But when you signed on for this life of glamour that is being a rancher, you signed on for this."

"A life of glamour," she repeated.

He jerked his head back toward the barn, and she trudged toward him. It was the weirdest thing. When she moved past him she could feel the hair on her arms standing on end beneath the sleeves of her coat. Could feel a prickling in the back of her neck.

She hadn't even been that close to him. He hadn't touched her.

It was just a strange awareness that settled itself over her like another layer.

She didn't feel quite as cold anymore.

"Got your horse ready for you."

He went into the stall and led her horse, Raisin, out to her, all tacked up. She frowned. "Thank you."

That was surprising. But then, maybe he had gotten out of bed a lot earlier than her.

"I have coffee," she said.

"Well, I can stop for a quick cup but then we need to get a move on. We're going to be battling daylight today. Sundown is at five."

"Sunup hasn't even happened yet," she said.

She poured some coffee into a cup and handed it to him. He smiled.

And she felt again like she was back in the barn nearly twenty years ago, helping her mom bring coffee to her dad and uncle.

"Is something wrong?" he asked, his blue gaze far too sharp.

She lifted a shoulder and offered him nothing. She wasn't the one who'd made it weird. He owed her an explanation. She didn't owe him anything.

She waited to see if he would ask if it had anything to do with what had happened between them last night. It didn't. Except, it was definitely part of why she felt weird this morning. She was sure of that. But she wasn't going to bring it up. She refused. It was up to him. He was the one who had…

She remembered that she had picked up a soda can and thrown it at his back.

Okay. She'd acted a little bit strange. And he had escalated it. But he was the one who had touched her. And that was the reason why her skin felt particularly prickly this morning. So, she felt like it was up to him to address that.

Instead, he took a sip of his coffee, while patting her horse on the rump. That the gesture felt pointed, particularly when his electric blue eyes met with hers, was likely her problem.

Or maybe it wasn't.

But either way, he didn't seem to be in a hurry to discuss any of it.

As they finished their coffee, mounted their horses and headed up toward the creek, Rose kept her eyes on his broad shoulders and back.

He was a brilliant horseman. She had always admired the way that he worked with animals. Today, though, the way that she looked at his movements, his body, felt different.

When he angled the horse, she noticed the way his hands gripped the reins. She knew how rough they were now. Because he had touched her face, her neck. Her collarbone. Yes, she had to catalog specifically every part he had put his hands on. It seemed important.

They were strong, too. The way he guided his horse with very little movement at all spoke of not only his strength, but his connection with the animal. With the very land itself. Because he seemed to know each dip and hollow in the path, in the hills, like he had a map written on his heart.

She understood. Because the same map was written on hers.

Because no matter how difficult the memories here at Hope Springs Ranch could be, those memories were the stuff of what she was. What had made her. And what sustained her now.

When his fingers moved slightly over the reins, she felt an answering whisper against her skin. A deep, low pressure between her thighs.

She jerked her eyes away from him, and forced herself to look at the view around her. That was the problem with all of this raw, natural beauty being quite so familiar. Yes, sometimes the clouds were spectacular, or the sun would break through in a particularly magnificent way, raining down golden glory. But often, it was easy for her to not look at all. And easy for her to get distracted.

By Logan's hands apparently.

But there was plenty to look at, even now, before the sun made an appearance. The air around them was a deep purple, the mountains a striking silhouette. The moon was still there, pale and fat, hanging on to its last moments.

And it still wasn't as compelling as Logan's hands.

"You're awfully quiet," he said.

"I'm not quiet," she said.

But the feeling of speaking was a little bit foreign, because she had barely spoken twenty words in his presence, and she realized how ridiculous her objection was as soon as she made it.

"What are you thinking about?"

"My parents." She went back to the earlier truth, not the present one.

A strange thing that it was easier to admit that than to admit that she was twisted up inside over what had happened the night before.

Either admission would've been true. But contrary to… every other moment in her life, talking about her parents felt preferable to talking about the other thing she was thinking of.

He understood, though.

And somehow, even in all the confusion between them, they still had that.

"What's got you thinking about them?"

"It's silly," she said. "I just remembered… This morning I remembered my mom and I bringing coffee to my dad. I had forgotten we used to do that. It's weird. Because I brought those same coffee cups and that same kettle outside for us a hundred times. And I haven't thought of that. But this morning I did. I don't know."

"It's not silly," he said.

"Memories for me are really few and far between. I was just a kid when they died."

"Yeah. But you know, they say all that formative years stuff is really important. So it doesn't matter that it wasn't very many, or that you were young. It mattered. It was important."

"Yeah. I just… I don't know why I was thinking of it today."

Something shifted inside of her, a companion to the shifting that had occurred yesterday. The answer to the question she wasn't asking.

Why was she thinking of it?

Because of the shifting. Because of the changing.

She gritted her teeth, grateful that Logan wasn't looking at her.

Grateful that he couldn't see the shifting.

"Do you remember my mom?"

The question was asked with a rough voice that made her heart twist.

He never talked about his mother. Not specifically. They all carried a shared grief. They didn't have to talk about it. But he didn't share memories. And when Christmas came around he retreated into himself, and he offered no explanations.

No one ever pushed, but she'd always suspected, always known that something about this time of year cut sharper and harder for him. She'd attributed it to his Christmas memories being different than theirs.

They were missing their parents at Christmas, it was true. But Christmas had been in the same house, with their siblings, and so that remained.

Logan's Christmases had been in another house, with only his mother. And maybe for him Christmas without her was so removed from Christmas with her he couldn't ever have it with enough joy to balance out the grief.

But he never offered, and she never asked.

She didn't know why he was offering it now.

"Yes," she said slowly.

Logan's mom had sandy-blond hair, and green eyes. She'd had an easy smile, and a soft voice. Rose remembered, because it was so easy to tell the difference between her mother, who had a low, loud tone and a robust laugh that echoed through the house, and Jane Heath whose voice was like a whisper with a song in it, and whose laugh had a quiet burr in it.

"She was sweet," Rose said. "And I remember that she made cookies. That was kind of her thing. When you guys would come over for dinner, she would always bring cookies."

"Yeah," he said. "She did." The roughness in his voice scraped against her heart.

His shoulders moved up and down, a heavy breath causing the motion.

Maybe if he had something of his mother at Christmas

it would be different for him? Those cookies. She'd always made cookies at Christmas.

"Do you have the recipe for her cookies?" she asked.

"Maybe," he said. "I have quite a lot of her things that I haven't really… I had it all put in storage. Except for a few pictures and knickknacks, those I have in the house. But you know, I moved in with you all after she died, and there was nowhere really to put the things. We were renting the house. So it's all in boxes in one of the barns, and I never really wanted to go through it."

"We should see if we can find them. You know, not so I can cook them, but I bet Iris and Sammy would do a good job."

He was silent for a long time. "That seems wrong somehow."

"Why?"

"I don't know," he said. "Just that… She's gone. So, seems fair enough that I don't get to have her cookies ever again."

Her heart twisted. She saw him more clearly in that moment. And it hurt.

"Well, it won't be the same," she pointed out. "It's just that it might make you feel a little bit closer to her. How could that be a bad thing? Seems like something she would have liked."

That was another thing she remembered. That Logan's mom had loved him. That she had been proud of him.

So proud. It had been obvious, even to a little kid. But she had understood, even then, that he had a very special bond with his mother. She had her mom and dad. He had her.

"Logan," she said slowly. "That must've destroyed you. To lose her. I'm sorry about what I said last night." It didn't matter now. That he hadn't been the one to bring it up. It didn't matter because what she'd said to him had been unforgivably cruel.

She'd been cruel the last twenty-four hours and she didn't like it. As if her personal pain meant she was somehow given a pass for being mean to other people. She didn't know why she was being like that.

Except that her heart had been a mess for the past few months. All the change. All the…moving on.

But it wasn't an excuse.

"It doesn't matter," he said.

"It does. I should never have taken something that… You do understand. You understand exactly what I've been through. And even more, and different because the two of you…because she was your whole family. You lost your whole family." She felt tears pushing against her eyes and she blinked them back. She didn't cry. And she certainly didn't deserve to cry now. She'd hurt Logan. She couldn't make it about her own pain. "To take something that personal to both of us and use it just because I was mad was borderline unforgivable."

"We've known each other too long to be doing unforgivable things to each other," Logan said. "I think it's all forgivable at this point. Don't worry about it."

When they arrived at the pasture, the cows were milling about and the sun was coming up over the mountains. Then it was time to work. It was a small group of cattle, so it didn't take a whole lot of manpower to drive them a quarter of the way across the ranch. But it did burn off the cold.

What it didn't do was distract her enough to make her quit looking at Logan. It was like driving by the scene of a car accident. Knowing that you shouldn't indulge yourself, the very worst part of you, and look at potential horror and tragedy, but too curious to stop yourself.

That part of her kept on looking at him. To see if it was any different to watch him drive cattle now than it had been before last night.

But it was different. When he eased that horse into a gallop, urging him on as they dogged those cows, keeping them in formation. The way his strong thighs held him in the saddle, the way every muscle in his body worked together as one... It was captivating.

And it was annoying the hell out of her.

And he wasn't going to say anything. Not about any of it. She'd felt bad, genuinely awful, for some of what she'd done yesterday.

But he'd *touched* her.

And he'd changed something. And he was acting like he hadn't.

When they finished, she was sweaty under her coat and her face was freezing cold.

They dismounted, and Logan let out a hard breath. She could see it in the air. "It is just not warming up today," he said.

"Fine by me," she said, defiantly wiping at her runny nose, refusing to behave any differently just because everything inside of her felt different.

"You look grumpy, Rosie," he said.

That caused her to scowl deeply. "I'm not grumpy."

"You look grumpy."

"Well, you don't know everything, Logan. Not even a little bit."

"I think you need to get some lunch, so that you quit being such a crab."

"I'm not a crab," she muttered, making her way toward the house.

Logan followed. And when she got inside it became clear that none of the…stuff between them was going to be defused by the presence of anyone else. Because nobody else was home. All the good it did her to live in a house full of people if none of them could show up when she needed them.

She stopped into the kitchen and jerked the fridge open, digging around for leftovers. She found a container full of the stew they'd had the other night. She got it out, and ignored the sound of Logan shuffling around in the fridge behind her.

"Is there enough stew for—"

"No," she said, cutting him off. "I'm hungry."

"That's not very nice."

"Maybe I'm not very nice."

She let the rest of the unspoken words in that sentence remain unspoken. And she waited yet again for him to acknowledge her feelings. Her feelings which were his fault. That she kept noticing his shoulders, his thighs, his hands.

He didn't.

She fulminated while she heated the stew. Then she looked up, and their eyes met. It was there. She could see it. Reflected back at her as if he had spoken. He wasn't oblivious. He was just pretending to be.

All of the things she thought he was ignoring…

Well, he was ignoring them. But he was doing it very deliberately.

She could sense it in the expression on his face, in the way he held himself.

She was desperate to figure out if he saw her differently, too. If today had been upside down for him. If it was something altogether new and wild. If maybe he wasn't talking about it because it had rearranged something in him the way that it had with her.

But she was too afraid to ask. Because there was no… She didn't even know what she would want if he said yes.

She didn't know what this meant. This close study of him, and the way he looked at her. There was a question inside of her, and she had a feeling that he was the only one who knew the answer.

She also had a feeling he wasn't going to give it.

Her phone buzzed in her pocket, and she dug at it, pulling it out. She frowned, not recognizing the number. "Hello?"

"Hi, Rose," came a somewhat familiar voice. "This is Elliott."

"Oh," she said. "Elliott."

"I hope this isn't a bad time."

"No," she said, getting a little bit of broth on her finger, and absently licking it. She looked over at Logan, who immediately looked the other direction. Her stomach clenched tight.

"The Christmas parade is coming up."

"Oh," she said. "I know all about that. I'm doing a booth. I mean, assuming I haven't got myself removed from the position."

"Oh. Right, because of Barbara."

"Yeah," she said. "Anyway. Yes, I know exactly when the Christmas parade is."

"I know you're going to be busy for part of it, but not the whole time, right?"

"No," she said. "We're going to be doing a pretty basic blacksmithing demonstration, and that will just be after the parade. So, I won't be busy the whole time."

"I was wondering if you wanted to go with me."

The air pressed itself out of her lungs. She didn't even know what to say to that. Her mind was like a shiny blank slate, and she had no idea how to respond.

"To go with you," she repeated.

She could feel Logan respond to that. She didn't even have to look at him to know that he had tensed up. It was the way that he was. The way that he radiated that sort of thing. She did look over then, and saw that he was doing exactly what she had thought he might be.

Did other people know when he reacted to things like that? Or was it only her?

It couldn't be.

It had to be something anyone could see. It didn't make any sense otherwise.

She blinked, totally derailed.

"Yes. As my date."

Her stomach sank, and suddenly she didn't want to eat. She didn't want stew or anything else. This was the first time she'd ever been asked on a date in her life. Coming from a man she'd been pushing toward her sister, a man she'd made her sister…like and be excited about. While she was being stared at by the man who'd told her so. The man who had taken her expectations of the world and herself and everything and turned them upside down.

It was horrible. Utterly, uniquely, horrible.

"Your date. I… Elliott, I thought you liked Iris?"

"What? *Iris?*" He sounded so incredulous. So incredulous that it made her want to eat the stew so she could throw it up.

"Yes, Iris. I introduced you to her. I thought that you would like her."

"You introduced me to your friend Logan too, but I didn't think you wanted me to go on a date with him."

"I…" She had. She had absolutely introduced him to Logan. But she had thought that it was obvious. And she had been so sure that he was interested in Iris. "You texted her to get her sourdough recipe," she said, as if that invalidated everything else he had said.

"Because you thought that I should have it. It was because of you."

"I… I am so sorry if I did anything to make you think that I was interested in you like that. I'm just not."

The silence coming from across the kitchen was as deafening as if Logan had dropped and shattered a bowl.

"You asked me to meet you at the bar," he said. "I thought you were asking me out."

She wanted to stamp and protest and say that it wasn't a very fair assumption since it was Iris he had been in contact with ever since.

"You called Iris," she said, and it sounded so very lame.

"To talk about you."

But there was no use arguing. He was saying that he liked her. And what was she supposed to do with that? How was she supposed to argue?

She wanted to argue, she just didn't know if there was any way to… Any way to do it. Because it wasn't like she could tell him that he was wrong about how he was feeling. She wanted to, but even she had to acknowledge that was a little bit ridiculous.

"I wasn't," she said. "I only ever wanted to… I just thought you would be good with my sister. That's all."

"I see," he said. "Well, I would be lying if I said that wasn't disappointing. Now that you know, though…"

"No," she said, horror twisting her stomach.

What was she going to tell Iris? All right, she had never got the feeling that Iris was head over heels for him, but this was… It was horrible. She'd been trying to do a nice thing, and she had failed so profoundly she couldn't even…

"No," she said again. "I… This isn't going to work. It can't."

"All right," he said, painfully decent until the end. "If that's how you feel."

"It is."

She hung up then, and she didn't want to look at Logan. She did not want to. Because this was more than just losing a bet. More than being upset because she had been wrong about something. She had very possibly caused harm to the one person she wanted to do something nice for. To say nothing of the fact that she had caused Elliott discomfort.

That paled in comparison to the potential hurt she might have caused Iris, though. She was trying to make herself care about Elliott because it seemed like the right thing to do. But mostly, completely, her worry was for Iris. And then, if she were honest, secondarily for herself because Logan was standing right there and he had borne witness to this whole thing. And he had told her.

He had told her a lot of things lately. And every single one of them burned.

"I take it that didn't go how you wanted."

"Please don't," she said. "Just don't."

Something in the air changed between them, and she looked up at him. It was just like last night, except there was no anger. But that same electrical current was there. That same shift in her soul.

She didn't know what the hell he was doing to her. And she was still too afraid to ask. Then, he took a step closer to her, and very suddenly she felt certain she knew what was going to happen next.

Like a key had slid into a locked door and turned it easily, opening it.

"You lost the bet."

She understood.

She understood, and she didn't move away.

CHAPTER EIGHT

THERE HAD BEEN a moment where he could've still turned back. But with one step toward her instead of away, he passed that moment by.

If he were honest with himself, he had passed that moment by back in the barn when he had backed her against the wall.

Maybe he had passed that moment by in the Gold Valley Saloon when they had gone up to the bar together to get beer and he had first lectured her on not understanding when a man wanted a woman. When he'd taken her bet and offered to teach her about when a man wanted a woman if she lost.

Maybe he had passed it by the first time he had looked at Rose and seen a woman, not his best friend's little sister. Not a child in need of protecting. But a woman. A beautiful woman whose strength and courage got under his skin. A beautiful woman whose smile and eyes and body played havoc on his dreams.

Maybe it had been too late all the way back then.

Either way, he pushed past his reservations now. Demolished them. Wrapped his hand around the back of her neck and pulled her forward. There was a breath where he stopped. Just one. Her eyes went wide. Her chest hitched upward, and her lips parted.

And then, he closed the distance between them.

The taste of her exploded through him, shrapnel from the impact embedding in his chest. He didn't know what he had imagined. That it might be gentle or easy because she was young. That he would have control over it because she was inexperienced, and he knew it.

It wasn't gentle. It wasn't easy.

And he did *not* have control.

Her mouth was so damn soft, and it was the softness that he thought might bring him down to his knees.

He would brawl with any man at a bar, even if he was twice Logan's size. He would be confident in his ability to win. Strength didn't scare him.

He would test himself against a sheer rock face, and he wouldn't be intimidated. He was a man who had survived so much there wasn't a whole lot that scared him. Wasn't a whole lot he thought might be able to bring him to his knees.

But this softness could.

This softness very nearly did.

It wasn't an avalanche. Wasn't an explosion. It was like the sun. Warming him through, melting ice in his veins he hadn't even realized was there. And it hurt. Like when your hands froze solid out working without gloves and you came inside and pressed them up against a heater.

It always hurt. When feeling returned to parts of your body that had lost it.

That was this kiss.

It wasn't what he intended. The bet had been to teach her a lesson, and hell…he'd had to follow it through. And part of him wanted to punish her for torturing him, for refusing to listen. He thought to crush her mouth beneath his and make her take the desire that rioted through his chest, whether he wanted it to or not.

Instead, he found himself just holding her there, her mouth against his, immersed in that softness, damn near devastated by it.

Then she moved.

A whimper beginning in the back of her throat, her hands coming up and taking handfuls of his T-shirt. He didn't know if she was planning on pushing him away or pulling him more firmly against her. He didn't give her a chance to make the choice.

He wrapped his arm around her waist and pulled her more firmly against his body, fitting her petite curves to his chest.

He could feel her fingers tightening on his shirt, could feel the way that she tugged him to her, even just slightly.

She wasn't pushing him away.

No, she wasn't pushing him away at all.

He angled his head, slipping his tongue between her lips, and she gasped, reeling backward and stumbling away from him. Her eyes were wide, her lips flushed pink and swollen looking.

It was the most intoxicating aphrodisiac he'd ever come into contact with.

Rose. Rose Daniels, looking like a woman aroused, flushed and turned on because of him.

He had seen Rose in a lot of lights.

He'd seen her dirty and exhausted from work. Cranky and favoring a leg with a strained thigh muscle after an unfortunate encounter with a spooked horse. Cut up from brambles and barbed wire. Laughing like a maniac while she raced him across the field. Cold and grumpy and wiping at a runny nose. Drunk. Yeah, he'd seen her drunk. He'd been the one to supply the alcohol. Silly and giggling in a way that she would never normally do as her inhibitions melted away with each sip.

He'd seen a lot of versions of Rose Daniels.

But never this one.

Of course, the companion to turned on seemed to be scared at the moment, and he didn't like that at all.

So much for teaching her a lesson. Apparently he didn't have it in him.

"Rose…"

"I don't…" She blinked hard. "I don't understand what that was."

"That's what it feels like when a man wants you," he said. "It's not all this pussyfooting around and texting your sister to get to you. I don't care what he thinks, he thinks that he wanted you, but he waited too long, and he let you get the wrong idea."

"You *want me*?" She asked the question in the same tone a person might ask if a bear was planning to eat them. Horrified. Shocked. Fascinated.

"I told you, sweetheart, you don't know what it looks like when a man wants you. If you did, then you would've seen it a while ago."

"How long is a while ago?"

"Doesn't matter. Fact of the matter is, you were playing with things you didn't understand, and I told you. I told you, but you didn't listen."

"I'm listening now," she said.

"Doesn't mean anything."

"What do you mean it doesn't mean anything?" Her voice rose a pitch, and he turned away from her, heading out of the kitchen. Rose followed after him, abandoning her stew.

"I've got work to do."

"You were going to make food," she said.

"Now I'm not."

"You can't do that. You can't just come in intending to make food and then not make it. You can't just kiss me and tell me you want me and then walk away."

"Which of these things is bothering you more? Are you truly that bothered by me not making food?"

"I am bothered," she said, tumbling outside the house onto the porch behind him. "In general."

"You'll manage it."

"I will not," she insisted.

"Rose, can you not make a spectacle out of this," he said when he got down to the bottom step. "You're going to get my ass kicked."

"I… I… He's not here anyway," she said, meaning Ryder, since that was who he had obviously meant was going to do the ass kicking.

"He could be back any minute. I'm not in the mood."

"You can't just walk away from me," she said. "We had a bet, Heath."

He stopped, then turned to face her. "I have to walk away from you. Or I'm going to do something that we're going to both end up regretting."

"I already regret things. But you didn't ask. I've never…" She tramped down the steps, stopping right in front of him. She lowered her voice, looking at him earnestly. "I've never been kissed before."

He chuckled, bitter and angry, and not at all with humor. "Honey, I know. Believe me. I know."

"Why? Because it was bad?"

"No. Because that's how innocent you seem. Because I've known you your whole damn life. Because I'm just a little bit too familiar with the daily schedule of your whole

existence. But it's not the first time I've ever kissed anyone. And that's why I hadn't done anything until today. I
shouldn't have done that. Just leave it alone."

"Leave it alone?"

"Yes."

"You said you were going to teach me if I lost the bet."

"Not like this," he bit out. "It was never supposed to be
like this."

"Logan, I didn't even know that I was attracted to you
until the other day. I didn't even know that I… That I could
be. And then you kiss me, and now you just want to walk
away? Now you just want to…"

"It's not about what I want. It's about what's best."

"Best would have been to never come near me at all."

"I know. But I can't fix that. So I'm making it right now."

"I didn't ask you to make it right," she said.

"Doesn't matter. You don't have to. I'll do it all on my
own."

"Why? Because of my brother? Is that what this is
about?"

"No. It's not about that. It's about me. I'm not your knight
in shining cowboy boots, Rose, and I'm not going to be.
And yeah, our relationship, the relationship that I have with
your brother, makes that a problem. If you were a different
woman? Well, then, maybe we could just have some fun.
But what we have here is worth too much to compromise
it for something that stupid. It always has been. It's why I
have never touched you before. I slipped up today. It's not
going to happen again."

He turned and began to walk away from her.

"You're wrong, though," she said.

Her words, as soft as her lips, had the same effect. They

hit him square between the shoulder blades like a knife, and twisted hard.

More powerful than a shout ever could have been.

"It will happen again," she said. "I'm sure of it. Because nothing has happened, for all these years, and now two things have happened, and now I know. I know what you feel. And now, I understand a little bit of what I've been feeling, too. If it wasn't going to happen, you would have never touched me in the barn. If it wasn't going to happen, you wouldn't have kissed me in the kitchen. Sorry. But I don't believe it won't happen again."

He closed his eyes, let out a long, slow breath.

"Honey, it won't. Because there's only one other place for it to go."

"Coward!" she shouted. "I didn't take you for someone who'd welch on a bet. I thought you were better than that."

"Rosie, I'm trying to be better than this. Don't make it impossible."

She didn't have anything to say to that, and because she didn't, he walked away from her. Feeling like an absolute ass. Not so much because he wished it hadn't happened. That would have been better. No. He felt like an ass because he didn't regret it. Because the taste of Rose Daniels would linger on his tongue until the day he died.

Because she was as sweet as he'd imagined. Sweeter, even. Everything he had ever wanted and more. He wished that he could regret it, but he couldn't.

And if his friend ever found out... Well, he would kick his ass.

And Logan wouldn't blame him.

But he would still hold on to the memory of that kiss.

His one taste of the illicit. His one taste of the forbidden.

It would only ever be one taste.

And it would have to be enough.

Rose was salty. She had been ever since that day in the kitchen. Somehow, she and Logan were supposed to do a blacksmithing demonstration, when they were circling around each other like two angry cats. She didn't know how that was going to work.

She wished that she had someone to talk to.

Somebody other than one of her sisters.

She'd felt awful when she'd told Iris about Elliott. Her sister's face had drained of color, and the look of absolute humiliation and horror on there would stay with Rose forever. She still felt so guilty and there was no way she could talk to her about the fact she'd kissed Logan.

She'd been kissed. She didn't think Iris ever had been.

Somehow, Rose Daniels had two men interested in her. And that hadn't been her plan at all.

Not that Logan was *interested* interested. But he *had* kissed her.

Maybe she could talk to Pansy. Yes, she would have to swear Pansy to secrecy, but she was much better off talking to her than, say, Sammy, who would immediately run and tell Ryder. It was a shame too, because she knew that Sammy had a lot broader knowledge when it came to sex and sexual attraction. Pansy… She was pretty sure the only man her sister had been with was her fiancé, West. So she probably wouldn't exactly be… Well, she probably wouldn't be pro jumping in and experimenting just for the sake of it.

But that had been on Rose's mind—when she wasn't just stewing in rage—for the past few days.

That was how she found herself walking down the newly decorated streets of Gold Valley, heading toward the police station when she very much should have been off working at the ranch. But Logan's avoidance made all that difficult.

Instead, with a sandwich clutched tightly in her hand,

she walked into the station, waving at Marlon, the secretary, as she walked back toward her sister's office.

Thankfully, Pansy was there, wearing her uniform and looking tough and smart as always.

Rose was so proud of her sister. The way that she had single-mindedly worked to get this position, to uphold their father's legacy.

"Rose," she said. "What brings you here?"

"Oh, I just thought I would bring you lunch." She held up the sandwich.

"Oh. West is on his way. He was going to take me out."

Rose's stomach fell in disappointment. "Oh."

"But I can sit for a bit. He won't be here for a while."

"Okay," Rose said.

"You can eat lunch if you want," Pansy said.

It was then Rose realized she only had one sandwich. "Oh. I kind of forgot to get myself something."

"Okay," Pansy said. "Since I'm meeting with my husband, you eat that sandwich, and then you tell me why you're actually here. Because if you had really come to bring me lunch, you would've remembered your own."

"It's just… I need to talk to you about…about men."

"Oh," Pansy said, looking vaguely appalled.

"I can't talk to Sammy. Not anymore. Because you know, she'll tell Ryder."

"Fair," Pansy said.

"And I don't want to talk to Iris about it. Partly because she doesn't actually know anything. And also because I just made a really big mess of something, and she's right in the middle of it."

"Do you mean the Elliott thing?"

"Yes. He liked me, apparently."

"Oh," Pansy said, this one with a more disturbed inflection than the previous.

"I know."

"Do you... Do you like him?"

"Oh, no," she said. "I really don't."

"I thought you wanted to talk to me about men?"

"I do. Not him. I was just saying... It's part of why I can't talk to Iris. Also, you're not a virgin."

"No," Pansy said slowly, shifting in her seat. "I'm not."

"I am." She waited for her sister to react. She didn't. "I don't know anything."

"I actually did know that," Pansy said.

"Well. I don't want to know nothing, not anymore. I walked myself into a really terrible situation, and I don't know what to do about it. I don't know if I should... I don't know if I should go for it, or if I should not, or what."

"Well, none of what you just said tells me anything I didn't already know, which is that you don't exactly have a rich sexual history. And you didn't tell me what happened, either."

"I got kissed."

"Well, that's good. Normal. I think, the lack of... I think the way that we did things isn't exactly..."

"I know," Rose said. "We are a bunch of weirdos. A bunch of weirdos who have avoided some very typical milestones because of our...our family stuff. But that doesn't mean that I feel ready for it now. Except I also... I really liked it."

"Your kiss?"

"Yes. But it's with somebody that I probably shouldn't have kissed. And I don't know what to do. I don't know what to do, because he said it's not going to happen again. But I think it could. I think it could if I...if I pushed him."

"Well, do you want to push him?"

"Kind of. But I don't know what would happen if I did. When he wants sex?"

"He's a man. If he kissed you, he wants sex."

"Is that how it was with West?"

Pansy scrunched up her face. "I don't really want to talk about my sex life with West."

"*Please.* I'm desperate. You told me… I mean, you told all of us when you slept with him. So can't you just… Can't I use your knowledge to my benefit, please?"

"I'll try," Pansy said. "But if it gets too awkward I'm going to have to tap out."

"Fine. I'll try not to be awkward." Rose had always been fairly forthright, while Pansy was a bit more guarded. Rose would have cheerily taken every detail her sister wanted to give. Because that was how you learned, after all. It just made good sense to share when you had something interesting to share.

"What do you need to know?"

"It's good, right? I mean, sex. It's fun?"

"I don't know if *fun* is the right word," Pansy said. "I mean, it can be. But it can also be…intense. It can make you feel connected to somebody in a way that you might not want to be. You know, you're talking to someone who figured she'd have a little bit of a wild time with the bad boy and ended up engaged to him. So maybe I'm not the best person for this discussion."

"You're the only person I have," Rose said. "And, okay, that actually is helpful. So, I know the two of you ended up falling in love. But you did want to just have fun with him. And it was fun."

"Yes. I guess. On the most basic physical level. Yes."

"What made you decide to…to do it?"

"I didn't exactly *decide*," Pansy said. Her cheeks turned bright red. "The first time just kind of happened. So did the second time. It kind of just kept happening. But West is just... I don't know. He's a whole thing."

Her sister did not sound unhappy about the fact that her fiancé was a whole thing.

"I think I might have to decide," Rose said. "I think I might have to... I think I might have to push him. But I'm not sure if I want to. How do I know if I want to?"

"If you don't know if you want to, then don't."

"It's not that... It's the consequences. I just... I don't know how I would go back to..."

"Who is it?" Pansy asked.

There was a sudden sharpness to her sister's eyes. A sudden stillness to her body that made Rose suspect Pansy might have a decent idea who the person was.

"If I tell you, you have to promise not say anything."

"Rose..."

"I'm serious."

"Fine," Pansy said. "I promise."

"It's Logan. He kissed me. He kissed me, and I liked it. But he infuriates me. And, he's not going to... I mean, it could never be a long-term thing with him, right?"

"Rose..."

"It's okay. I don't want it to be, I'm just saying I get that...with how things are the fact it would have to end would make things complicated. But I keep thinking if I'm going to learn something about sex..."

"Sleeping with a guy who is practically your brother is maybe not the best place to start."

The words caught Rose off guard. Because she had caught Ryder and Sammy making out and had immediately recoiled in horror and accused them of practically being related. It was funny to hear somebody else say it to her.

"He's not, though," she said. "My brother. That's the thing."

"He lives at Hope Springs. He's there on every holiday. You work with him every day."

"I know," Rose said.

"If he breaks your heart…"

"He won't," Rose said.

"You don't know that," Pansy said. "Because you can't actually know how you're going to feel until you actually… Until you actually do it. And then it will be too late."

"I wish I could talk to Sammy," Rose said. "Obviously she knew how to have sex without catching feelings."

"You could talk to Sammy, but she would tell Ryder, and he would kill Logan before you ever got a chance to touch him."

"I know," Rose said. "And isn't that part of the problem? This town is so small and everyone is so protective of me. Even Logan. He wants me. I know he does. But he wants to protect me from himself, which is basically the dumbest thing I've ever heard."

"It's not dumb," Pansy said. "It's responsible. Because he understands what all of this could make you feel. And you don't. My advice…" Pansy sighed heavily. "My advice is to listen to him. Because he knows what he can give."

Rose frowned. "Didn't West…"

Right as she said that, the door to the office opened. She turned, and her eyes collided with electric blue. Something twisted in her stomach, and then her brain caught up with what she was seeing. It was West. Her sister's fiancé. But for a moment, she had seen that blue and all she had thought was… Logan.

She had thought before that the two men's eye color was similar, but it had never impacted her like this. Obviously. Her cheeks heated, getting prickly.

"You guys talking about me?" West asked.

"No," Pansy said. "Everything isn't about you." She got up from her desk and moved past Rose, where she was still sitting resolutely.

West wrapped his arms around her sister, kissing her passionately. And Rose felt...prickly.

"I didn't realize it was going to be a table for three," West said.

"It's not," Pansy said cheerfully. "Rose was just going."

"She didn't look like she was going."

"She was," Pansy said.

Then she stretched up on her toes and whispered in his ear.

"Good to see you, Rose. We'll catch you later," he said.

Rose watched her sister and her future brother-in-law retreating quickly, and became more and more angry. It was clear to her that they were off to do some kind of amorous nonsense. After she had given Rose a puritanical lecture.

And she hadn't even given her the chance to finish her sentence.

West had been very clear about what he could and couldn't offer, too. It didn't seem fair that Pansy would tell her she needed to listen to what Logan had said when Pansy herself clearly hadn't listened when West had warned her off.

The problem was... The problem was... She just didn't know if she wanted to take the step.

She felt increasingly sorry for herself, sitting there with a sandwich in her hands that wasn't hers. She had gotten mustard on it, because Pansy liked mustard. And she didn't.

So here she was with a sandwich she couldn't even eat. And she hadn't liked the advice she had gotten. Not at all.

It would have been better if Pansy would have told her to go for it so Rose could have argued against that.

Instead, she felt sullen and rebellious, and on the verge of making a decision that might compromise everything she was. Everything her life was made out of.

Maybe that was dramatic.

It was one kiss, after all.

It was one kiss, and she could let it go.

But it had opened up a flood of thoughts and ideas inside of her that she never had before.

Being near Logan was like being near a furnace, and avoiding him was a feat that took complicated dance steps given the way their lives were arranged.

Maybe if she did nothing it would fade. Maybe if she did nothing she would be able to regroup and go back to the way things were. But the problem was she doubted it.

It will be worse if you kiss him again.

Or if she slept with him.

She looked around her sister's office. At all the things that Pansy had achieved.

A career. A fiancé.

Rose swallowed hard. For the first time, *she* felt genuinely left behind.

She hadn't felt that way. She had focused on the fact that Iris might feel left behind. That she might feel alone in the aftermath of her siblings finding love. Especially as an older sister.

And Rose had resolutely not thought of herself.

Because it wasn't even fair of her to feel it yet. Not when Iris wasn't…solved.

Stupidly, sitting there in a plastic chair, holding a sandwich, with her sister's achievements plastered on the wall in front of her, and their father's before her, she wanted to cry.

Rose was proud of herself. Of the work she did on the ranch. She was. That wasn't even it.

She just felt the same. And changed all at once.

She didn't know how those two things went together. But they did. Because Rose, Rose herself, was in the exact same place she had been a week ago. But she felt entirely different. Nothing had changed, and it was the change in her that made her feel so painfully aware of that.

That made her feel so unsatisfied.

So...sad.

She didn't like it. She avoided this. Avoided thinking about herself and what she wanted and what she didn't have.

She wanted to talk to Logan about it, and she couldn't.

Because that kiss had not only taken her peace of mind, it had taken her confidant from her, too. It had taken a lot of things from her. She couldn't talk to Sammy. She couldn't talk to Iris.

She couldn't pretend that she wasn't curious about all the things she had never explored.

Couldn't pretend that she was just waiting around until she found a man she was attracted to.

There was one. But he frightened her. Or at least, what might happen frightened her.

Talking to Pansy hadn't gotten her any closer to a decision.

She pushed herself out of the chair and walked back out of the station. She meandered outside and walked down the sidewalk, making her way toward Main Street.

The redbrick buildings were festooned with Christmas decorations. Dark green bows wrapped around support beams and balcony railings. White Christmas lights draped over everything. Red ribbons tied around wreaths that hung on doors, and the big tree already set up in its place, awaiting the parade, and the Christmas tree lighting that would happen afterward.

There was a familiarity to it that usually gave her a sense of comfort. But not today. Today it made her ache. Because it was another thing that was the same while the inside of her, the things that made up who she was, felt entirely different.

It was like the town was trying to goad her. A resolute monument to the fact that while she might feel different, she wouldn't be brave enough to do different.

She would come to the parade on Saturday, she would do her demonstration with Logan. They would pretend that nothing had ever happened.

It would be the same. The same, the same.

And maybe someday she would coordinate the parade. She would be Barbara Niedermayer. Bitter and angry and demanding that things stay the same because the sameness of the town might make her feel not so ashamed of the sameness in herself.

And a young impetuous person might call her out for being so inflexible. And that person would get told off because Rose was an object of pity, and everyone should know and respect that.

That cut Rose down to her heart. That she'd been the one to hurt Barbara, maybe. That her words might have caused her pain.

When she wasn't...

Better. She'd gone around recklessly causing harm and wherever it came from... Why did she think she was better than Barbara?

She thought she might be on the same path anyway.

That future was bleak. And right now, it felt like a very real possibility. But the alternative was to potentially upend the life that she knew. The life that she loved.

Rose already knew life didn't come with guarantees. She already knew there was no safety. No guarantee it would all work out in the end. Because she'd lost her parents. The source of all the security she'd felt as a child.

She already knew that sometimes in life a change, an event, was heavy enough to ruin everything. That sometimes things couldn't be fixed or repaired. That some things were permanent.

And that was just the way it was.

Even seeing the future as grim as it might be, Rose felt like she might be too afraid to do anything about it.

Because at least that future was one she could see.

A future that stretched past kissing Logan again...

She couldn't see that. She didn't know what might happen. She didn't know who she would be on the other side. That frightened her.

She stopped on the street corner, and a troop of carolers wearing Victorian dress exited the kitchen store, singing gaily about silver bells, right as a frigid wind picked up and wrapped itself around Rose.

She stood there while the music filtered through her, while the wind chilled her to the bone.

And she had to look at herself the way those carolers might see her. Pale and large-eyed and frozen there in her tracks.

Not a tough cowgirl. Not a bold, bright force who tried to bring cheer and goodness to the people around her.

But a frightened animal ready to race back into her burrow at the first sign of trouble. A woman who got overly involved in the lives of the people around her so that she didn't have to deal with her own.

A girl who felt tender and bruised because she feared she might have a crush on a man who had the power to devastate her.

But the carolers weren't looking at her. They were just singing.

The town rolled on, as it always had.

It was only Rose who felt changed.

And there was no one who could help her with the decision she needed to make about what she was going to do next.

Because nobody else would ever understand what she was feeling now.

It was a choice she had to make for herself.

To run away, to be afraid, or to be new.

She was afraid she didn't have the courage to be new.

CHAPTER NINE

IT WAS A fairly miserable day for a parade. Gray clouds had collected in the sky, rolling one over the other creating a patchwork of color that ranged from mist to the color of a donkey's muzzle. The sky promised to break open later, and Logan only hoped that it would wait until after the event.

Or not.

It wouldn't be the worst thing in the world if the whole thing got rained out and that meant he could go to the bar and drink. Instead of firing up the forge and trying to work alongside Rose.

The last few days had been what Logan imagined torture might be like. Like sensory deprivation. Or being kept thirsty, with a big glass of water right in front of you, just out of reach.

Yeah. He imagined it was like that.

He should never have touched her. But then, he knew that. He had known it then, and he had still done it.

He might have known it, but what he hadn't done was think ahead. Hadn't thought past the moment when his mouth might touch hers. He had wondered what it would be like. Had—for all the years before this one—told himself that he couldn't ever let it happen. But then he did.

He'd done all this warning himself, all this self-flagellating for finding her attractive. But he had never thought to where it might leave him if he got to the place where he acted on the attraction.

So now here he was.

It was hell.

Because a kiss was one thing, but his body wanted more, and there was no way he could ever...

Rose was innocent.

I've never been kissed before.

Her words echoed inside and he closed his eyes for a moment. Trying to breathe past the temptation.

He wasn't in a position to be the first.

The thought of that sent a kick of arousal through his body and he gritted his teeth. Called himself ten kinds of son of a bitch. Though, it wasn't the first time. It still hadn't stopped him from kissing her, so he didn't know why he was bothering with the castigation.

It hadn't kept him from committing that first most deadly sin.

Volunteers had set their booth up, and because of that, Logan had managed to avoid Rose so far for this endeavor. And he had a bit of time before he had to be there yet. The parade itself was about to begin, and he didn't need to sit out on the street and watch it.

He'd had to park way off Main, up by the little patch of grass and playground that had been put in about ten years ago. He walked down the hill toward Main, and saw all of the parade participants lining up and getting ready.

He never went to the Christmas parade, so he hadn't seen the spectacle before.

Girl Scouts, dance troupes, bagpipe players, ROTC, the garden club and the Rotary. The equine drill team from Gold Valley High, a classic car club with members who had clearly come in from surrounding areas, all being facilitated by the local church youth group, who were raising money to go to Disneyland.

Logan had never been part of groups like this growing up. He and his mom had been a two-man team and that was all he'd needed. He had never played sports, hadn't taken his enthusiasm for adrenaline and riding to the rodeo like Jake and Colt had. Hadn't ever been part of the church, though after his mom died he'd gone to midnight mass with the Daniels, because they went, and he tended to do what they did.

He wondered what it would be like, to be part of a strange community like this one, bonded together by a common interest. They were bonded together by tragedy.

It was a timely reminder, he thought, as he continued to walk down the sidewalk, his hands stuffed in his pockets. He was part of the Daniels family because they had lost together. But he wasn't bonded to them by blood. Rose was.

And if he did anything to hurt her, he would be the one out on his ass. And he didn't have anything else. Anyone else.

His soul was bound up in Hope Springs Ranch, his years of work. A lot of his money went back into the place, just like Ryder. He owned a portion of it, it was true, and he could always sell it back to Ryder and make his own way if it came down to it.

But he built his life around that place, around that family.

He'd decided a long time ago that biological family didn't matter. He'd gotten used to tuning out the biological family he knew he had in town. It had been a little more difficult over the past few months, sure. But he told himself, over and over again there was no point getting wound up about it.

He had a lot of things he was trying not to get wound up about right now. Instead of heading straight to the parade route, straight down to the booth, where he feared Rose might already be, he pushed open the scarred black door to Sugar Cup and walked into the rustic coffee shop.

It was all roughhewn wood, aged barn floors and a chalkboard menu, with a chandelier hanging down from the ceiling. It was somewhere at the intersection between practical café and avocado toast. He had to admit, he didn't really mind the avocado toast, considering they still served coffee the way he liked it.

The usual barista wasn't around, so the cook, a large, broad man with a beard, and his hair tied up in what a person might be tempted to call a man bun, but wouldn't considering who it was attached to, took the order.

The door opened, and in scampered a petite figure, clasping her hands in front of her, rubbing them together, obviously to ease the chill.

Damn that Rose Daniels. She had the exact same solution for avoiding him that he'd had for avoiding her.

She saw him. And he could see that she was strongly considering scurrying right back out, and not even pretending that she wasn't hiding from him. Then she didn't, God knew why. He watched as the same steel came into her eye that he'd seen a dozen or so times before. When she was approaching a particularly recalcitrant horse, or dealing with a frightening bull that she had to get moved, scary or not.

Yeah, Rose Daniels was about to approach him the way she did every problem animal. Filled with piss and vinegar and damn well certain she would get her way.

"What are you having?" he asked, figuring the best way to deal with her was to pivot.

Because again, he'd seen this before.

Come at Rose head-on and she'd lock horns with you till one or both of you was tuckered out. Regardless of the fact that she didn't have horns, and occasionally her foe did. Sidestep, though, and sometimes you could catch her off her guard.

"Coffee," she said.

"Nothing peppermint? 'Tis the season."

"Keep your girly drinks," she said.

"Now, Rose, we both know you don't mean that, because you like your coffee with enough sugar to send a unicorn on a hallucinogenic bender."

"Fine," she said, scowling. "Peppermint mocha."

"I'm buying."

"Why?"

"To be nice."

Her eyes glittered like beetles. "*Why* are you being nice?"

"Can't I be nice?"

"No," she said definitively. Certainly.

"Watch me."

He turned to the counter and ordered from man-bun-not-a-man-bun again.

"Let's have a seat," he said.

"I was going to watch the parade," she responded, the inherent stubbornness and her tone telling him that that was not in fact what she had been intending to do, but she had changed her mind upon seeing him there.

"Were you?"

"It's cold," she said, rubbing at the end of her nose.

And he found that kind of thing just so damned cute it made him question everything that he was. For as long as he could remember, he'd liked the look of women. He liked the look of most of them, but he had to admit a certain fondness for the kind of girl who put on a pair of tight jeans and lip gloss, her hair teased to make her a little closer to

Jesus. He liked them cowgirl pretty, with rhinestones and a little bit of flash.

Rose was a cowgirl, it was true. The kind with dirt under her nails and holes in her jeans that had come with wear and tear, rather than purchased that way from the store. She was also cute. And he would have said that cute really wasn't his thing. Shiny, flashy, curvy, sparkly. Not cute.

But with Rose, he appreciated the cuteness. Like when she tried to warm her own nose.

Though appreciating Rose's cuteness was a lot like appreciating the cuteness of a badger. Sure, it was fuzzy. Relatively small. But if you got right up close to it, it might mess you up. And think nothing of it.

"I know," he said. "You don't like to be cold."

Silence stretched between them, tense as anything. All he could think of was wrapping her up in his arms, opening up his jacket and letting her burrow against his chest.

Okay, that was some shit. It was one thing to have sexual fantasies about her. It was quite another to have some kind of domestic, cozy fantasy about giving her his body heat.

But the way that her cheeks turned pink he had to wonder if she was thinking the same thing.

This was a problem. Looking at her and knowing that her thoughts might mirror his own. Looking at her and being pretty damn sure she felt the same thing.

For a long while he'd been pretty damn sure she didn't.

But then they had kissed.

"No," she said finally. "I don't."

"Peppermint mocha," the guy called out Rose's drink.

"So, I don't actually believe you were going to go watch the parade," he said, picking up the cup and handing it to her.

She took it from him, and their fingers brushed.

He felt the impact of the touch all the way down to his cock.

"Well, maybe I am now."

"To avoid me?"

"You're not supposed to say anything about that," she said.

"I'm not?"

"No," she said, taking a sip of her mocha. "We're pretending it's not happening."

"It has to get talked about eventually."

"Does it? You're the man—aren't you supposed to advocate for us never talking about feelings or anything of the kind?"

"We work together. We are about to do this blacksmithing demonstration together. How long do you suppose we can feasibly pretend that this isn't happening? That we are not acting like we can't be in the same room? I mean, that's the whole point of never doing it again. Making sure we can be in the same room."

Suddenly, a little sliver of suspicion lodged itself beneath his skin. "Are you doing this on purpose?"

"Am I doing what on purpose?"

"Are you trying to prove your point? Your whole...thing about how we could do it. By making it impossible now?"

"No," she said. "I don't have the ability to be that manipulative. Not when I'm in the middle of...intense confusion."

"It doesn't need to be like this," he said, not having any idea if it actually did have to be like this or not. Because he sure as hell didn't feel normal. He had slept with... He didn't even know how many women. One kiss with one woman should not be messing with his head to this degree. Or to any degree.

He was tempted to apologize, but when he went to open his mouth, he was sure that it wasn't an apology that was going to come out at all. But then the door opened, and in walked Pansy, hand in hand with her fiancé.

West Caldwell.

He didn't put a lot of thought into West. At least, not beyond his relationship with Pansy. He liked the guy. And if he had some weird feelings of envy wrapped up in who he was, he just ignored those, too.

"Hi," Pansy said, looking between the two of them.

There was something in that expression, pleasant though it was, that made his stomach twist into a knot.

Pansy knew.

He didn't know how he was so certain, only that he was.

"Hi," he returned.

West grinned, and Logan felt a shift inside of him.

"Howdy," he said.

For some reason, he could feel a keenness to Rose's gaze just then. He didn't need that much study from the Daniels women. It was strange. Pansy was glaring at him to figure out what his intentions were toward her sister, and he didn't know what the hell Rose was trying to see.

"Were you headed out to watch the parade?"

"No," he said. "Rosie wanted to get warm before we had to go stand out and do the demonstration."

"Before you went and stood by a forge," Pansy said.

"Put the interrogation away, Officer," Rose said. "We're having coffee."

"Police chief," Pansy said. "Not officer."

"So touchy," Rose responded.

"Yeah, but she's mean," West said. "So you don't want to anger her."

"Please," Rose said. "I was born angering her. I will die angering her."

"Yeah," Pansy said. "You might want to revisit the wording there. Or you may die irritating me a little bit sooner than you counted on."

"As charming as this is," Logan said, "I just want to drink my coffee in peace."

"I don't think we're allowed to do anything in peace with the Daniels women around."

He was uncomfortable with that comment, and the parallels that West was drawing, on multiple levels.

"Do you want my wrath, too?" Pansy asked, giving her fiancé the beady eye.

"Never," he said.

"We're going to go watch the parade," Pansy said.

West ordered their drinks—just coffee—which came up immediately. "See you after," West said.

He could still feel Rose looking at him while the two of them walked out of the coffee shop.

"You told her, didn't you?" he asked.

"I had to talk to somebody."

"She looks like she would cheerfully gut me."

Rose ignored that. "I need to ask you something," she said, looking down at her mocha, and then back up at him.

"Do you think we should maybe move away from the counter?"

"Sure," she said, taking a few steps away, and sitting at one of the two-person tables against the wall. "So, does this work?"

"Sure," he said, feeling skeptical about her intentions.

"I need to know. Is Hank Dalton your father?"

SHE HADN'T BEEN SURE, until she had seen West standing there across from him and had put the pieces of it all together. The way that West's blue eyes had impacted her so much when he had walked into the police station the other day. The way they stood. The way they smiled.

They weren't identical. But there was a resemblance.

And if she knew one thing about Hank Dalton it was that he did have children constantly coming out of the woodwork. A daughter had shown up a couple of years ago, and had ended up married to one of the Dodge brothers, a widower who hadn't seemed interested in any sort of happiness until McKenna had come to town.

Then of course there was West.

And it seemed feasible that there would be more. Because why wouldn't there be.

"I don't have a father," he said, his face suddenly becoming that implacable granite, which she was learning was his retreat.

"Sorry, Logan, but you and I both know you can't give me that. I do know where babies come from."

"It's true. As far as anything matters, it's true. My mother did everything for me. She taught me to throw a baseball. She taught me to do my own laundry. She taught me to sew so I could fix my own damn socks, and she taught me to drive a stick shift. She's the one who bought me condoms and told me to treat my girlfriends with care. And my father... My father didn't give her anything. He hurt her horribly. I would never... I would never betray her memory by speaking his name."

"Logan..."

"The man who fathered me didn't want me. He broke up with my mom when she wanted more and she tried calling, but she was always blocked by his wife. And one time she banded together with some other women who had his kids, went to see him. His wife blocked them then too, said he didn't want the kids. Offered a payout, and she took it because she wanted me to have something. But it was too little too late, Rose. She died so soon after she got that money. After all those years of working and working…"

"So he is your father. Because if he weren't it would be easy to just say no."

"It doesn't matter."

"Logan," she breathed. "West is your half brother. You didn't say anything. He's been here… He's been here all this time and you haven't said anything. You could have started building a relationship with him."

"I have a relationship with him. He's marrying a woman who is practically a sister to me. So, he'll be like a brother to me anyway."

"Don't give me that. You haven't gotten close to him. Not at all. I mean, you're cordial to him, but I haven't noticed… That's deliberate. It's deliberate because he is your half brother and you don't know what to do with it."

"Rose," he said, his tone full of warning. "Do not meddle in this. This is not just you trying to match your sister up with someone. This is my life. I swear to God if you get your hands in this…"

"What? What will you do if I get my hands in this?"

"Just don't," he said.

"Don't. That's your answer to everything. Just don't, Rose. Don't do anything. Don't push you. Just be a manageable farmhand. What? Do you look at my ass and then say the rosary to try and atone? Everything is fine as long as I don't come near you? And then you can sit back and brood in your feelings about how you feel about West. But did you think about how he might feel? He came here looking for family. Basically, you get to know everything, and decide exactly how all your interactions are going to go. You know what? It's bullshit, Logan. You're a coward."

"Talk about bullshit, honey," he said. "You think that you get to make demands of me at your leisure just because you had a revelation about who West is to me. Well, it's not news to me. I get it. And I get that my decision to have nothing—and I mean nothing—to do with Hank Dalton, or any of the rest of the Daltons impacts on him. I get it. You don't think I thought it through? You're talking to me like I might not have made my decisions for my own reasons. But I did. You can be damn certain of that."

"I'm sure you did," she said. "I just can't believe it. I can't believe you would be so… That you would be so stubborn. So callous… I mean, what's the point? Your mother is gone, Logan. And I don't think she would've wanted you to turn away from the family that you have left."

"You don't know what the hell my mother would've wanted. You don't know how bad Hank Dalton hurt her. I do. He was married, Rose. He had no intention of ever leaving his wife. My mom…she would cry at night. She loved him. She missed him. She also couldn't risk anyone in town knowing. I could never let any of them know, Rose, I wouldn't betray her like that. Then people would know she'd been with a married man and she was so ashamed. And Hank? Where's his shame? When it comes to Hank, he's that kind of man. It means nothing to him. It cost him nothing. He runs around hurting his wife, hurting other women. He doesn't care."

"You don't know that. You don't know what Hank does or doesn't care about…"

"His infidelity is pretty damned infamous, Rose."

"Yes, but West has gotten close with Hank. Maybe he has changed. I'm sure that…"

"I know a little bit about all of it from West. Because he's talked about it. He still doesn't sound like anyone I want to know. And I don't want to get involved with someone, anyone, who would treat my mother the way that he did."

"But maybe he wouldn't now."

"Doesn't matter. That's the thing. You have to treat people right. The whole time you're alive, because then they might die. You might die. And you don't have any time to make up for it. And if I were to go to him now…my mom was proud, Rose. He broke up with her, he told her he didn't want to be with her and only later she found out she was pregnant with me. She didn't ask him for a damn thing until she had to. She hated that she violated her own moral code, getting involved with a married man and hoping he'd leave his wife and kids for her. You can't know how much it hurt her. But I do. I remember how she punished herself. Never dated, never let herself find love. I remember how afraid she was people might realize I was a Dalton. Might judge her the way she judged herself."

"I understand that, Logan, I do. But West…he didn't do this to your mom. If life is so short, then maybe you should make a relationship with your brothers. With your sister. There are so many Daltons, you have… You have this whole family."

"I had my mom. She was my family. And now I have your family," he said. "They've been there for me. That's the most important thing."

She looked at him, at the hurt written so clearly across his face. And she wondered if there was more. "Why didn't Hank come for you?"

"I don't know, but I wouldn't have gone with him anyway."

"He didn't come for you."

"No. He damn well didn't. But don't think for one second that matters to me. It doesn't. I wouldn't have gone with that bastard anyway. I would rather have been with you all. With Ryder. I owe him big. It's why I worked the ranch. It's why…"

"Why you won't touch me."

"You're a little brat, Rose, that's why I won't touch you."

The lie settled between them. She knew it was a lie. Because he had betrayed the way that wanting her tortured him. He had shown her. It was too late for him to take it back. She knew. And because she knew, he couldn't pull this on her.

But then, she supposed that went the other way, as well. He knew that she wanted him. And…there just wasn't a whole lot of defense to be had there. They both knew each other just a bit too well.

"Well, maybe if life is short I should start fucking you now and worry about the consequences later?"

She stilled. He had said it to be mean. He had said it to push her.

Except… Language aside, it didn't sound so bad.

Though, she didn't really know what all went into fucking. Making love sounded a little bit more like something she could handle. A little more like something she could wrap her mind around. Because it seemed gauzy. The other sounded very physical. A little bit harsh. She was interested. But she had some concerns about whether or not she could withstand it.

"Don't look at me like that," he growled.

"What? You were the one who said it."

"You're supposed to get mad at me, dammit. That was disrespectful."

"Was it? Sounded like a promise to me. And now you're telling me it's a promise you had no intention of keeping."

"You couldn't handle it."

"Let's make a deal. I can't meddle in your life, and I can't tell you that you should have a relationship with your family—when you clearly should—maybe you don't get to tell me what I can and can't handle."

"But I know."

"Blah, blah, blah," she said. "You know an awful lot for an emotionally constipated dick who won't even tell his half brother who he is."

"Great. So glad we had this talk."

"If I've figured it out, then he's going to," she said. "He's marrying Pansy. If he doesn't figure it out, she will. I'm not sure that I can keep it a secret from her."

He reached across the table and put his hand over hers. "Keep the secret." Something burned in his blue eyes, and it wasn't anger. It wasn't superiority, or any other things that she could get easily mad about. That was annoying. Because she would really like to be able to go ahead and stay angry at him. To keep on fighting.

But she couldn't yell at sincerity.

"I will," she said. "But the original statement stands. He's going to figure it out. Whether by himself or through Pansy, you know he will. I…I didn't notice until we kissed. And then West walked into the police station. At first I thought it was you, and it felt like my stomach bottomed out. She's going to see you. She has to."

"I imagine she knows him well enough to not get him mixed up with another man."

"It isn't that you look like him. Your eyes are that same blue. And there's more. It's the way you hold yourself. The way you smile. It's like it's mixed in with your blood."

"It's not like it is. It is."

"Logan, I wish so much that one of my parents was still out there. Yours is."

"Well, that's just evidence of the cruelty of the world," he said. "Because if Hank dropped dead tomorrow, it wouldn't hurt my feelings any. In fact, I'd trade him to bring your daddy back in a second. Your father was like a father to me. He mattered. My mom mattered, your mom mattered. Hank Dalton doesn't mean anything to me. Blood doesn't mean anything to me. Not with him. Not now."

"West?"

She could see that was a regret.

"It doesn't matter."

"It does. You might not want it to matter, Logan, but I know it does. It's okay."

"You're suddenly a safe space?"

"I don't know. It doesn't feel very safe between us right now. But what it is... I don't know what it is. I'm never going to let you do something that I think might hurt you. I trust it's the same with you to me. We've got each other's backs. Through anything, right?"

"You know I've got your back."

"So maybe we can just trust each other there. Maybe we don't agree. Things might not be safe. But they are as inevitable as the Christmas decorations on the street outside. And the mountains around the town. Things between us just are."

"I'm glad you feel that way."

"It's just sex," she said.

"You don't know what that means."

"Well, maybe I need to learn."

"I can't keep track of this conversation. Did you want me to reconcile with a father who never wanted to know me? Or did you want me to take you to bed?"

"Can't I want both? Your emotional and physical well-being?"

"Sadly, I don't think you know enough to help me find either."

That stung. The rejection stung. And even though she was pretty sure that what he said was a lie, and he knew it, it still stung.

"I'm going to go to the booth." She kicked the chair back and stood, making her way out of the coffee shop. And he didn't go after her.

CHAPTER TEN

IT WAS DIFFICULT for Logan, Rose and their mutual irritation to fit in the booth. But somehow they managed. They were both heating metal and hammering before the parade ended, getting things ready to go, the pounding of iron on iron a welcome ring in the air over the top of Rose's highly unusual and blessed silence.

He didn't need her opinions on the way that he chose to handle the family that he decided not to think about. It was *his* choice, dammit.

Rose didn't have the right to say a damned thing. She didn't understand. She couldn't possibly. She had been a kid when their parents had died. So young that she didn't have the kinds of memories that allowed guilt and blame to take hold. And anyway, she didn't have the cause to. Not the way that he did.

But the other thing she didn't have was memories of how his mother's life had been.

He did. He remembered. He remembered, always, the wound his mother carried that his father had refused to involve himself in their lives. That she had never been able to get access to him after she had found out she was pregnant.

Stopped at the door by his wife. And then, again, years later when she had tried with some other women who had children by Hank to get what they were owed, they had all been stopped again.

He knew that she was ashamed of that. Of the fact she had taken a payoff, because Hank Dalton's wife had offered that if they would go quietly.

He'd known she was ashamed she'd taken the money until the day she'd died. They'd needed that money, no question. Still, his mother had felt as if she had sold his relationship with his father for the proverbial thirty pieces of silver.

He remembered her ducking into a supermarket aisle or a store when she saw Tammy Dalton coming.

He'd overheard Ryder's mom in the kitchen with his once. While his mother had cried.

"The embarrassment would be worth it to me, if he wanted his son. It's not fair he has those other boys that get to have a dad, and he doesn't. He always sends his wife out to handle me. I haven't even spoken to him since before Logan was born."

"It's better for him to have us," Linda Daniels had said. "All of us, than one stupid man who doesn't know what he's missing. He's a sperm donor, that's it. And Logan will always have us. And so will you."

Logan had known who mattered before then, but it had all been cemented in that moment.

Logan had never cared about Hank. And he'd told her so. His mother had done everything she could to take care of him. And to take care of him well.

It had been all he could do to stop himself from driving across town, going to that big, beautiful Dalton ranch and defacing their property.

He'd been so angry when he was a teenager.

And then his mother had died.

The only anger he'd had left had been at himself.

Past that, he realized that the best thing he could do was forget. Forget that the Daltons were anything to him.

It was strange, the way that West had come into his life. Strange and wholly unexpected. But he realized that the likelihood that one of the women his mother had gone with was West's. That there had been a connection between their mothers, and never with them hadn't seemed strange until West had shown up in town, and ended up part of Logan's day-to-day thanks to his relationship with Pansy.

He'd never wondered about his half brothers before that. At least, he hadn't much let himself. His mother had wanted to keep the more sordid details of her relationship with Hank, and Hank himself, away from Logan. And he'd respected that.

After her death, he felt honor bound to not go make something that she couldn't make in life.

No. He had never wanted to go fling himself at Hank Dalton's mercy. Tell him that his mother was dead and he didn't have anybody.

He couldn't think of anything more pathetic.

That was why he had forgotten.

West made it harder to forget.

He was used to ignoring Gabe, Jacob and Caleb Dalton. They'd grown up in the same town, gone to the same schools some years. He'd known. He suspected they didn't. And if he had sometimes wanted them to know, had sometimes felt the mean and awful urge to tell them so that their happy family could be shattered—especially after his mother's death—he'd ignored it.

And if he'd felt something like grief when Caleb and Jacob's best friend had been killed fighting fires alongside his half brothers, he'd pushed it down. If he had felt something like regret when he'd heard through the rumor mill that his half sister had come to town and found a place in the family, he ignored that.

If he felt any kind of mystification over West showing up in Gold Valley and being welcomed by the Daltons in just the way McKenna had been, he just pushed it away.

He'd made his decision years ago.

Fact of the matter was, that bastard children were being accepted into the family left and right... Yeah, it made him question why when his mother had died Hank hadn't come for him.

He hadn't appreciated Rose asking that question because it stabbed at a wound he didn't like to acknowledge existed.

Rose had brought out a whole lot of things he liked to pretend didn't exist.

And there she was, working and sweating, stripped down to a tank top, even out in the cold because the fire they had going from the forge was blazing hot. And he admired her strength. Her body. Lean muscle that was packed into every part of her frame. She was solid in places, soft in others. The epitome of feminine strength.

And he found her sexy as hell.

He couldn't deny that. No matter how much he might want to. And he really, really wanted to deny it.

It was impossible.

Even after she had uncovered a secret he pretended he didn't even have.

Not even Sammy knew.

And she was the one person he had come closest to confiding anything in over the years.

Because she was someone who knew a piece of that pain.

Still, they didn't speak.

Instead, they pounded iron, huffed around each other, and maneuvered past each other's bodies like they might get a worse burn by touching each other than they would coming into contact with some of the molten metal they had around the booth.

He had a feeling that was true enough. It was a hell of a thing.

The parade ended, and people began filtering over to the booth. Somehow, he and Rose managed to talk about how a forge works, and a bit about how to fashion horseshoes. They managed to play off each other. Managed to somehow seem like they weren't in a state of being appalled with one another. Difficult as that was to believe.

It was when West and Pansy came over to the booth that things got hard. Because Rose all but arched her back like a pissed-off cat, and Pansy was still looking at him like he might debauch Rose over an anvil at any moment with the whole town acting as an audience.

He had to admit that was a damn sight more appealing than he wished it were.

But he was a sick bastard. He admitted it. There was nothing to do but admit it.

It was a bit much to deal with his half brother, the sister of the woman he wanted, and the woman he both wanted to kiss and throttle all at once, with an audience present, however.

"How's it going?" West asked, his arm wrapped tightly around Pansy's waist.

"Good," Rose said, not looking at him. Not even a little.

"A little warm back there?" Pansy asked, referencing Rose's tank top.

It was then Logan realized he was still in a coat. Possibly because he wasn't in a space where he wanted to strip off any layer of clothing in tight quarters with Rose.

He'd tried. He'd damn well tried.

To keep away from the Daltons. To honor his mother's memory.

He'd tried to keep away from Rose.

He was failing at both and he didn't know if he had the strength to keep on with the trying in full view of the fact that there was almost no use.

Maybe Rose was right.

Maybe there was no going back.

Because if there were, then he never would have kissed her in the first place.

Because if he really had the self-control he'd need to never touch her again it would have had to be strong enough to keep him from kissing her at all.

"Just a bit," Rose said, wiping the back of her hand over her forehead and leaving a trail of soot and ash behind.

He felt the impact of that in his gut. Down lower.

What was it about her? Wearing dirt, wearing ash, wiping her damned nose, that appealed to him? It was a question he hadn't much asked himself because he'd been so busy trying to pretend that none of it was happening.

That if he ignored it, it might go away.

And all the while, all these last months he'd given Ryder advice on how to deal with Sammy. Had walked around like he had some kind of expertise on the subject of feelings. And how wanting the wrong woman could be just fine.

When he didn't think that was true for himself, and he didn't see how he ever could.

"You?" Pansy asked, the question pointed right between his eyes.

"Oh, I'm fine," he said, gritting his teeth.

She narrowed her mouth into a skeptical line. "Are you?"

"Just dandy," he shot back.

"Be sure you stay that way," she said, a very clear warning.

Rose bristled beside him. He could practically see her hackles go up. Feral little wildcat.

"Don't you have some citizens to check on?" Rose asked.

"I'm doing my part to make sure no one does anything stupid," Pansy said.

"Best get off to police some kids, then," Rose said, waving a hand. "No one here needs your intervention."

"I hope not." Pansy directed that last part at Logan.

For his part, West looked vaguely apologetic as the two of them walked off into the crowd.

"She's impossible," Rose muttered, replacing her angry look with a grin when a group of people walked by. They didn't stop, and her smile immediately flatlined, then turned down. "She has to stop thinking she's police chief of me personally."

"I mean, you're a citizen of the town so I think technically she is."

"Fine. So, if I graffitied Sugar Cup or...or carved my name on the wall in the bathroom of the Gold Valley Saloon..."

"You know why they do that, right?" In spite of himself, he asked the question.

She turned wide eyes to him. "No. There's a reason?"

He laughed, but it came out more of a cough. "Um. Yes. You do it if you've hooked up in there."

"No."

The awkwardness between the two of them lifted for a moment while he could see Rose taking a mental catalog of names she remembered seeing there. "Olivia Hollister..."

"I mean, I'm sure her husband is to blame for that."

"She just seems too...too prim."

"But *he* isn't."

Rose frowned. "So that's how it is then. This sex thing.

It makes you crazy. Makes you carve your name in bathrooms. Makes you…do that in bathrooms."

"Since the dawn of time, basically," Logan said. "Which is why I told you, you don't really know. You think you do. It's not a lack of respecting you that has me turning you down. But to my mind it would be like letting a driver without a license behind the wheel of a car. Or letting someone with no experience on one of the stallions we have on the ranch."

Her lips twitched. "Are you calling yourself a stallion?"

He snorted. "I'm not a gelding, that's for damn sure."

She was silent for a long moment. "All right, say your analogy holds. If someone wanted to get on the back of a stallion, let's say, with no experience, wouldn't you rather be right there to…instruct?"

"I'm lost now."

"I'm going to do it someday," she said. "And I think I'm a little too…"

Suddenly, her eyes went glassy. If she'd been any other woman he'd have thought they were tears. But Rose didn't cry.

"Everything feels a little messed up right now. And I don't know if it's everyone pairing off or if it's Christmas or…or kissing you. Maybe it's everything. But I thought about what you said to me. Why I was meddling in everyone else's business and not my own. It's because I don't like thinking about my own feelings."

He huffed. "Join the club."

He turned back to the forge and made a study of stoking the fire.

"Well, I really don't like it. But I've been wallowing in them the past week. I hate it, Logan. I feel guilty about Elliott. I'm angry that you were right. That I didn't recognize what was going on. That I didn't even have the… I'm twenty-three, I'm not a kid. I should recognize it. I shouldn't have gotten my first kiss in my brother's kitchen years after I had my first beer. And well, come to think of it you gave me my first beer so it makes even more sense."

"Oh, please, God, tell me you are not asking me to teach you about sex."

"That was the bet."

"The bet was me…teaching you about chemistry. Explaining things to you, not…actually…showing you."

"Maybe I'm a tactile learner. I need hands-on examples."

"Stop it. That isn't going to happen."

"Why not?"

"Spoken like a virgin."

"Fair enough," she said. "I *am* a virgin. Hello." She smiled broadly at the people who approached the booth, which effectively put their conversation on hold while they went into their spiel about horseshoes and blacksmithing again. When the family left, she turned back to him.

"I just don't see what the problem is. You want to. I think I want to…"

"You *think* you want to."

"Well, I haven't done it. So, it's really hard to say."

"So, answer me this. Do you just want to because I'm the first man that's ever shown any interest in you that you've noticed?"

"You're not the first. There was Elliott."

He snorted. There was not enough derision in the sound to express how much he felt. "Okay."

"I'm not at all interested in Elliott that way," she continued, as if he hadn't snorted. "And I don't need to trial and error that. I have immediately no interest."

"All right. So, between me and one other guy that is the

human equivalent of a pair of pleat-front khakis, you are more into me."

"Rude. Also, I'm not sure how many people are required to go through a list and compare and contrast and decide if there's another person out there they might want more than the one in proximity. Most people just do it."

"My point is," he said, "I think this might have more to do with opportunity for you. And what you're not considering is the consequences."

She blinked at him in utter confusion. "Well, use a condom."

He just about pitched over the edge of the booth and landed on the poker he was gripping in his hand. But he didn't have time to react. Because another group approached, and they had to do another bit in between this current nonsense they were engaged in. He gritted his teeth through the whole thing. And as soon as they left, he rounded on her. "What the hell do you mean talking like that?"

"I'm being pragmatic. That's what you do to prevent *consequences*."

"Pregnancy," he said. "Which is not the only consequence."

"It's my leading concern."

"I wouldn't let you get pregnant. That's kind of a given."

"Apparently Ryder and Sammy didn't think so."

"They're different," he said. "Anyway. Sammy wanted a baby."

"So, I got the feeling that whatever happened with them wasn't really…that kind of thing."

"I haven't put that much thought into it," he said.

"I didn't *want* to. But seeing as I walked in on them, and there's not enough bleach for my brain. But I don't think

of you as a brother. I never have, really. I mean, I feel…
I guess I feel safe with you. I always have. You… I don't
know. Like I said earlier. There is an inevitability to it. A
certainty. I've always felt that way about you. Like you
would always be there for me no matter what. Like I was
safe with you." She blinked. "I know it sounds silly, Logan,
but that kiss brought a lot of stuff up to the surface for me.
And it's not really about being horrified that it's you. At
first it was. When I started noticing you. After the… After
you touched me in the barn."

"You keep making it sound like I did something really
inappropriate," he growled. "I put a hand on your face."

"I felt it everywhere. Doesn't that tell you something
about how I feel? Yeah, it kind of blew my mind. Because I
didn't look at you that way. Because you were always a man.
But somewhere in there I became a woman, and I just never
changed the way that I was looking at you. But then… Then
I did. And now it is what it is. I want you. And more than
that, I know what it is to want somebody. But it has also
forced me to confront some of the crap that I have, the…
the reasons I don't like to think about my own feelings."

"Why is that?"

"Because I just couldn't? Because if I did, then it would
ruin everything for everyone else. I just didn't want to be a
burden. But I just was one by default. My parents had me
because they chose to. I never question whether or not they
wanted to take care of me. It was their life. Our life. Ryder
didn't choose me. Neither did you. Or Iris, or Pansy. Colt
or Jake. I was just this little…useless thing. And I don't
like thinking about it. I don't like feeling lonely, and I don't
like feeling needy. But sometimes I think I just am. I don't
know how to have all those feelings and not be a burden on
somebody else. I've tried to not…ask for too much or want

too much. I've tried to… I've tried to help. I never wanted to take more than I already had just by being young. So when you needed bandages… I bandaged you."

The sadness in her voice, the depth of it, made him feel like he had fallen on that poker and driven it right through his chest. "We make you feel like a burden?"

"No," she said. "You never would have. But that doesn't mean I wasn't afraid. And thinking about…men and relationships and all of that…it brings all that up for me. Plus…"

"What?"

"I can't be settled. I can't be with somebody before Iris."

"Why, because you're younger?"

She said, "I mean, I can't leave her to be the last one in the house without someone. And I just… I wanted to fix that. And I thought, I can deal with my feelings later, but maybe I can't. And… I think I need help. And you promised."

"You lost the best. It was supposed to be your concession, if I let you off the hook you should just…let me."

"I don't want to."

"Rose," he said, feeling weary and defeated.

Because the woman he wanted more than any other was begging him to take her to bed, but the reasons were all wrong. The problem was the right reasons didn't really exist. Not between the two of them. Because he could not offer her forever, and Rose was the kind of woman who should have it.

That thought stopped cold in his head.

That was just a thing he'd been telling himself to keep from touching her, but the truth was… Rose would sleep with more than one man.

Of course she would. He didn't expect her to marry the

first man who touched her. She was an all-in, both boots in the mud kind of woman. She harbored real insecurities in her heart, and she'd shared those with him today. Had told him she felt like it had kept her from dating, but he knew her.

When she did date, the guy would kiss her and she'd shove him into the bedroom. Maybe just to see. To satisfy curiosity.

It was how she was.

A doer.

What she deserved was a man she could trust. A man who cared about her. A man who would show her what good sex was so she never settled for less.

A man who satisfied her curiosity to the fullest extent and then some.

Damn, the thought of it made him ache. All the ways he could satisfy Rose Daniels.

The idea she deserved marriage with sex had kept him away from her. Kept her safe. But he'd just demolished that with a healthy dose of reality.

It would be some man, someday.

Why not him?

He wanted her.

She wasn't perfect. She was a snarling little brat sometimes. She'd been terrible to Barbara. She'd gotten pissed off and said horrible things to him. And that didn't make him see her as less. But it made him see her as a person. Just a woman, and not one who needed to be set up on a shelf.

Human, just like he was.

She made mistakes, and she'd make more.

And couldn't he be part of her mistakes?

Why the hell not? Why couldn't he give her this? Why couldn't he give himself this?

He didn't have the strength to say no. Because he was just a man.

"Come to my place after this," he said, the words scraping his throat raw.

But they were spoken, and with it his decision was made.

Her bravery faltered, her eyes wide. "Really?"

"Yeah," he said. "If you want a lesson, Rose, I'll give it. But you better be prepared to want to learn it."

He could see her weighing it. All her brashness had walked her into something she didn't know a damn thing about. Yes, she was a woman. And yes, he damn well respected her as one. But that little bit of uncertainty highlighted the gulf in their ages and experience, which was the real reason he shouldn't have told her to come to his place. Not Ryder and any loyalty to him.

But it was too late now.

He'd decided, the moment he'd first started feeling things for Rose about the time she was nineteen or so, that he would never, ever act on the lust that twisted his gut into knots.

That when he'd started noticing the fit of her T-shirts over her breasts, the way her smile lit up her face, the way her dark hair showed flashes of gold in the sun, he'd just push it down the way he did all the feelings he didn't want.

He lived less than five miles from a father he'd gone out of his way to never meet. From half brothers he never spoke to.

When he decided on something, he stuck to it.

Changing his mind took doing.

Or, took a taste of her lips.

And now his mind was changed. Going back wasn't an option.

She bit her bottom lip. "Should I bring something?"

"No." Just her. That was all he needed.

"Wine?"

"No. Don't bring wine. You're not allowed to lower your inhibitions, dull your senses, or anything else that will make you act out of character. You need to show up and be you."

"What about cheese? Cheese is not especially mood altering."

"Why the hell are you offering me wine and cheese? You've never been into fussy stuff."

"I'm not fussy." She frowned. "I'm just trying to be classy."

Trying to bring class into their ill-advised sex lesson? Shit, he didn't want class. He wanted it dirty and sweaty and everything he'd been aching for the past five years.

"I don't need you to be classy," he bit out. "Be you."

There was a flash of stark vulnerability on her face that made her look younger, and made him feel like an asshole.

"That's why I need it to be you," she said softly.

"Why?"

"Because you know me. You want *me*. That means something to me."

Discomfort shifted his gut. "Well, I'm glad," he said.

"The crowd is really thinning out," she commented.

"And I bet we can take a break," he said decisively.

They needed to get out of this booth for a minute, and if the girl was coming over to his place for sex…well. He ought to take her out first.

A half-assed attempt at being a gentleman.

"Why?" she asked.

"Because. I think we should wander around a bit. I'll get you some cider, come on."

He strode out of the booth, and she grabbed hold of her coat, scampering after him. "Cider?" she asked.

"Yeah," he said.

"You don't like Christmas," she said.

His stomach twisted. "No. But I like you. So. I want to walk around with you."

A small smile curved her lips upward and he felt himself smile in response. He couldn't help it.

They walked side by side, not touching. She flexed her fingertips and he could tell she felt that same kind of restlessness that he did.

It was funny. The way he could feel her indignation. He'd been able to do that for a long time.

But he could feel the way she wanted to touch him now. Could feel just how much she wanted him to take her hand. But he couldn't do it here. Because whatever happened between them, it was going to have to just be the two of them.

This was on his terms.

She might be getting something out of this, but his was his fantasy.

His downfall.

He'd decide how it went.

The cider booth was being run by Glenda, the owner of the Mustard Seed Café, who also had chili hot chocolate. There were also candied cinnamon-spiced nuts. He bought two ciders and a paper cone full of the spiced nuts, handing them to Rose.

They wandered after that, Logan not feeling the cold or seeing much around him.

Rose walked beside him with the cone of nuts in one hand, and her cider the other.

He felt like a high school boy trying to impress a girl, and he didn't like it one bit. He had that tension in his limbs he could remember from that age, too. That intense anticipation. Dates from when he'd been a kid. When the high school football game ended they'd get in his truck and would they park for a while? How far would she want to go?

He'd taken safe sex seriously even back then. His mom had given him condoms once he'd grown to over six feet tall at the age of fifteen. He would never leave some poor girl pregnant, she'd told him. The condoms were insurance, not permission.

He'd already had some. He hadn't told her that.

There was something about this moment with Rose, the anticipation, that brought him back to those years and he didn't like it.

He had to be a lot better than a horny sixteen-year-old for her.

But damn if he didn't feel like one.

For her part, Rose seemed oblivious. She tilted the cone up to her mouth and shook it, dumping some into her mouth. "These are good," she said around a mouthful.

His stomach tightened. "Glad you like them."

During their brief circuit, they ran into Pansy and West. Pansy eyed them both suspiciously. Rose took another defiant mouthful of nuts and chewed them ostentatiously as she stared her sister down. They also went by Iris's booth, where she and Sammy were serving baked goods.

"Ryder went off to get me a cheeseburger," Sammy said. "You just missed him."

He wasn't that broken up that he had missed Ryder. All things considered.

He recognized Rose's body language getting awkward again.

It must be Iris. This whole thing really did have Rose all wound up. He did feel sorry for her, but it was a mess of her own making. A mess she had dragged him into. A mess they were now about to both be tangled up in.

"How's the booth going?" he asked.

"Good," Iris said. He didn't think it was his imagination that Iris seemed…a little bit chilly. So, maybe Rose wasn't completely off base with her discomfort.

"Great," he said. "We're just taking a break."

"Yeah," Rose said, shaking her diminished nut cone.

"We haven't had time for a break," Iris said. "We've been busy."

"Great," he responded. "Well, we won't keep you, then."

"Bye," Sammy said, waving them off.

When they were out of earshot, he turned to Rose. "So she's really mad at you?"

"I think so," Rose said. "And I don't know how to begin to fix it."

"Do you think she liked him that much?"

"She was starting to. And it's all bad because I know she's never put herself out there like that before. But… When I… When I told her…her face, Logan. And she's been chilly ever since. And I don't know what to do about it."

"Well," he said, "we can't fix it right now. And you can't fix it until she tells you what's going on."

"I know," she said."

"So, I guess that just leaves us with only ourselves to worry about."

Rose looked up at him, her eyes shining bright, filled with some unnamed emotion.

It wasn't really excitement. It wasn't really fear.

It was something else altogether, mixed with a kind of admiration he didn't think he deserved.

"I guess so," she said.

"Come on," he said. "Let's get back to the booth."

There were still a few hours of torture left to go before he'd finally have Rose, naked in his arms.

He'd waited five years.

He could handle a few more hours.

Then she would be his all night.

CHAPTER ELEVEN

THERE WAS A time in every woman's life when she looked at her underwear drawer and found it lacking. At least, Rose assumed this was something that happened to every woman. She had never looked at underwear before and considered what someone else might think of her in them.

It was a little bit annoying, knowing that beyond cleanliness, she doubted men considered it at all. Or maybe they did. She didn't actually know. Their options were limited, sure. But maybe there was some consideration given to if they were going to wear standard tighty-whities or something a little bit more provocative like a pair of tight black boxer briefs. Again, making assumptions about which would actually look more provocative.

She had seen men in underwear on underwear packaging, but that was about it.

Whether he was worried about it or not, she was going to see Logan in his underwear. And he was going to see her in hers.

She stared at her underwear drawer, as if it might magically make something sexy appear.

Nothing. Not a single scrap of lace.

Show up. Be you.

Yeah, he said that. But hers were plain white and from a variety pack. Both the panties and the sports bras.

Her hands felt numb. She didn't know why. She opted

for the underwear that had a slight bit of scalloped edging on the waistband and legs, and delicate pink roses. Again, from one of those packages. It had probably come with white and gray, something serviceable that tended to be Rose's go-to. She was grateful now for the hint of floral.

The bra...

Well, she decided to put on a real bra that clasped in the back. She did have two of those. A nude color and a white one. She went with white, just because it matched the panties.

She had never wondered what a man might think of her underwear, or her body. And now she found herself staring in the mirror above her dresser— a dresser that had once belonged to her mother—and giving her body a critical once-over.

She had a decent rack. Kind of narrow hips, and muscular thighs from all the riding that she did. Her arms and midsection were toned. Not bad, all things considered. She'd never been near any kind of waxing. She hoped he didn't mind that.

The thought made her brain short-circuit, and she knew if she didn't get dressed and get away from the mirror immediately she was going to talk herself out of this whole thing.

Waxing.

And Logan seeing anywhere that she might need to wax.

Her hands went from numb to sweaty and numb in record time.

Then she slapped her hands down on the top of the dresser and decisively grabbed a pair of jeans and a red sweater. It was her Christmas sweater. One of the nicer things she owned. Not a T-shirt, not plaid, and not a work jacket.

She left her hair down.

Then she turned and started to walk out of her bedroom, down the stairs and into the living room. The dogs were shuffling around down there, making more commotion than she would have liked.

"Settle down," she hissed.

That was when Sammy came in from the kitchen with a bowl of ice cream in her hand.

"Are you going out?"

"I... Yeah," Rose said.

Prickles crawled up the back of her neck and she gritted her teeth, hoping the prickles didn't bloom into a full-blown blush that bled into her face and made it painfully obvious that she was up to something.

"Where?"

She tried to think. It couldn't be the saloon, because there was every chance that someone from her family would be there.

And if she wasn't there, then they would wonder where she was.

Maybe this was the real reason she had never had sex before.

Maybe it wasn't her profound emotional issues.

Maybe it was just the problem of having a large family in a very small town.

There weren't very many corners for her to hide in. Her family filled up too much of the space.

"Meeting a friend. From high school," she said.

She had a couple friends in high school on the drill team. And she did often meet up with them for dinner or a drink when they came to town, usually around the holidays, so it was plausible.

Most of them had moved away, of course.

"Oh," Sammy said. "Fun. Are you having dinner out?"

"Yes," she said. "Probably Italian. But maybe we'll be fancy and go to the Gold Valley Inn. I can always go for steak. So."

As lies went, that was a pretty good one. Because she wasn't being decisive, and she wouldn't be likely to run into her family at either venue.

"Well, see you later."

"Maybe," Rose said. "I… If I end up having too much to drink I might crash at my friend's house. You know. Because her parents live in town. So we can walk if we need to."

"I can come get you," Sammy said. "I'm constantly designated now."

"No. It's okay. I know that you might be tired. It'll probably be late. And… Anyway. I might be out all night."

Sammy stared at her. Rose realized that she had probably overextended herself. Just a step too far. But Sammy wasn't going to call her on it. And after a couple seconds of staring, Rose fully realized that.

Sammy might not believe her, but Sammy was going to allow her to have her secret.

"Okay," she said.

And now Rose also knew that she had to drive.

But if she drove, then her truck was going to be outside Logan's.

But if she left her truck, then they would know that she should be here.

She gave Sammy a wave, and then ducked out of the house, making her way to her truck. Ultimately, she decided to park it behind one of the barns, and make her way on foot to Logan's. Good thing she hadn't brought wine and cheese, because she would have been laden down. And already, she was panting with exertion by the time she got there. She had very nearly run.

Maybe that wasn't the best idea. To arrive at her potential lover's cabin sweaty. Out of breath.

Right now, though, she felt like she was outrunning some of the reality that she had been smacked with upstairs while looking in her mirror.

Like the subject of waxing. And what he would be expecting to find beneath her underwear.

She could see his cabin, the lights on, the porch clean but barren of any kind of decor. The main house at Hope Springs Ranch was completely decked out. Wreaths and lights and Christmas bows. But then, most of that was Sammy's doing.

Not that they didn't do Christmas decor at the ranch. They did. And they had, from the very beginning, when their parents had died. Ryder had been determined that things wouldn't fall apart more than they already had. He'd gotten a Christmas tree that had been too big for the living room. They had to cut the top off, and it had served as a mini tree that had sat on the kitchen table.

It had been ugly, gaudy and shiny as hell during the darkest time of their lives.

They had always made time for Christmas.

Logan never had. He'd always withdrawn during this time of year.

She would focus on his lack of Christmas decoration. Because it was easier than...well, just about anything else.

She swallowed hard and made her way up the steps to the house. Should she knock? She didn't know.

She was still standing there, debating...well, everything, when the door opened.

Somehow, he was taller and broader than she remembered. Which was ridiculous, because she had just seen him a couple hours ago. Oh, and pretty much every day of her life.

And there was no way he had changed in the time since she'd last seen him. But maybe it was just because she was so aware of the fact that all that strength, all that height and breadth and muscle was going to be…

Touching her.

"Come on in," he said, his voice gruff.

It was only that gruffness that gave her any indication that he felt something out of the ordinary.

So she came in.

She had been in his cabin any number of times, but right along with him feeling bigger than usual, it felt smaller.

Earlier today when he had initially made this offer, she had felt triumphant. Especially when she had been staring Pansy down, daring her to say something. Daring her to tell Rose that she didn't know what she was doing.

He had walked her all around the booths like he was proud to be with her. And sure, there wasn't anything particularly unusual about it given they were together all the time, but it had made her feel special in some way or another.

But wandering around town with spiced nuts and cider and feeling like she had won some kind of game was all fine and good with the barrier of the public and the outdoor air all around them. They were inside now. And they were alone.

She had been alone with Logan countless times. But this felt different. Heavy. Weighted. It didn't take a genius to figure out why. And if anything scared her, really scared her, it was that. That it felt different now, when all they had done was kiss once. That it felt different now with just the promise of sex between them.

It made her wonder if it would always be different.

But if so, then there was nothing that could be done. It was already different.

And her heart was pounding so hard she was dizzy with it.

It wasn't just that he looked larger. Taller. His face looked different. Harder. Like it was carved straight from granite. His mouth was held in a grim line. She was… mesmerized. By the glint in the blue that was so sharp she thought it might cut her. He was… He was a beautiful man. And she didn't know how she had spent so many years with him and not seen it. Truly seen it.

His face was perfectly sculpted, square jaw, straight nose. Right now, it looked rough with stubble, and she found it fascinating. Compelling. Wondered what it would feel like beneath her fingertips.

She swallowed hard.

"You're staring," he said.

"Yeah," she said. But it didn't stop her from staring. Instead, she continued her visual tour of Logan. Looking at him like…like a potential lover, and not like an inevitability.

She had told him that she felt like he was safe. And she had. But there had been naivety in that statement.

She hadn't understood what it would feel like when they were alone. When there was nothing to stop her from reaching out and touching him. Nothing to stop him from touching her.

Like that night in the barn.

But there would be no reason to stop. She wasn't here for it to stop.

She suddenly wished that there had been spontaneity to

this. That maybe the kiss in the kitchen had become more. Instead of all of it becoming this determined decision.

She waited for him to say something. But he didn't. Instead, he took a step toward her, took her chin between his thumb and forefinger, and brought his mouth down on hers. She shivered, melted beneath his firm lips. It was different than that kiss in the kitchen. It was different than anything.

In part because it wasn't blunted by the shock of Logan kissing her. He had kissed her once before, she had come here to be kissed. And then some.

There was an edge to this. Danger.

Even though he held his body apart from hers, the only place they made contact her chin and their mouths, there was an intensity that wound its way through her body.

He tilted his head, taking the kiss deeper, sliding his tongue into her mouth, against hers.

The friction shocked her, sent an arrow of pleasure straight to her center. She gasped, and he took the opportunity to go even deeper, which she hadn't realized was possible.

Then he took her into his arms.

Wrapped her up completely in him. His heat, his strength. She had the barest impression that it would be different to be near all his strength, all his intensity, when it was wrapped around her, but she hadn't really understood.

Then he groaned, cupping the back of her head, his other arm hard around her waist like a steel band. Her breasts were crushed flat against his chest, and she could feel his hardness pushing against her stomach. Evidence of his desire for her.

But it was more than that. It wasn't just the physical signs of how much he wanted her that she felt.

She had always felt his emotions. Always.

The bristling of his disapproval, the hot flash of his anger. She had always been so in tune with him. But she had never noticed this before. Wanting her. Maybe it was because she was blind to things like this. He'd said that she was.

Maybe it was because it was only since he'd kissed her that he wanted her. Maybe he could have wanted any woman the same way. He was a man, so she had to concede that that might be true.

Show up. Be you.

He wanted her. He'd said that. So she had to believe that it mattered. Believe that this intense, white-hot, electric need that she could feel coming off him as sure as she could feel heat radiating from the engine of her truck when it stalled out on the road on a summer day, was for her.

That she was special.

That he wanted her. Her. That she wasn't just a responsibility that had been foisted on him. But an object of desire.

Of choice.

Suddenly, she realized why he had wanted to know for sure that she wasn't just using him as a stand-in. She wanted to tell him. Wanted to tell him, but that would require separating from his mouth, and she didn't want to do that, either. No. She didn't want to do that. She wanted to kiss him like this because it was a high. An injection of adrenaline that made it impossible to feel nervous. Impossible to feel uncertain.

That was when she found herself being walked backward, taken down to the couch. And he was over her, strong and solid, consuming her like he was starving.

She couldn't think anymore.

She had turned into liquid heat. And liquid heat couldn't think. Couldn't do anything but feel.

She found her sweater being stripped up over her head, and she forgot to worry about if her bra was plain, or if he might like the look of it.

Because that was when he finally separated from her, and the look in his eyes was one of pure fire. He growled. Really growled, like a feral animal, moving back down to her and kissing her neck, the scrape of his teeth on her skin sending a flash of desire between her thighs.

Teeth.

Oh.

Well, now she knew. And she wanted more.

It hurt. Both his teeth and the way it made her want. And she didn't understand how hurt could be good. But it was. Right now, it was.

She had thought that they might talk. But they weren't talking.

She had thought that he might outline what they would do. But he didn't.

He just kept on kissing her. Kissing her until her mouth felt swollen, until she thought her heart might gallop out of her chest. Until his magic hands dispensed with her bra and she barely even noticed, let alone remembered to be embarrassed.

He sat up for a moment and he shuddered. His big, muscular body that she knew was hard as granite. She didn't have to be here making out with him to know that. She had watched him tangle with animals that outweighed him by ten times, and he hadn't shaken. But he did now. Looking at her.

"You're so beautiful," he said, his voice rough, thick, like he was drunk. "Rosie, do you know how pretty you are?"

It was the intensity of those words that shocked her. Almost as much as the content. "I've never thought about it," she said, honest as possible.

"Well, hell," he said, chuckling. "I think about it all the damn time. How pretty you are. Usually, though, I'm thinking about how pretty you look in your jeans. Can't wait to see you out of them."

Her heart was like a whole team of wild horses thundering over her breastbone, so hard she was sure that it would crack. He thought about it all the time? She didn't even ever think about how pretty she was. And suddenly, she wanted to catch up. Not to her own beauty, but to thinking about his. It seemed more important than her own nudity. Seemed more important than anything else.

She shoved her hands beneath the hem of his shirt, her fingertips making contact with hard, hot skin. She gasped, slid her hand up higher, marveling at the feel of the hair that covered those muscles. Served as a reminder of just how different they were. Masculine to her feminine. And she did not spend a whole lot of time pondering her femininity. But the overwhelming intensity of his masculinity sure did it.

She pushed his shirt then, desperate to get it off. Desperate to see him. And he obliged her. He reached behind his head and tugged at his shirt collar, pulling it up from the back and casting it to the floor. "How do men take their shirts off like that?" she marveled. "It's the most amazing thing I've ever seen."

"I'm sure you've seen plenty of men take their shirts off."

"Not this close," she said.

And then, they couldn't talk anymore, because he was kissing her again, her hands pinned between them, flat on his chest, which was as rough and hairy and muscular as his stomach.

Then he was kissing her neck, down to the curve of one

of her breasts. He looked up at her, electric blue hitting her like a lightning bolt. And he kept on looking at her as his mouth migrated down to the tip of one of her breasts, as he drew her nipple deep into his mouth. She gasped, arching back, her stomach pitching hard. She had not been prepared for that. For the intense need that would flood her when he did that. Then with his hand, that work-rough, calloused hand, he cupped her other breast, pinching her nipple hard between his thumb and forefinger.

She started to move her hips against him, finding his hard thigh and trying to use it to soothe the ache that was building inside of her.

"So pretty," he murmured against her skin, raining kisses over her tender body, leaving her feeling electric. As if all the nerves in her had come online when his lips touched her. Parts of her that she hadn't even been aware of were suddenly taut and aching, begging for his touch.

Already, this was not what she had imagined.

It was so much more complex. She had thought of it as some great mystery of the universe. In answer to a question that she had. But so far, all she had were more questions. About herself. About him. About how he made her feel these things.

And all the while, he kept looking at her. She was so deeply aware that it was Logan touching her like this. Logan holding her in his arms and making her want things she had never even fantasized about before.

In her head it had been a formal lesson. In her head, she had thought she might sit for a while. Maybe chat a little before it all started.

And it was the deep, wrenching difference between that vague imagining she'd allowed herself and what was happening now that kept her from catching her breath.

Or maybe it was him.

Logan. How many times had she made jokes about sex with him in the room? About his sex life even? About him going off and hooking up with a woman. And she had no idea what it meant. Not really. Because she hadn't imagined him touching some other woman's breasts. Hadn't imagined him sucking her nipples into his mouth. Making her weak with wanting and helpless with desire.

If she had been able to imagine *this*, she never would have been able to joke about things like that. Not ever.

He was right. She hadn't known what she didn't know.

It was such a wealth of ignorance. She was the Scrooge McDuck of it. Swimming around in a pool of innuendo and not having a clue what it all was.

Suddenly, it was like a lock had clicked inside of her, and out had come the flood of understanding.

And they'd only just gotten their shirts off.

"I need you," he growled. "Dammit, I really do."

She knew that he was serious. That there was more to what he'd said than just sexual flattery or anything like that. That it wasn't just part of the thing that people said when they were about to have sex. But that it was some kind of deep truth that had come from the center of all that he was. And because he was Logan, that mattered.

The way he looked at her, like he knew the answers to all her questions, made her whole world feel tilted on its axis. And suddenly what had been inevitable earlier today felt deeply uncertain now.

It felt like the whole world was fragile now. Like all the mountains around Hope Springs might crack and collapse. Those mountains that were her guide when she was out on the ranch, her horizon line that she counted on to find her way. Those sentries that were centuries old and had stood guard around the land for generations suddenly compromised over this moment.

She didn't know what he needed from her.

So she nodded, put her hands on his chest, slid them up around his neck, and kissed him. And she found herself lifted up from the couch, her denim-clad thighs wrapped around his waist as he held her tightly, kissed her as they walked from the living room, right into his bedroom.

Logan's bedroom.

It hit her then that whatever she had thought about the two of them, there was a barrier between them. Because she had never been in his bedroom. If he were like a brother, she would have been. Because she'd been in her brother's bedroom a hundred times. More than. If he were family, she would have been in his room, like she had been with all her family.

If he were a friend like Sammy, there would have been no reason she hadn't gone into his room.

Whether her or him, there was some reason she hadn't been, though. Not even for a moment. Not even stepping in for thirty seconds while he looked for something. While she waited for him to get ready for the workday.

His bed was big.

Perfect for this kind of thing.

She wondered how many other women had been in it.

She didn't know why she should care.

"I don't bring anyone here," he said.

She startled, and for a second she was afraid she had spoken her misgivings out loud.

"I didn't like the look on your face," he said, taking hold of her chin again, between his thumb and forefinger. She was beginning to like that. "I don't just bring women here," he repeated. "Too personal."

There was a wealth of meaning in those two words. They were personal. And there was no pretending they weren't.

Neither was there any pretending that she didn't feel intensely relieved by them.

But he mattered.

She knew him about as well as she knew anybody. And he knew her, too.

Then they started kissing again, and when he pushed her back on the bed, he kissed away the nerves that started to twist her stomach. His hand moved down her body to the waistband of her jeans. He undid the button there, then slid the zipper down, pushing his hand between her legs. Her rose-bedecked underwear provided little protection from those firm fingers, and she gasped when he pressed down with the heel of his palm, sending a shock wave of pleasure through her body.

He stroked her through the thin cotton until she was panting, until she was working her hips in time with the motion. "I can feel how wet you are through your panties," he said against her lips, and she looked at him, her eyes flying wide. "That's a good thing, honey," he said. "You want me. I think you might want me almost as much as I want you." He slipped his fingers beneath the elastic on the leg of her underwear and his skin made contact with hers. She gasped at that first intimate touch. And then she moaned, unable to help herself. His hands...

His hands should be illegal. Those hands that she saw put in hard hours every day. She knew what had caused every callus, every scar because she'd been there. To know those hands were touching her, where no one else ever had.

Those hardworking man's hands.

"Feel what you do to me," he said, the words sounding

tortured as he grabbed hold of her hand and put it on the front of his jeans. He was so hard. And so…so big.

Her face was flushed, sweat on her brow. It wasn't nerves, though. Anticipation. The way she felt on the heels of an exhilarating ride on her horse. The way she felt after putting in hours of satisfying work.

Except it was that and then some. Plus adrenaline. Plus this intense sort of desire that was unlike anything she had ever known.

Then he pushed a finger inside of her, the invasion utterly foreign, and completely breathtaking. She bucked against his hand, almost embarrassed to betray how much she wanted him. How much she wanted more.

"It's good," he repeated. "I love how much you want me. And you do, don't you? You'd do anything I asked right now, wouldn't you?"

She would. She would hide a body for him if he needed her to. If only he would just keep touching her like this. She could only nod, a whimper escaping her lips.

"Good," he said. "Touch me."

She pressed more firmly against his denim-clad erection. And he shook his head. "Not like that."

She understood then. With clumsy fingers, she undid the front of his jeans, pulled his underwear down. She hadn't been prepared for the sight of him. Touching him had not given her a clear enough idea of just what she was dealing with.

He was… He was beautiful.

She'd never seen a naked man before. She'd had no idea she would find one beautiful. All her experience was babies, classic art and animals. And none of that had indicated she would find male anatomy any particular kind of aesthetically pleasing.

But Logan was.

And her body responded, her internal muscles clenching hard.

"See there? You might not have known what you wanted, but your body sure as hell knows," he said.

And again, he seemed to know exactly what she was thinking without her having to say a word.

She curved her fingers around him, shocked at how soft his skin was. How hot he was. And how hard.

She slid her fingers up and down, exploring him slowly.

"Dammit," he said, the word ground out through his teeth. "I can't handle it, Rosie."

"I just want to touch you," she whispered.

"No," he bit out, removing her hand from him.

Then she found her jeans being tugged hard down her legs, her white flowered underwear going down with them, like a flag of surrender.

"Logan," she said.

He gripped her hips roughly and spun her around, then she felt his teeth clamp down on one butt cheek. She yelped and he gave her a smack, right where his mouth had just been.

"What did I tell you?" he asked roughly. "I told you this would bite you in the ass."

But before she could respond, he turned her again and buried his face between her thighs, and then his mouth was on her.

Between her legs.

She moved her hands down to push him away, but then he growled, gripping her thighs and pulling her harder against him, and she found herself lacing her fingers through his hair as his tongue made her his prisoner as it slid over her sensitized bundle of nerves.

She couldn't do anything. She was weak. Boneless.

All she could do was make greedy, guttural sounds that she was sure weren't the kinds of sounds a woman was supposed to make when a man... Well, hell, she didn't know.

She had never even thought about a man doing this to her.

And now Logan was.

Logan.

And suddenly, it was all more than she could take. Desire crashed over her like a wave, and she clung to him, to his head, as he continued lapping at her while she called out his name. He didn't stop. He kept on going. Kept on going until she was begging for a reprieve, because she couldn't take any more. She was too sensitive. All over. And yet, somehow she still felt unsatisfied.

And she knew what she needed. She needed him.

She didn't have to say anything.

Wordlessly, he moved away from her, making his way to the nightstand and opening the drawer.

"You said you don't bring women here," she said when he reached inside and pulled out a condom.

"I don't," he said. "But I knew you were coming tonight. So I put it in a centrally located spot."

Possessiveness gripped her heart. She didn't want to think about him touching another woman. Didn't want to think about that box of condoms that he'd already had, she was sure, because it was open, after all. And he might have moved it thinking of her. But when he had opened it for the first time, he probably hadn't been.

"It's just you," he said. "It's just you tonight."

He pushed his jeans off the rest of the way, tearing open the packet and rolling the latex over his length. She couldn't stop staring. At the way his strong hand gripped his own body. It was mesmerizing. He was mesmerizing. Broad shoulders, muscular, defined body. Every time he moved there was a chain reaction in those dips and hollows, an action creating a reaction in that perfectly structured form.

He came back to the bed, kissing her. She could taste her own desire on his lips, and heat flooded her. She would have expected shame. But he clearly enjoyed her arousal so much that she couldn't feel ashamed of it.

He put his hand between her legs again, pushing a finger inside of her, and then another. "I can't promise it won't hurt," he murmured.

"It's okay," she said, her throat getting tight.

Now, they were talking. But she couldn't say she liked it. The wordless passion was a lot more comfortable. It made her eyes feel less scratchy and her mouth feel less dry.

He cursed, harsh and hard. "I can't, Rose," he said. "I can't wait anymore."

He gripped himself, positioned himself between her legs, nudging the entrance of her body with that blunt, thick head. He started to push inside, and she gasped, clinging to his shoulders. It didn't hurt. Not really.

But she shivered as she took him in, inch by inch. He was so thick, so hard. And she was…invaded. Conquered.

He closed his eyes and he shuddered. And she felt it. Felt it echo inside of her. It was too much. She wanted to run from it. Wanted to fight against it.

He was in her.

He'd warned her. That it was so much more than she could imagine.

She hadn't understood, not really.

Until now.

And she already felt all these things that he did. She didn't know how she was supposed to survive Logan actually being inside of her. And she hadn't thought of that. She was breathing too hard. Terrified of the great, swelling feelings in her chest, the pressure building behind her eyes.

But then he kissed her. And it wasn't a fire like before. It was sweet, like honey. Soothing. And with that sweetness he began to create that desire inside of her again. Overtaking the fear.

Then, he began to move. Deep, hard strokes that taught her about new places inside of herself each and every time.

Until she was desperate again. Until her entire world had become Logan, and the feelings he created so deep inside of her.

Until the only word she remembered was his name. And she said it over and over again. More times than she could count.

Then he said her name. Only once. Like a curse and a prayer all wrapped into one. "Rose."

And she shattered.

She clung to him, her body pulsing around his. And then she felt all that great strength crumble beneath her fingers. As he shook and shattered, giving in to his own release, his body pulsing deep inside of her.

She had been right.

The mountains were in danger of crumbling.

The most inevitable, certain mountain in her life just had. In bed with her. In her arms.

Buried deep inside of her.

Something felt fundamentally altered. Fundamentally changed.

And she was suddenly desperately, deeply afraid, that she would never be able to have that landscape back the way it had been.

That she might have lost her horizon line forever.

CHAPTER TWELVE

HE'D BEEN AFRAID to sleep. But after Rose had turned to him a third time, and they had both been left sated and exhausted, Logan had dozed. And when he woke up, he realized why falling asleep had been a bad idea. Because it was in that moment where he had a bit of distance, and time to rest his brain, where he truly realized what he had done.

Rose must have realized it too, because it wasn't the gray light of dawn that woke him. It was her. Padding around his room with bare feet. He opened his eyes just in time to see her pulling her jeans up over her ass.

An ass he had grabbed last night. Multiple times. And bitten once. Well. Twice. An ass that was even more beautiful than he had let himself imagine.

Dammit.

What the hell had they done?

Well. He actually knew the answer to that question, because everything they had done flashed through his mind in full, vivid color.

He had said that he was going to teach her about sex.

That hadn't been a lesson. Hadn't been a forfeit taken for losing a bet.

It had been a conquering.

A final exam without any chance to learn the source material.

It had been amazing. But he had been selfish. Rougher than he should've been. More demanding.

Three times.

And she'd given as good as she'd gotten. He'd lost count of how many times she'd shattered.

But she'd been a virgin. What the hell had he been thinking?

"Where are you going?" He hadn't meant to ask that question. He had meant to…apologize maybe. Instead, he could only focus on the kick of regret that he felt over the fact she put her jeans back on.

"I don't have work clothes," she said quietly. "I need to go get some. I need to get into the house without anyone seeing."

"Why?"

"I'm still in the same clothes from last night. Anyway. I told Sammy that I might be out with friends. So…I can just tell her that I got drunk at the bar and fell asleep on my friend Lacey's couch. It's not that big of a deal."

"Right."

Not that big of a deal. Everything inside of him felt like it had been demolished with a wrecking ball.

"I'll see you for work."

She turned toward him, and his gut tightened, his dick instantly getting hard. She was topless. And she had the most beautiful breasts he'd ever seen. It wasn't the size, though they were generous enough. The shape. The way they fit in his hands. The color of her nipples, and the way they tightened when she was aroused. Or cold. He wasn't exactly sure which she was now. But she was something.

"I… Yeah. I'll see you at the barn." She nodded decisively, a very Rose move, then went into the living room. He got out of bed, not bothering to grab any clothes, following her, getting there just in time to see her pick her bra up from the ground.

"You don't have to leave."

"We have work to do."

She looked at him, and even in the gray light he could see color mounting in her cheeks. He looked down. He was sporting an erection, and wasn't doing anything to hide it.

"Sorry about that," she said. "You know we have work."

It took him a minute to realize what she was apologizing for. "Are you...apologizing for my...?"

"Yes. Sorry about your penis. Anyway. I'll see you."

She dressed quickly, and scampered out like a frightened rabbit with a fox on her tail. And he supposed it was a fair enough move, all things considered.

Fox. Hen.

He had already eaten her up, though. So, the running was happening a little bit late.

After that he decided to get in a cold shower, and get dressed, doing his damnedest to not replay the events of the night before.

That had been a mistake.

Liar.

He gritted his teeth.

Yeah, he was really good at telling himself all the things he wished that he believed.

That Rose was some virgin princess who deserved better than a rough roll in the hay with a guy who couldn't offer her more than good sex.

That he felt guilty for what he'd done. That it was a mistake and shouldn't happen again.

Yeah. That was what a decent guy would think.

As he stepped out onto the porch and put his cowboy hat on his head, looking out at the ranch, this place that was his in part because of Rose's brother. Because of the bond that they shared, which should have been something he wanted to honor a bit more. It was all the same.

All of it. Nothing had changed since he had stripped Rose Dalton naked on his couch. Since he had taken her virginity in his bedroom. The sky was still blue, the mountains were still tall and strong. It was just the inside of him that felt different.

Or perhaps, grimly aware of what he was.

Hank Dalton's son, whether he wanted to be or not.

Because if he asked himself what Hank Dalton would have done, with a pretty little thing that showed up on his doorstep... Well, the answer was everything Logan had done.

Except, Hank Dalton wouldn't have used a condom.

At least there was the condom.

He went out to the barn, but Rose wasn't there. And so he got to his chores, expecting that she would show up at some point.

He didn't see her. All day. Not until he came in the house at dinnertime, the smell of some kind of spicy baked good hitting him with force, right at the same time Rose appeared in the living room, making him crave a whole different kind of sweet.

"Didn't see you all day," he said.

"I was busy," she said. "Ended up getting caught in the far pasture. Sorry about that."

He would've been tempted to think that everything was normal. Except for the set of her shoulders. Usually, Rose had a particular look to her. Stood defiant, her posture straight. Instead, she was bowed in slightly, and that was unusual.

But almost the instant that he noticed it, she had corrected it, looking at him with defiance he couldn't ignore.

That little brat was going to pretend that nothing had happened.

All of the nothing that they had done flashed into his mind. Naked skin and gasps of pleasure. The way that her skin tasted against his tongue. The way that soft body had felt beneath his hands.

Yeah, there was a reason this had been something they couldn't do. Shouldn't do.

It was just that he didn't care anymore. It was done. And he wasn't going to play around with it.

Maybe because you're thirty-three and not twenty-three.

Well. Maybe. Wouldn't hurt her to get a dose of maturity.

But there was nothing he could say because then Iris was in the room, greeting her sister with a much warmer smile than they'd gotten yesterday.

"Hi," Iris said.

"Hi," Rose said, and if he didn't know Rose, he would have said that her greeting was shy. Hell, he supposed it was.

"I made your favorite," Iris said. "Fried chicken and mashed potatoes."

Rose lit up. "You did? Thank you." She looked hopeful.

Food meant a lot to Rose. And in general, said a lot about the family. Iris and Sammy had been cooking for all of them for years. But particularly Iris, who had learned at a young age, and it made sure that things that had felt like home to them when their mom had been alive carried on.

It made him think of his mom's cookies. That conversation he'd had with Rose. He pushed it to the side.

He couldn't tell for sure if this was Iris's attempt to bury the Elliott hatchet. Which, in Logan's opinion, wasn't even worth being a thing. That guy wasn't anything to get worked up about.

And it turned out that Logan did in fact have a position to criticize him from. He'd been sloppy, and he'd been lazy. He'd settled in the middle, had taken the non-committal route. And then Logan had taken the object of his desire's virginity. That was what happened when you messed around.

He cleared his throat and moved past both women into the kitchen. He ignored the faint scent of Rose that followed after him. Not the flower. She didn't smell like a flower. She smelled like woman. Skin. Dust, hay, horse. Ranching was his passion, the land was in his blood. And Rose carried the scent of both on a body that was enough to drive him to sin.

Had, in fact.

Yeah, not responding to that scent, particularly now that he was even more in tune with the bit that was just her, was a damn miracle.

But maybe this was his one Christmas miracle. Maybe God was granting him the strength to get through this dinner without losing vital body parts. Anything could happen, he supposed.

Sammy was already sitting at a set table, the matching plates, which he still wasn't used to, in place, along with serving bowls filled to the hilt with food.

It was impossible for him to list all the ways this family had taken care of him. But food, home-cooked meals in the midst of tragedy, had been one of them, and it had been vital.

A great time to think about everything they all meant to him. When he was in the middle of a very unrepentant fall from grace. Yeah, there was no part of him that was repentant. Not now. He had half a mind to turn Rose over his knee and spank her for being a little brat and pretending nothing had passed between them, that was for sure.

And that idea sounded a hell of a lot more appealing than he had expected it to. But then, getting his hands on her in any way sounded appealing. One sex session had hardly dealt with five years' worth of fantasies.

No. Far from it. If anything, it had just whipped up more. A hell of a lot more.

The coward sat at the far end of the table, keeping her distance from him. He hadn't taken his seat yet, but when Ryder entered the room, he decided not to push it. Not just yet.

Trust Sammy to go ahead and fill any silence, and she did, which Logan appreciated, since he and Rose clearly weren't in talking moods. And if Sammy took a breath, the rest of them were bound to notice about Rose. Rose was typically pretty chatty. An understatement, really.

Rose was the one who liked to interject a harebrained scheme or an innuendo. The idea of turning the tables on her and throwing an innuendo out there now that she might actually understand what one of them meant, really and truly, amused him. But then, it was Rose. And there was a very real danger she would get frustrated and announce to Ryder that Logan had despoiled her, which might end in his inglorious death by drowning in a bowl of gravy, right next to Iris's famous mashed potatoes.

He didn't particularly want that for himself. Mostly because he wanted a chance to get another taste of Rose.

He was less interested in the gravy.

"Did you have a good night last night?" Sammy asked.

The hair on the back of his neck stood on end, and he

looked at her, realizing she was directing the question to Rose.

Rose fidgeted. "Yeah," she said.

"I didn't see you come home."

"I told you I might crash with Lacey," Rose said, which he noticed was not an affirmative statement that she had crashed with Lacey.

It was, though, the story that she had said she was going to give, the one she'd said she'd given Sammy on her way out.

He could only give thanks that Pansy and West hadn't come to dinner tonight. Because Pansy would have smelled the bullshit in this story. Sammy might, but Sammy didn't know about the kiss. Of course, Sammy knew about his feelings. But Sammy would have confidence in his self-control where Rose was concerned.

Sammy believed in the good in people. Lucky for him.

"The cousins will be here in a couple of days," Ryder commented. "Colt and Jake are going to sleep in the bunk-house."

"Like old times," Logan said.

"Unless you want to put one of them up in your cabin," Ryder said.

Logan snorted. Okay, under normal circumstances, he would. Should. But he didn't particularly want anybody staying in his cabin right now. Because he wanted the luxury of having Rose in his cabin when he felt like it. And having Colt or Jake adjacent was not going to work.

"Yeah, I'll pass," Logan said. "Anyway, they're only going to spend the night here half the time."

Classic. Turning it around on someone else. A go-to asshole move. Making it about the fact that they probably wanted to go out and get laid, not about the fact that he wanted to stay here and do it.

"True enough," Ryder said. "And I imagine you don't want to share your sole bathroom."

Right. That would have been maybe the better excuse. That the cabin only had one bathroom, and wasn't really suited to sharing with anyone that you weren't pretty intimate with.

The thought of intimacy brought him back to Rose, and he looked down at her end of the table.

She was looking at him. But the minute that his eyes connected with hers, she looked away, studying her fried chicken with deep interest. Her cheeks turned pink.

She was very bad at this.

Pretending that nothing had happened just enough to make him mad, but not actually managing to cover that something was up. Basically the worst person a man could ever sneak around with.

And he intended to do a whole lot more sneaking.

Hey, how else would she learn?

"There's going to be so much testosterone in this house," Sammy grumbled.

"Hey," Ryder said. "It culminates in a wedding. I can't think of anything more estrogen fueled."

"Really?" Sammy said sweetly. "Was it estrogen that drove you to build me a fairy canopy for our wedding, Ryder?"

"That was love, woman. And you know it."

That actually did make his stomach turn over. But it wasn't guilt. No, he had accepted that there wouldn't be any of that. But there was something... Looking at that, the connection that Ryder and Sammy had, it was enough to make anyone ache.

They'd spent their lives in this makeshift family, doing their best to fill the gaps left by dead or inadequate parents. But that was what it was. Filling gaps. The best that they all could. Ryder and Sammy had somehow found a piece that fit completely. And they'd found it in each other.

Pansy had managed to find it with someone who hadn't been part of their little clan. And still, they'd found a way to complete each other.

He'd made a lot of decisions in his life, and they'd all served to make sure that he was off in his own corner, licking wounds that the rest of them didn't even know about. He'd kept distance between himself and the rest of them.

He didn't regret it. Mostly. What he'd done had all been for good reason. A tangle of reasons that he could barely follow back to the beginning now. But the truth was, it had made him who he was. What he was. And there was no going back from that.

He didn't mind. Mostly.

Until he saw things like that, like Ryder and Sammy, and he wondered what it might be like to have someone who knew you that way. Who knew all those things about you and wanted you just the same.

He gritted his teeth and turned his focus to his meal.

Rose didn't say a single word to him. She managed to talk to everyone else, but she didn't talk to him. And by the time they were finished, he was in a damned foul mood.

"I'm tired," she announced. "I'm going upstairs."

She pushed her chair back from the table and took her plate to the sink. He could feel the dare radiating from her body. The triumph. She thought she had escaped him. That she wasn't going to have to answer to him at all. That was what she thought.

He could read her well enough to know that.

They might not fill all the gaps in each other, but he knew Rose Daniels. Better than just about anybody, he was sure.

And she couldn't go pulling things like this without him knowing exactly what it was she was doing. Running the hell away from him.

And she figured that if she announced boldly to her family that she was going to bed, he was going to let her do it.

But on the tail of Rose's departure, dinner ended, and everyone began to disperse. And no one thought anything of him heading upstairs. Ryder wouldn't have even noticed because a football game had started, and he was basically absorbed by that. Logan had never been into sports in quite the way his friend was. Ryder coached the local high school team now, and when he'd been younger, had been on a path to a college scholarship for football until his parents had died. Then he had to stay in Gold Valley and make sure everyone and everything was taken care of.

Guilt arrived then.

But not over what he'd expected it to. No. This was old guilt. The guilt that lived here in the Christmas season, woven all around him like strands of tinsel. Guilt that he never really thought about. Because it was like the blood in his veins. It was just there. Pumping through him. And he was rarely aware of it. But then, there were moments. Moments like this, when it hit. And then, it tended to hit with the intensity of a gale force wind.

Sammy and Iris were in the kitchen still, having tea and eating cake. So, they weren't going to notice anything, either. And the fox was in the henhouse. So, he did what any good fox would do.

He played like a gentleman for one moment, knocking on Rose's door.

"What?"

He took that as permission to enter. He pushed the door open and ignored her wide eyes.

"What are you doing in here?"

"Making sure you don't forget."

He closed the door behind him, and then closed the distance between them. He couldn't remember the last time he'd been in Rose's room. At the moment, he couldn't remember if he ever had been.

It was just like her. Serviceable, but with touches of femininity. Some nice, classic furniture that he assumed had come from her parents. A full-size bed with a whole mound of pillows, mismatched pillowcases, though. But Rose would care a lot less about the pillowcases, and a lot more about having a lot of blankets and a lot of softness all around her.

She was tough. And she worked harder than any man he'd ever known.

But she liked her creature comforts. Didn't like to be cold.

Instantly, he pictured her with a cherry-red nose and a scowl on her face as she had been the other day, and all the arousal that he'd been holding at bay all evening flooded him.

Because somehow, he wanted this woman almost especially when she was essentially her.

She opened her mouth like she might protest, but he pulled her into his arms and stopped it with his mouth. He kissed her, kissed her with all of the frustration that had been building up inside of him through dinner. Kissed her hard and long and deep. Because maybe if he did, she would feel that great, empty thing inside of him that had opened up during dinner watching Ryder and Sammy together. Maybe she would understand.

Logan wasn't the half of anyone's whole. He had worked for too long to whittle himself into a solitary shape that couldn't much function with anyone else. But he wanted her.

But he needed her to understand all the same.

She whimpered, wrapped her arms around his neck and arched against him.

But this was his hard limit.

He wasn't taking her down on that plush bed. Was not screwing her with her brother downstairs watching football.

No. Even he had a line.

He pulled away from her, and she looked up at him in irritated wonder.

Yeah. She was irritated.

"What was that?" she asked.

"You know full well what that was. I wasn't going to let you pretend nothing happened between us."

"Why not? We should pretend that nothing happened between us. It happened. It's done." The jut of her chin was particularly stubborn just then, and he wasn't sure if he wanted to scold her or kiss her again. Maybe both.

"It's not done," he bit out.

"It should be," she said. "Because we gotta get back to who we are. To what we do. I can't sleep with you every night and then go sit at dinner like that. I can't do it again. It's fine. And I'm not hurt. But I don't want to go sneaking around, either."

He huffed a laugh. "Only because you're not used to sneaking around."

"And you are. I'm sure."

He hadn't had to do a lot of sneaking around. His guardian had been an eighteen-year-old boy. Yeah, Ryder hadn't wanted them screwing things up too badly when it came to school. And he hadn't wanted them doing drugs or drinking too much or anything like that. But he'd look the other way when it came to a few beers because he had to, since he was always having a few of his own.

And he'd definitely look the other way if there was a girl involved.

Unless it was a school night. He been kind of a stickler for that. But as he shouted at him once when his grades had been bad, he wasn't going to support a deadbeat. So he had to do something to improve his own life.

Logan had graduated from high school. But only barely. And anyway, his solution had been to become a rancher. Not that ranchers didn't need or didn't have smarts. It was only that given there was a whole lot of connections involved in the position he'd gotten, they hadn't been necessary for him.

"Doesn't matter. This isn't about anyone else," he found himself saying. "It's about you and me. And this is unfinished."

"It isn't," she said, wrapping her arms around herself. For about one second she looked vulnerable. And then, on a deep breath, she seemed to find herself again. "I'm good. I mean, I feel like I learned everything I set out to learn. Questions answered. Thank you."

"The thing is," he said, "I didn't have questions about sex. I had questions about you. I've wanted you. I still do."

"To what end?"

The question stabbed him right through the chest, and twisted hard. "Does there have to be an end?"

"There will be. Might as well be now."

"I don't agree."

"Too bad. I didn't ask you. Get out of my room."

He didn't have to be asked twice. But he could see that she was lying. Lying about wanting it stopped. She didn't. She wanted him, the same as he wanted her. But the thing with Rose was you could lock horns with her endlessly.

And he had no desire to get into that again. He wouldn't have to. He didn't know how he knew it, only that he did.

"Suit yourself," he said. "But I want you to remember one thing. I didn't do this just to satisfy your curiosity. I did it because I've wanted you for the last five years. Because wanting you has kept me awake at night. Because for the last five years it's been a damn struggle to work with you when all I wanted to do was pull you in my arms, pull you down underneath me. I tried to keep my distance, Rose. But in the end you wouldn't let me. I have self-control to spare, and I could have gone on never touching you. You did this. You asked me for it. And now I just think you're cutting it off because you don't like the fact that you're not in control. Because I made you feel things and you don't like it. You think on that."

Then he turned and walked out of her bedroom, moving quickly down the stairs, because if he didn't get the hell out now, he was going to change his mind. Going to turn around and go right back to her childhood bedroom and hope that Ryder shouting at the TV when his team failed to get a first down would drown out the scream when she came.

He kept his head low as he walked into the living room, heading straight for the door.

"Hey," Ryder said. "I didn't know you were still here."

"Headed out," he bit out.

"Why don't you stay? Grab a beer. Watch the game."

"No. I got an early morning ahead." It was a lie. But maybe he would do something to make sure it wasn't a lie. Maybe he would manufacture some chore and get his ass out the door before five just to make this true. So it wasn't just about him running to a cold shower because he wanted a woman who had just cut him off, and he was furious as hell.

"Suit yourself," Ryder said.

He had to leave quickly after that, because if he didn't, he was going to end up laughing hysterically. There was no suiting himself. Not now. Not in this. If he had his way, he would march right back upstairs and take Rose into his arms again. Carry her down the stairs behind her brother and out the front door, back to his cabin, where he would lock her inside and spend the next few days…

What? What the hell are you going to do?

To what end?

Yeah. She'd asked that. And it was the one thing he didn't really have an answer for. Because the first thing he wanted to say was why did it have to end?

Well, he didn't even know what Rose wanted. Not in terms of this kind of thing. Relationships. Did she fantasize about getting married and having children?

The thought made his throat dry.

Rose. Getting married. Having children.

No. It wasn't for him.

He'd had a family once.

He wasn't going to make another one.

He'd depended on one person in his whole life. And she'd depended on him right back. His mom had been his whole world. The woman who had devoted herself to raising him. His world had fallen when he'd lost her. And the thing that haunted him, and always would, was that it had all happened because of how he'd tried to love her.

He would never be able to get rid of that. That feeling

of being so excited about something, so proud. And having it turn to death in the end.

Didn't matter if thinking it was his fault was martyrish or thinking it would happen again was some kind of magic thinking. It was still there. Inside him. Likely where his ability to love another person right would have been.

He'd wished things were different a lot of times, for a lot of reasons.

Tonight, he wished they were different for Rose.

But it didn't change things. It never did.

No matter who he made those wishes for.

CHAPTER THIRTEEN

SHE WASN'T USUALLY INDECISIVE. Rose was big on leaping before she looked. She got an idea, and she went with it. She also wasn't used to regretting her actions. But she had been seriously regretting several actions for the past few days. One of the big ones was meddling in Iris's life. And that was something that she needed to address.

The other thing was that she hadn't addressed it at all yet, because she had been so consumed with her own stuff.

Then there was her own stuff. Yeah. She regretted what had happened with Logan. She regretted turning him away last night, too. She felt so fragile, so delicate, and she had no idea who she could talk to about it. Because it was Logan, it made things complicated. She probably would have just told her sisters if it had been any other guy. But Logan? If she told Sammy she would tell Ryder. Ryder would find his burdizzo and castrate Logan like one of their ranch animals.

Pansy had not been supportive at all just knowing that Logan had kissed her. If she found out what else they had done…

She sighed heavily. She was still avoiding him, and she didn't want him to know that she was avoiding him. Eventually, she was going to have to deal. But he'd made it clear that he wanted more. And she didn't have a handle on her emotions. She felt small. Embarrassed. Everything that had happened between them had been wonderful. Off the charts, amazing wonderful. A combination of riding her horse at full speed and Christmas morning, somehow combined. Exhilarating, magical. But she hadn't expected the emotional reaction that had followed.

She'd woken up early in the morning, and everything from the night before had flashed through her mind. One of the first things she thought was that she needed to get away. Because if he was gentle with her, if he was nice, if he kissed her, well, if he anything… She might cry.

She had been running away from him, and from tears for the last two days. She worried that she was getting to the end of that. That she was either going to end up weeping at a really bad time, or was going to end up grabbing him and either yelling at him or kissing him.

She wasn't sure which thought disturbed her more.

It was lunchtime, and she had managed to stay away from him for the day. She was sure that he had packed a lunch, and she went into the kitchen to collect something there.

But the house wasn't empty.

It wasn't Logan that she saw standing in the kitchen, it was Iris.

"Oh," she said. "Hi."

"You don't have to be weird," Iris said.

"I'm not being weird."

"You nearly jumped out of your skin when you saw me."

Well, some of that was because she was worried that the other person in the kitchen might be Logan. But she wasn't going to say that.

"You just startled me. That's all." She sighed. "I'm sorry. I'm so sorry that I meddled in your life."

"Don't. Just don't do that."

"But I am," Rose said. "I'm sorry that I thought he liked you, when he liked me."

"I really don't want to talk about it," Iris said. "The fried chicken was a peace offering and a hope we wouldn't ever speak of it."

But Rose needed to speak of it. "I didn't even think you liked him very much."

"Rose, please," Iris said. "It's embarrassing enough without having to go over it."

"Why are you embarrassed?"

"Because! I…I would never have liked him. I would never have gotten involved. But you're right. I'm alone. I'm always alone. And he seemed interested and no one else ever has been, so even though I wasn't immediately enamored with him I thought I should make myself have stronger feelings. And I did. I did and then he *didn't like me*."

Rose's horror grew. Expanded. She'd thought her sister was maybe heartbroken, but this was actually worse. She was humiliated. Rejected by someone she'd forced herself to have feelings for. "Iris, I'm so sorry…"

"You know that's not even the worst part, Rose. And it's pretty terrible, but it's not the worst. Do you know what the worst thing is?"

"What?" Rose asked, her throat going tight.

"Khaki pants. Water filtration. That's what you think of me. That is the…the great and exciting guy that you wanted to hook me up with. And I don't even know what to make of that. I don't know who I'm more disappointed in, Rose, you or me. That you think that's who I am. That that's what I want. Or that I let myself think that it was maybe what I should want, and went along with it. And I know that I am insulted down to my bones that I lowered myself to try and feel something for him, and he didn't even like me at all. So really, go ahead and apologize, but it's going to take a while for all of it to settle. I'm not mad at you. Not really. I'm just... I just had this crazy couple of weeks where suddenly I thought maybe my whole life was going to be discussions about water filtration systems over dinner." She shook her head. "And not only that... that I hoped for it. For just a while. That I thought maybe it was the best I could do. That I needed to just settle, and that maybe it was going to be... That I should be happy and like it. Because what am I doing with my life, Rose? I cook and clean for the ranch. But Sammy is here now and she and Ryder are married and I just live in the house. You at least work the land. I don't..."

"Iris," Rose said. "I did not mean to insult you by setting you up with him. I thought that you would want somebody who was stable. Somebody nice. I didn't see him as beige or boring, that's not it. So many men out there are...they aren't together like you. You took care of me. I didn't want you to be taking care of some guy. I thought you should have someone who had his ducks in a row. Someone who... someone who would take care of you."

Iris's expression changed. "Rose, that's... It's sweet of you. And it makes me see it a little differently, that's for sure. But I'm not looking for someone to take care of me. I don't need it." She let out a long breath. "It's just... I need to think about some things."

"Like?"

"I don't know. I don't know, maybe... Maybe I should buy a bakery."

Rose hadn't expected that. "A bakery?"

"Yes. I've been thinking about it. Ever since we saw that Sugarplum Fairy went out of business. I've been thinking about starting my own business. I would need a lot of capital. Money to invest and a business plan, and a lot of things that I don't know anything about. And really… None of us do."

"But we would all help you," Rose said.

"I know you would," Iris responded. "Look, Rose, I never doubted that what you were doing you were doing because you loved me."

"But I hurt you. I didn't want to do that."

She didn't think that she could possibly feel…worse. But she did. She felt like she had been stripped of an entire protective layer. Probably left it somewhere back in Logan's room. And now here she was, having to really face down the implications of what she had done by meddling in her sister's life.

"I'm so sorry," she said. "I didn't understand what I was doing."

She reflected on the intimacy that she had shared with Logan. In her mind, setting her sister up with a guy was so much more simple than she realized it was now. She was saying: Here, I think you should get naked with this man. Let him touch you. Let him inside of you.

Oh, there were so many ways that Logan had been right about her and all she didn't know. It stung now. Now that it was too late for her to go back and do better. Be different. Understand.

When she thought of it in those terms, of course pleat-front khaki Elliott was a terrible choice. Of course Iris didn't want a man who was thinking about water filtration when he touched her.

Sex was… It was intimate and raw and terrifying. It was the most incredible thing she had ever experienced. It wasn't something she could just go get a lesson in.

She had been an idiot to think so. And Logan had been right.

And maybe, just maybe, that was actually why she was so upset. Because everything he had said to her was true.

That she didn't know what she didn't know.

She had no idea what she was asking him for, and so it had been easy for her to walk herself into something she didn't even understand.

"Are you okay?" Iris asked.

"I… How did you end up asking about me? See, this is the problem," Rose said. "I just wanted to do something for you. But I'm sorry that I didn't ask you what you needed. You've always been there for me. You've always been there for me, and so often in this family I feel like…like I was everybody's burden to carry. I'm older now, I don't have to be a burden. And here I went and made myself a burden without even meaning to." She sighed. "I'm sorry. Can I help you with the bakery idea?"

"I don't even know where to begin."

"Neither do I. But we can find out. And I'll help you. I'll support you in whatever way I can, even if it's just… carrying things. Or painting walls."

"I think I am a long way away from painting anything," Iris said. "It's just… It's just a tiny little idea. In a germ of one. It's probably not worth thinking much about right now. But… Yeah, I don't know. I just think it might be nice. To do something new. To do something bigger."

Rose opted not to say that the concept of doing something had possibly spurred her into doing the most rash, ridiculous thing she had ever done. It wasn't the time.

And given the way that everything was, she supposed it wasn't the ideal moment to confess to her sister that she'd had amazing, earth-shattering sex with a man who did not in fact wear khakis.

Oh, no. She really didn't need to get into that with Iris.

All of a sudden, she heard the thundering of footsteps down the stairs. It was Sammy, with the dogs hot on her heels. "It's an emergency," she said, rushing out the front door.

"What?" Iris and Rose asked in unison, moving after her.

"Ryder texted me and said that there was an accident."

"What?" Rose repeated, moving as quickly after her sister-in-law as she could.

"Logan turned the tractor over on himself and he's stuck. Ryder is trying to lift it up, but it's stuck. And we're going to need help."

Everything in Rose's mind went blank. Logan was hurt. The tractor had rolled over on top of him. People died that way.

No. That wasn't fair. She couldn't lose Logan. They couldn't lose Logan. They had already lost so much. And the idea of their family having to go through anything more was… No.

She pushed all the thoughts away as the three of them ran toward the barn, following Sammy, who was moving as quickly as a woman in her advanced stage of pregnancy could.

When they came to the place where the tractor was tipped on its side, and she could see Logan's leg sticking out, she screamed his name. She wasn't even conscious of making the decision to do it. And then she overtook Sammy, her boots pounding the ground, her arms swinging wildly back and forth.

When she rounded to the other side of the tractor, she could see that he was conscious.

"You're alive," she said.

"Yeah," he answered. "If I was dead there would be no point in calling 911. And really, there's no point anyway except I've got to get out of here."

"I'm going to hook my truck up to it," Ryder said. "I've got a winch. Just need to get back up on its side."

"And not make a mistake," Logan growled. "Because I don't really want you cutting my leg off if you drop the fucking thing back down on me."

"I'm not going to cut your leg off," Ryder said. "It's not any different than hauling anything else out."

"Except I'm under it."

"How the hell did you manage that?" Rose asked angrily. She had half a mind to bend down and hit him on the exposed shoulder. "You dumbass."

"Took the corner too hard," he said. "I'm not going to die or anything."

There was a wild look in Ryder's eyes, though, and it was that that scared her. Because her older brother was nothing if not absolutely steady. Like a rock. And if he wasn't steady, then maybe there was real cause for concern.

"I don't want to move him," Ryder whispered to Rose. "You know, in case he has a spine injury or something. I don't know. I can't tell." He shook his head. "I've just heard stories. You know, adrenaline blocks pain. So, he's yelling at me, but I don't trust that to mean he's not injured."

She swallowed hard and nodded.

"I don't want to move him," Ryder said. "But I'd like to get the tractor off him."

"Maybe we should just wait for help," Rose said.

She hated that he was stuck there, underneath that tractor. Hated that he might be in pain at all.

She lowered herself down to her knees and looked at his

face. His handsome face, which looked so different now than it had a few days ago.

She knew her brother was right there. But she figured he wouldn't think anything of her touching Logan when he was pinned underneath the tractor. She put her hand on his cheek. And ignored the fact that *Ryder* wasn't on his knees with his hands on Logan's face. That perhaps it showed they had a different relationship, no matter the situation.

Ryder was hooking a winch up to his truck, and attaching the other end to the tractor.

"If you die," she hissed, "I will kill you."

"Well, dying is not on my agenda for the day," he said, looking up at her, that startling blue making her stomach tight, even now. "Should have been nicer to me last night, though."

"Don't push it," she said.

He laughed, and it sounded rusty, and she hated that.

It was only one minute later that a fire truck came up the driveway, lights on, no sirens. And by then, Ryder had the tractor hooked up to his truck.

The EMTs came, and took stock of Logan.

"Looks like it's missed most of him," said the woman, a dark-haired, dark-eyed petite creature that Rose vaguely remembered from school. Juniper Rainville.

"Well, that's good," Rose said, realizing she was sitting flat on her ass in the dirt, and not quite able to bring herself to move.

"Should I try to pull it off him?"

The other EMT, a young guy that Rose didn't recognize, turned to Ryder. "I mean, you might as well. We could call for backup and pull it off, but if you think that'll work..."

"Should," Ryder said, engaging the winch.

The tractor began to rise up off Logan, and as it did, the

paramedics slipped a spine board beneath him, strapping him down and pulling him out from beneath it.

"I'm fine," Logan said.

"Yeah, but in the interest of not causing damage, we have to treat you like you might have a spinal injury," Juniper said. "So be patient."

"I'm not going to the hospital," he grumbled.

"Maybe you should," Rose said, pacing back and forth and staring down at him while the EMTs checked him out.

"You want to pay my bill?"

Rose pinched the bridge of her nose while they looked in his eyes, checked his spine for trauma.

"I recommend you go to the hospital," Juniper said. "Just to be safe."

"All right. But in your opinion am I gravely injured?"

"I can't diagnose you."

"Isn't there paperwork I can sign and not go?"

"Yes," she said.

"Then I want that paperwork. Because I'm not going to the hospital."

"Why not?" Ryder asked.

"Because I'm fine," he said.

"You're just being stubborn," Rose said.

"Seriously," he said, having finished being checked over, and moving himself into a sitting position, then standing. "I'm fine."

He winced as he tried to put pressure on his leg.

"Are you sure you didn't break it?" she asked.

"It did look like he managed to mostly get his body in a gap," Juniper said. "He's lucky. Because if anything would have made real direct contact he probably would have wound up with some crushed limbs. Or worse."

"Nothing is crushed," Logan said. "Believe me, shock

might be a hell of a thing, but it's certainly not going to have me standing on a crushed femur."

"I'll get you that paperwork," Juniper said. "You have to promise that if you have any severe symptoms you'll take yourself to the doctor."

"I don't have to promise a damn thing," Logan grumbled.

Rose felt slightly at her wits' end. She didn't know how to react to this. As a friend, she was scared. As his lover, she was something else entirely. The feeling that was rolling around inside of her chest was somewhere on the border of hysterical and unreasonable. And she didn't know what to do. Didn't know how to react at all, so she found herself sort of frozen.

She knew that Sammy and Iris were fussing, and that Ryder was examining his tractor. And Rose was just kind of standing there, her ears buzzing. She felt so… She was already such a disaster. And then a tractor had fallen on the man. A tractor.

And she had no idea what she was supposed to do in response to that. It was like… Was he being punished? Was he being punished for taking her virginity? Because that didn't seem fair. He hadn't taken it. She had given it to him. With joy, at that.

So, surely, God wouldn't drop a tractor on him for that.

He had done great work that night.

And she had rejected him. But she felt like she had been scraped out inside. She felt like she were dying a little bit. Like she might have been crushed underneath that tractor. And that made her think that rejecting him had been the best thing she could have done for herself. Because if she felt like this now, how would she feel later?

There couldn't be a later.

For that very reason.

Except…

"I have to go," she said. And suddenly, she found herself running again. Running like she had done to his accident. Running and running like a coward.

And in her mind, flashes of another time she had run filtered through her mind.

There was an accident.

Mom and Dad…

She ran and ran. When she stopped, she was breathing hard, and she realized tears were running down her cheeks. Her lungs burned from the cold air. She stopped at the base of a tree and sank down to the ground. She was already dirty anyway. And she cried. Cried out all the tears that she had been holding inside of herself since that night with Logan. Since last night when she had told him no. Since this morning when she had talked to Iris and had to face how badly she had hurt her sister.

Since she had seen him lying on the ground pinned underneath the tractor.

And for good measure, she cried some tears she thought might have been building inside of her for the last few years. Because sometimes she felt lonely. And there was no way to say that. No way to say that sometimes she just felt like there was a big hole inside of her chest and nothing would fill it. Nothing. Not ever.

Because she loved talking to her sisters and confiding in them, but sometimes she just missed her mom. And she usually didn't let herself. Because how could she? When everyone had done so much for her. Everyone had done so much for her and it seemed like being sad about what she didn't have wasn't fair. It seemed like it minimized everything they had done for her. Because of course they missed their parents, too. They missed their parents, and they'd also had to take care of Rose. And it felt like a terrible repayment to be sad. To feel like she was missing bits and pieces of something vital.

It wasn't anybody's fault. Iris and Ryder and Sammy could not have done any more for her. Pansy couldn't have done more. Logan...

She pressed her fists to her eyeballs. Trying to stop the tears. She hated this. She hated it more than anything. All these feelings that were welling up inside of her. These feelings that she usually did such a great job of ignoring.

She cried and she hid. Until she felt like a coward. Until she felt...better.

She had felt fragile for a while now. And there was something about crying that made it feel like that fragility had drained out of her. Like it was done. Like she had drained some kind of poison from her body and left herself feeling stronger.

And she wondered if maybe this was the big change that really needed to happen. Finally thinking about her own feelings.

Finally admitting that she had pain.

That it was okay to feel loss. That it didn't make her a burden or ungrateful or any of the other things she was so afraid of being.

She sat there until it was starting to get dark. Which it did so early this time of year.

Then she stood, pushing herself up, away from the tree. She felt a little bit guilty about leaving Logan. Because he might have been in some kind of serious pain. But she wouldn't know, because she had run. Of course, someone would have come to get her if he was hurt badly.

Finally, when she had herself a little bit together, she

trudged home. When she came into the house, dinner had just been set out on the table.

"Where's Logan?" she asked.

"He was feeling kind of done in," Iris said, looking at her curiously. "He went home."

"Oh. Did he... Does he have dinner?"

"No. I bet he wouldn't mind if you brought him some. Are you okay, Rose?"

She stared at her sister for a long moment. "I think so."

"He's okay," Iris said, her tone so gentle it made Rose want to cry again.

"You know how it is," Rose said, looking down. "You know. Because... Sometimes you think everything will be okay, but..."

"People die," Iris said.

"Yes," she whispered. "People die. When you don't expect them to."

"He's not going to die," Iris said.

She nodded. Then she looked up and caught her reflection in the glass on the microwave, and could see that her eyes were puffy. So no wonder her sister had looked at her like she had grown another head. "Allergies," she said.

Iris nodded. "Sure."

"I'm going to... I'm going to take him his dinner."

"Good," she said. "I'll tell Ryder and Sammy where you are."

"Thanks." Rose collected rolls, and filled a plate with meat and sides. Then she headed back out of the house, not really thinking. Not really thinking about anything. What she would say when she got there. How she would explain her reaction to the whole thing. None of it.

All she was thinking was that he wasn't going to die. She repeated that. Over and over.

"Not dead," she said out loud as she knocked ferociously on his cabin door. He jerked it open, and she froze.

His shirt was halfway unbuttoned, and he looked tired, grumpy and slightly disoriented.

"I brought chicken," she said.

And then she found herself being dragged into the cabin.

CHAPTER FOURTEEN

HIS BODY HURT like the devil. His head hurt like the devil. Everything hurt.

And then, Rose had appeared at his door looking whole-some and carrying a home-cooked meal, and all he could think was decidedly non-wholesome thoughts. About a thousand of them. All flashing through his mind in bright, brilliant Technicolor in the split second between when he opened the door and when he dragged her inside.

He grabbed hold of the plate of food and set it down on his coffee table. She stared up at him, her eyes glittering.

"Why are you here?"

"Dinner," she said.

"Bullshit."

"You got hurt," she said. And then, something happened that he didn't expect. Ever. In fact, he would have been less shocked had the sky opened up inside of his cabin and a thunderstorm had begun in the living room.

Her face crumpled. Her lower lip quivered. And then Rose, his tough, strong Rose, began to cry.

He bundled her up into his arms without even thinking.

"You rolled a tractor on yourself," she said.

"I'm okay," he responded.

"But you might not have been."

"I know. I thought that. As it tipped over on its side. I thought... You hear about this stuff. This is how people get themselves killed. Doing what they've done hundreds of times, and not paying attention, or being careless at just the wrong time."

"Was it because of me?"

"Rosie, I think you're pretty damn sexy, but I did not roll a tractor over on myself because I was distraught that you said you wouldn't sleep with me again."

"That's not what I mean," she said, angry now. "Did I distract you?"

In all honesty, probably. He wasn't exactly sure what he had been thinking about before the tractor had tipped over. But he knew what had flashed through his mind as he'd gone down to the ground. Her. Her face. The way it had felt to have her hands on his body. And a shocking bolt of grief that he might not ever feel them again.

"Are you here because you feel guilty?"

"No," she said. "I'm… I'm upset. I needed to see that you were okay."

"I'm fine," he said. "Sore as hell. Then it's going to hurt even worse tomorrow. But I'm fine."

"Eat dinner," she said.

"I don't want to eat dinner, Rose."

"Eat dinner. Have a beer. I'm going to run you a bath."

He froze. Heat filtered through his veins. His gaze sharpened, and he looked at her. "A bath?"

"A bath," she returned.

And she treated him to a stern glare that sent a bolt of desire right down to his cock. But she didn't stick around to allow him to question her. And he decided to just let her go. If Rose was here to take care of him… Well, damn him to hell, he was going to let her. Whatever shape that took.

He'd taken control the night they slept together. He didn't regret it.

But he was curious what she might do if given the chance to take the lead.

He sat down on the couch and picked up the plate of food that she'd brought. It was quite a pile of food. Chicken and mashed potatoes. He dug into it, and realized then that he actually was starving. Who knew that near-death experiences whipped up an appetite? He went to the fridge and grabbed a beer, opened it up and settled back down on the couch. He rested the bottle on his thigh and grimaced. Yeah. He might not have taken the full brunt of the tractor, but the way he had braced himself for impact had knotted his muscles up tighter than he'd ever felt them.

And he'd definitely been hit by parts of the machine, even if it hadn't been the full weight of it. His hip bone hurt like a son of a bitch, all down his leg. His shoulder ached— he wasn't quite sure why. He had the vague impression that he might have landed shoulder first before the tractor had come down on top of his lower half.

He grunted, then took another bite of food. What a day.

He heard soft footsteps, and he looked up. And damn near just about dropped his plate. Because there, standing in the doorway, was a large-eyed-looking Rose, wrapped in a white towel. She had it rucked up underneath her arms so there wasn't much to see of her breasts. But it just barely skimmed her hips and thighs, revealing a very healthy length of beautiful, shapely legs.

She was a thing of beauty. Athletic and sculpted from all the hard labor she did. And he remembered well what those legs felt like around him. The girl knew how to hang on. All that horse riding she did. Made it fun to ride her, that was for sure.

And apparently, there was no amount of traumatic injury that could damage his sex drive where Rose was concerned. He went from feeling sorry for himself to basic bro in a split second.

"The bath is ready," she said.

She looked shy, and for some reason, he found that even sexier.

That he knew she was strong, that he knew she was confident in about a thousand kind of ways, but that she was a little hesitant in this.

Hesitant, but still here. Hesitant, but still naked.

"Are you offering me pity sex?"

She lifted a bare shoulder. "I didn't say you were getting sex."

"That's cold," he said.

"I'd say it's up to you to make it a certainty, wouldn't you?"

"Are you asking me to seduce you?"

"Couldn't hurt."

"Well. Given my current physical state, it might. But I'm willing to take the risk."

He set the food down and stood, making his way over to her. He started to wrap his arm around her waist, but she put her hand up, stopping him midmotion. She put her hand on his chest, letting her fingers drift down to the first closed button on his shirt.

She undid it slowly. Maddeningly slowly.

His whole body felt like it was on fire. He was pretty sure everything was still keyed up from that fall. Adrenaline mixed with pain. And the brush of her fingertips against his skin. Just a bit. Just enough…

It about set him off.

She undid the next button. Then the next, her eyes never leaving his.

And all he could do was watch. Because it was Rosie.

His Rosie. The object of his fantasies. Everything had been so harsh and sharp and real that night they'd been together. It had been a fantasy. It had been the most incredible experience of his life. And he had been damn certain he had experienced it.

Still. This felt like something more. Something different.

Maybe it was because that first time she had come to him, and no matter how much she had told him otherwise, he had known that she didn't know what she was getting herself into. And her reaction following it had only confirmed what he had been afraid of.

That she would find herself overwhelmed by it. By the connection between them. By everything. But she was back now. Even knowing how it was. And that was a hell of a thing.

She unbuttoned his shirt the rest of the way, then grabbed hold of either side of it, tugging him into the bathroom. She closed the door behind them. Locked it.

"We're the only people here," he said.

"My whole family lives on this ranch," she whispered. "If anybody comes walking in for any reason…"

Point taken. While he was willing to defend what was happening between them if he had to, he didn't exactly relish the idea of anyone catching them in the act.

He pushed that thought away, because it was enough to dampen a little bit of the arousal he was feeling. And he didn't want anything to dampen it. Because it was just too damned good.

"Now," he said, his voice getting rough, "you can drop that towel."

"Can I?" she asked.

She pushed his shirt from his shoulders, and he let it drop to the floor. Then her face contorted. "Logan…"

"What?"

"You look like you got…well, you look like a tractor fell on you."

"Funny story."

Her fingertips traced over his pectoral muscle, down his stomach where he winced, and so did she, as she ran her fingertips over a visible, dark bruise that came up over the waistband of his jeans.

With her eyes on his, she started to undo his belt. This was an old dance for him. A woman taking his jeans off. But it felt new. With her. Felt like something else entirely. Something he'd never experienced before. He didn't quite know what to do with that. Not even a little.

Because they weren't just a woman's hands. They were Rose's hands. Because he was looking into Rose's eyes. She was familiar, but this wasn't. She mattered. This mattered. His Rosie.

She licked her lips as she undid the button on his jeans, as she lowered the zipper. His whole body tensed, and he grimaced. Then she pushed his jeans down his hips, and there was no hiding just how deeply she affected him. He was hard as iron, and it was obvious.

She leaned in, kissed his mouth. Her body wasn't pressed against his, she held herself separate. And her kiss was soft, sweet. He would be tempted to call it innocent if she weren't in a towel and he weren't desperate to be inside of her.

Then she kissed his neck, and he shuddered. His chest. And she kept on going. Those soft lips pressing to every inch of his skin on down. Until she was on her knees in front of him, and he had to grip her hair to keep himself from falling over. She looked at him, her fingertips playing over that deep, purple bruise on his hip. "It could've been so much worse," she whispered. She kissed him there. On that bruise. So close to where he ached for her, an ache that now surpassed any of the physical pain that he felt from his accident, and he nearly doubled over.

"I don't know what I would've done," she said, the words choked.

"What you always do," he said, the words strangled. "Survived. Gotten on just fine."

"You might get on after stuff like that happens," she whispered. She looked up, from that position on the floor, and it was like a punch to the gut. "But you're not the same. Not ever."

"I don't suppose."

"And the hole is never filled."

He swallowed hard. The idea that the loss of him might leave a hole in Rose's life that could never be filled was one he both liked and disliked in near equal measure.

She kissed him again, close, but not close enough.

"Quit teasing," he ground out.

"I haven't kept you waiting long," she responded.

"You kept me waiting for way too damned long," he bit out.

Five years' worth of it.

And then, she kissed him right there. Betraying all that sweet innocence as she did. Every tentative movement of her mouth over his shaft. It took her a while to get her tongue involved, and when she did, he saw stars.

If he was in any kind of pain from the accident, it was gone now. Because his entire world was now focused on her mouth. And when she took him inside, he thought he might go ahead and die. He leaned back against the bathroom wall, hands buried in her hair as she pleasured him. This was one fantasy he'd never let himself have. Because he was a filthy animal, wanting his friend's sister the way that he did, but he had never let himself fantasize about her doing this.

So having it happen, having that mouth on him...

If he had died when that tractor rolled on him, that would have been a tragedy. If he died now, he could die pretty damned happy.

He could feel his control slipping. And he didn't want it to be over. He tugged her hair, and she pulled away from him, her eyes looking glassy.

"Not like that," he said gruffly.

He looked over the counter and saw a condom. God bless her. She had sneaked one out of his room. He grabbed hold of the towel, and let it drop to the floor. For a second, she blushed. And he thought it was the prettiest thing he'd ever seen.

He hauled her against him, and kissed her, then reversed their positions, pressing her body against the wall.

And then it was his turn to get down on his knees. He hooked her legs up over his shoulders, and he pressed his face right there, tasted her exactly where he knew she would want him most. He tasted her until she was shaking. Until she was shouting out his name. Until he thought he was going to explode from needing to be inside of her.

But he had to make sure. He had to make it good for her.

And when he felt her shatter beneath his mouth, that was when he reached for the condom. He sheathed himself, standing and positioning himself between her spread legs before lifting her against him again, pinning her to the wall and thrusting home.

She gasped, and he couldn't hold back the roar building inside of him. It was frantic after that. Affirming or something. He didn't know. All he knew was that he was reduced down to this thing between them. To where they joined. To what she made him feel.

To the earth-shattering intensity that existed between them. To the overwhelming reality of what it meant to be inside of her.

And then he kissed her. And there was nothing innocent in that kiss. It was carnal, and it mimicked their lovemaking. Deep and hard and long. Until he felt her break. Until she began to convulse around him, shuddering out her pleasure in a way that echoed through his body.

He could feel it. He could feel it the way he could always feel what she did.

And then, it was too much for him. He followed her over that edge into a shared oblivion that left him feeling rocked. Drained.

Too soon, he felt the ache return to his leg, the pains returning to his body.

He dispensed with the condom, then picked Rose up, in spite of all that pain. He could only credit lingering adrenaline—from his orgasm, not his accident—for his ability to do that. He deposited her in the tub, bringing her down on top of him as he sat in the water.

They didn't speak. He just held her.

She turned slightly, curling into him, rubbing her cheek against his damp chest.

"I'm okay," he said finally.

"Obviously," she said.

"Sorry I scared you." He pushed some damp hair away from her face.

"Don't do it again," she said. "I don't like having emotions."

"Yeah. So say we all."

"I really don't," she said grumpily.

"You like me," he said.

She elbowed him in the stomach. He caught her arm and flipped her over so that she was facing him, her full breasts crushed to his chest, all slick and sexy. He started to get hard again. "That was naughty," he said.

"It must've been," she said wiggling. "Because you're getting…"

She blushed again.

"How can you blush about me getting hard when you're lying naked on top of me?"

"Because I'm not used to your… I'm not used to that."

"How messed up is it that I think that's cute?"

"No more messed up than anything else in our lives."

And that, he thought, was maybe the most salient point to be made about their situation. Who was to say what was right? Or messed up or normal.

"This is a little different than the time that I bandaged up your hand a while after our parents died."

She said the words so softly, he barely heard them.

"What?" he asked.

"Do you remember that?"

She looked at him with such intensity, such sincerity, and part of him wanted to lie to her. "No."

He couldn't lie.

"But I don't remember very much about those days," he said. "It's all kind of a blur."

"That's probably why you cut yourself. On the fence. I helped put a Band-Aid on your hand. I asked you when they were coming home."

His chest tightened. And a memory scratched at the back of his mind. He knew then why he hadn't remembered. He hadn't remembered deliberately. It wasn't something he wanted to recall.

He could see her all the same, even though it was difficult for him to picture the child that Rose had been when the woman loomed so large in his mind.

"What did I tell you?" he asked quietly.

"That dead is forever."

It was amazing, how easily that old despair could fill his chest. How quickly he could be overtaken by that grief, as if it had all happened yesterday, and not seventeen years ago.

"I'm sorry," he said.

She wrapped her arms around him underneath the water. He tightened his hold on her. She shifted, her cheek moving on his chest, until it came to rest right over his heart.

"Don't be sorry," she said softly. "It wasn't fair. That we had to do that. Go through it. That you had to explain it to me. That I had to understand it. But I'm glad that you were there."

He put his chin on top of her head and rested it there. "Me, too."

"I'm glad you are here for this, too," she said quietly. "For me."

A weird kind of symmetry to that. That he could be the one to teach her about grief and death and sex also.

They had chosen to deal with the first two things. But at least this was something they'd wanted.

"You've always been there for me," she said softly. "It was really important to me that I was there for you today. I'm sorry that I ran away at first."

He looked down at her. "You're always there for me. I couldn't do half the work I do without you there. You're like… I don't know. A really good tractor."

She burst out laughing, the sound reverberating off the close bathroom walls. "That is the worst."

"I'm sorry."

"Well," she said, her tone sly, "I am on top of you. Also like a tractor."

"That's not what I meant."

"What did you mean?"

"I couldn't get my work done without you."

"Well, why am I the tractor? Because I'm the girl? That makes me seem like an implement. Rather than implementer."

"Fine. You're the best ranch hand a man could ever ask for."

"Ranch hand." Then, something wicked came over her face. "I could give you a hand... If that's what you really want from me." She slipped her hand between their bodies and wrapped it around his hardening length. "How's that? Ranch handy?"

"That's not what I meant, either," he groaned. "But I'll take it."

"What I should probably do is assist you into bed."

"Not a half-bad idea. As long as you get into it with me."

"Admit I'm the rancher. And you're the ranch hand."

Well, he was basic, after all. So the only answer to that was for him to put his hand between her legs and stroke her, tease her the way that she was doing him. "What do you think?"

She sighed. "I think we complement each other pretty well."

His chest burned then, with the desire for something more. Something he couldn't put a name to. And for the first time in his memory he wanted to give something to someone else.

A gift.

There was so much damn baggage involved in him giving someone a gift.

But Rose…his Rose. She was in his arms all soft and warm and slick and he'd give her the world if he could.

The whole damn world.

He'd gone to a Christmas parade for her.

He'd give her a gift, too. And he knew just the thing.

CHAPTER FIFTEEN

THINGS CHANGED AFTER THAT. Rose gave up trying to impose limitations on what was happening between them. She also never asked him again what the endgame was.

Because she didn't want to think about it.

As long as she was living in the moment, she didn't care.

The two of them worked together like they always had. And then at night, she sneaked off to his cabin.

The more she stared at the stark, determinedly undecorated space of his cabin, the more she was determined to find his mother's cookie recipe and give it to him as a Christmas gift. But she was also a little afraid that it might upset him. She didn't want that.

He didn't do Christmas. He didn't do gifts. She knew that. But he'd done the Christmas parade with her. And she wanted to believe that maybe for her...maybe with her he'd be willing to make something new.

She wanted to give him something. Something real. Because every so often she would look at him and the full scope of what he meant to her would hit her like a...well, like a tractor falling on top of her. Which, based on the lovely color of his still healing bruises, was quite a lot of impact.

West and Pansy's wedding was getting close, and it was also the time of year that Colt and Jake came to town to spend Christmas with them.

Rose felt slightly guilty about how distracted she was.

It was tough to care about Christmas, or even her sister's wedding when she was so consumed by her affair with Logan.

Affair. Was that the right word? She didn't even know.

"Are you listening?"

Rose looked up from the pot of jam that she'd been stirring and made eye contact with Iris. Sammy and Pansy were staring at her, too.

They had gotten their berries from summer out of the freezer, and were making jam and pie filling. More jam to send off with the boys when they left again, and prepping the pie filling for dinner tonight, and through the next couple of weekends.

They went through so much food when everybody was here. And Rose wasn't really the best person to assist with the cooking. But she did.

Not because it was women's work really, or anything like that. She did enough of the ranch work that she didn't feel like she had to go work in the kitchen, too.

But she loved spending time with her sisters, and Sammy.

Of course, a little bit less during times like this when she felt like she had been caught out at something.

"No," she admitted. "I wasn't listening."

"Are you scheming?" Sammy asked. "Because I thought we put a moratorium on your scheming."

"I don't have anything to scheme about."

For once it was true. She wasn't as consumed with anybody else's life because she was so wrapped up in her own. She had been avoiding that. For a very long time. Because it was… Well, caring so much about what was happening in her own life was scary. Potentially painful.

But she was in it. There was nothing to be done. And right now she was… Well, she wasn't even upset that she was so consumed with her own life. Because her own life was interesting. And sex with Logan was amazing. She was enjoying herself. There was nothing wrong with that, was there?

"Well, as long as you promise not to scheme," Sammy said.

"The only scheming I'm doing is figuring out how to eat as much of this jam with a spoon as I can without Iris noticing."

"Don't do that," Iris groused. "I'll have to box your ears."

"What does that even mean?" Pansy asked.

"You used to threaten to do it to me all the time," Rose said. "And you don't know what it means?"

Pansy shrugged. "No. But I figured it sounded frightening and that was what mattered."

"And you're the person keeping the streets of Gold Valley safe." Iris shook her head. "Shocking."

"I think we've already established that I'm vaguely shocking."

"How are your wedding plans going?"

"Two weeks until the wedding, so they should be pretty well finalized," Pansy said, looking pleased. "Though after all this I'm starting to think you and Ryder had the right idea."

"Shotgun wedding?" Sammy asked.

"Pretty much. I wish he had gotten me pregnant. Then we could've just done it."

"Right. But where does a pregnancy fit into your first year as police chief?"

Pansy sighed. "It doesn't. I figured two years in the new job, and then I can have a baby."

Rose and Iris exchanged glances. Babies were very far from both of their minds. For a moment, though, Iris's face softened and Rose wondered.

A baby.

She had never wanted kids.

But as soon as she thought that it felt… Well, she didn't know. Not strictly true. She had never thought about kids. Maybe that was the truth of it. It instantly set her mind to wondering what kind of father Logan would be.

Her stomach clenched painfully.

No. She did not want to think about that. That was ridiculous. What she'd said to him when she had been setting Pansy and Elliott up was true. She was not thinking about pairing off. Not permanently. Not just yet. Maybe never.

It was just something she had never thought about. And she would have to give it a lot of thought before she even knew if it was something that she might consider.

She hadn't really imagined Pansy ever getting married and having a baby. She just had never seemed the type. And her soon-to-be husband West didn't really seem like the type either, if she thought about it.

Her brother, Ryder, didn't, either. He was the biggest father figure in her life, so it wasn't that she didn't think he'd be a great father. She did.

It was just that she didn't think he would have wanted to be one. Not after spending all that time raising them.

And she knew that he had always thought he didn't.

Until Sammy. Sammy had always seemed like an earth mother type. Definitely a nurturing, maternal person.

Sammy and Pansy were completely different from each other. So were West and Ryder. But they were doing the same things.

The common bond, she was forced to conclude, was falling in love.

It seemed to make you want different things than you did before.

She didn't know quite what to do with that realization.

Jam making bled right into dinner preparation, and with all hands on deck they went a little bit crazy. Iris made the most beautiful sourdough, and Sammy helped put together a spectacular roast.

Pansy and Rose made themselves responsible for the green salad. And then scooted off to the store to buy beverages. Which was often Rose's function.

She should have realized it was a mistake, though, to bundle off with her sister. Because the minute they were alone in Pansy's little car, she turned to her.

"What's happening with Logan?"

"What makes you think anything is happening with him?"

"The fact that you didn't just answer my question."

"Well… *Well…*"

"Are you sleeping with him?"

"Don't ask me that!"

"Why not?"

"Because I am," she grumped, "and I don't want to tell you about it."

"Oh… Rose…"

She could tell that her sister was genuinely upset by the information.

"Why do you care?"

"Because I'm afraid you're going to get hurt. And I'm afraid it's going to… Did you think about what it might do to us? To our family?"

Anger and guilt twisted at her heart in equal measure.

"You're not actually worried about me," Rose said. "You're just worried that if something goes wrong between Logan and I things will change. You changed things already, Pansy, that's not fair at all. Why do you get to change things and I don't?" Irritation was moving through her like a freight train going downhill. Picking up dangerous speed.

"And what about Ryder and Sammy? If something had gone wrong between the two of them it would have destroyed everything. Sammy was prepared to leave."

"I didn't know about them."

"I did," Rose said. "I caught them kissing, and I had to keep it to myself. I knew about it, and I didn't lecture them."

"Well, both of them know about sex. You don't."

"I do now," Rose groused. "Logan's good at it. And he's taught me a lot."

She was mad now. So she wasn't going to preserve Pansy's delicate sensibilities. Far from it, it made her want to get into exactly what Logan had showed her in great detail.

"A man who can lift hay bales as easily as he can, can get up to some pretty athletic stuff."

"I'm familiar with the virtues of sex with a cowboy," Pansy said dryly. "You don't need to fill me in on the details."

"Well. Just making sure that you know."

They got out of the car, and went into the small market. Rose pushed the cart, but angrily, and Pansy went about selecting chips.

For her part, Pansy seemed committed to ignoring the fact that she had made Rose angry. So Rose decided to fume with all the force of her irritation. And Pansy just doubled down on ignoring it. It was so irritatingly reminiscent of interactions she'd had with her sister when they were younger. And it was over something so…so adult. But somehow it had regressed them.

They overbought, essentially filling the cart with chips and soda, then not speaking to each other as they paid. Rose piled the chips onto the conveyor belt and dared the young man working behind the counter to comment with his eyes. He didn't.

They loaded their treats into the car and Rose stewed while Pansy drove.

"I'm not a child," she muttered.

"I know," Pansy said. "It's not that I think you're a child. But I do worry…"

"I know. You're super worried that this is going to mean we all lose Logan." She looked out the window. "I don't want to lose him."

"It's not that simple," Pansy said. "I'm not just worried about that. I'm sorry if I sounded that insensitive. It's not… It's not that simple. I'm worried he'll hurt you, and I'll hate him. I'm worried that we'll lose him, sure. I'm worried about that hurting me, but I'm worried about it hurting you, too. We are all woven so tightly around each other, Rose. And I guess I just worry that if the wrong thread gets pulled at we could all unravel."

"I don't think we're that fragile," Rose said stubbornly. "Look at everything we've been through. Everything. And look at how much has changed in the last year. You're getting married in, like, a week. We added West to the family." And she didn't even get into the fact that by introducing West to the family Pansy had introduced a lot more strife and change than she realized.

It wasn't her secret to tell, and she had promised Logan that she wouldn't. And she realized then that in some ways Pansy was right. Things would be changed by the fact that she had slept with Logan. They already were. Because maybe before her loyalty would have been slightly split. Maybe before she would have felt like her sister needed to know that her future husband was Logan's half brother. That West coming into the family had already effected the change that she was so afraid of. Maybe she would have wondered where her allegiance should lie, and she might have put it with her sister.

But now. No, now she felt a burden of responsibility for what Logan had entrusted her with.

Yes, part of it was that she had guessed. But she had guessed because of the intimacy that she felt with the man. Even before sex. And telling his secret felt like an abuse of that intimacy.

She didn't want that. She felt...oddly protective of him. He might be nearly ten years older than her, and a damn sight more experienced, but he felt like he was hers. In this regard, at least. And she wanted to protect him with all the snarling, feral allegiance that she felt to him.

Theirs might not be the easiest of relationships. Just in that they still sniped at each other while they worked sometimes, and she pretended some nights that she was going to resist him, go to her own bed rather than going to his. She never did, though. She never did because she wanted too badly to be in his arms.

And maybe it was even more special because of that. Because there were some hard, sharp edges, just like life itself.

He was the strongest man she knew, and when he held her in the aftermath of the storm that inevitably erupted between them when they came together, he was gentle, his strength leashed as he cradled her like she was a precious thing.

It made her want to protect him. To protect that part of him that she was pretty sure only she saw.

The gentleness.

She saw the rest, too.

Stubbornness. Pride. He was the most hardheaded man in existence. A man who had grown up in the same town as his estranged family and never acknowledged them. A man who was content to let the people he was closest to in the world believe he didn't know who his father was, while his father lived a short drive away.

A man whose half brother was part of their family now, and he still wouldn't budge on his stance.

Yeah. She saw those parts of him clearly.

And still, she felt loyalty to him. To his decisions about that whole thing.

"I don't know," Pansy said. "Don't you ever think that Hope Springs is kind of a magical world? And if we do the wrong thing we might…break it."

A deep sadness filled Rose. One she had difficulty identifying. "*You* got to change. You got to try something. Is it just because it's Logan that I'm not allowed to? That you think me growing up might break it?"

"I'm sorry," Pansy said. "I don't think anything I said came out right. Of course I don't want you to not grow up. But yes, I guess it did catch me off guard that it was with him. Because he's like a brother to me, but you are my sister."

"Logan is… He's not like a brother to me," she said, staring out the window as the trees blurred into a green indistinct shape.

"Well, obviously."

"No. I mean… I don't know what he is. But he's always been more to me. Different to me. It's not like I had a crush on him or anything. I didn't." No, the way that she felt for him couldn't be called a crush. "Sometimes I think he's like the other part of me. The way we work together… It's like two sets of hands. And he's always driven me crazy like no one else ever has. I can feel it. When he's mad at me. When I annoy him, I can feel little prickles of irritation coming off him in waves. I've always thought it was funny. So, I try to do it more. And when we are together…" She started breathing a little bit faster, embarrassment and excitement warring within her. "It's like I feel what he's feeling, and when we're together like that…"

"Oh, no," Pansy breathed.

"What?"

"I think you're in love with him."

Fear grabbed hold of Rose and twisted her heart. Hard. "I'm not," she said.

"Yeah, that sounds like love to me, Rose. Sorry."

"I don't love him. I mean, I do love him. But I'm not… I'm not in love with him. I don't… I'm twenty-three."

"So what?"

"I haven't even ever thought about being in love. I never dreamed about it or fantasized about it or even wanted it."

"Because you had it. Already."

She felt like a big crack had just been wedged into her chest, each word of her sister's expanding it.

"I've never thought about getting married or having babies or any of that."

"You don't have to. I'm just… I'm sorry. I've made a really big mess of this. If you're not ready to think about it that way, then don't."

"How did you get from it's not a good idea to you're in love with him?"

"Because if you're in love with him it changes everything. Because then you fight for it, Rose. You fight for it, and you don't worry about what your stupid older sister says. And you don't worry about whether or not it makes sense. Or whether or not it might hurt. You fight for love."

"Did you?"

"With myself," Pansy said. "And West fought for it. He showed me that I could, too. That I needed to. I was afraid. Really afraid. Because everything we've been through hurt so much. And…" She laughed. "I guess I'm still a little bit afraid. Look at how I freaked out about you and Logan. You're right. I let myself have love, and then I worried about you. About maybe it being a little bit too much happiness for all of us. But we can't stay stuck where we're at. Everything does have to change. I mean, look at Ryder and Sammy."

Rose nodded slowly. "Sure."

"Did I freak you out?"

"Yeah, this whole episode kind of freaked me out. Thank God we got twenty bags of chips."

"I mean, I always feel thankful for chips. Empty calories can fill a lot of voids."

She nodded and tried to laugh. Because they were back at the house, and she didn't need to be looking shell-shocked. Even though she kind of felt like it. When they walked into the house, Logan was sitting there in the living room with Colt and Jake.

Their eyes caught for a moment, and she knew there was nothing she could do. And anyway, it didn't matter, because she was caught up in bear hugs from her cousins, and even one from their friend.

"Hey, squirt," Jake said to Pansy.

Pansy was the smallest, even though she wasn't the youngest, and she knew that their cousins liked to harass her about it. "I'll tase your ass," she said, poking Jake in the ribs.

"Rude," he said.

"You're always rude," Pansy said. "Why can't I be rude?"

"Why don't you go out and help us bring chips and drinks in," Rose said. "Instead of just being a useless jerk."

And they did. And she was able to push her feelings about Logan from her mind. Because all of this felt familiar. It felt good to have a full house.

Fuller even than normal.

Ryder and Sammy were here, of course. Then there was Iris, Pansy, West, his half brother Emmett and the rodeo boys.

It was customary for them to all bring their presents and dump them under the tree at this point, and everyone had done so. Rose felt bad because she didn't have anything yet. She had been way too wrapped up in the newness of her relationship with Logan.

There were gifts beginning to collect under the tree. Logan hadn't brought any because he never did. He never, ever participated in opening presents on Christmas. Never gave any and never wanted to receive any. But she wanted so badly to give him something, and she didn't know if it was the right thing to do.

She began to obsess about it. Got consumed by it. She downed half a bag of chips without even enjoying it.

She loved having everyone home. She really did. She was annoyed with herself, beyond annoyed that she was obsessing about Logan. And the fact that they couldn't just sit together. That she couldn't just ask him about the present. That she didn't know how to interact with him in front of everybody without giving them away. And that she wasn't sure she even wanted to, because it felt stupid to be near him and not be able to touch him.

It felt stupid to be hiding like this. Except, if everybody knew, then they would just react like Pansy. And it was maybe even dumber to let everybody know what was happening, because it wasn't like…

She thought of her own words.

To what end?

They had quit thinking about that. Or, at least she had. She had shunted it off to the side, but the whole conversation with Pansy had brought her back around to it.

The idea that she might have feelings for him that she didn't want.

The idea that when things ended between them it would ruin the family.

And if both of those things were true… And what would it do to her?

She squeezed her eyes shut, and they felt scratchy and painful. So did her lungs. So did her heart.

After dinner they all went into the living room and ate pie, and she knew that she should be comforted by all of the talking and laughing going on around her.

But she was just… She was just so preoccupied.

Suddenly, the hair on her arm stood on end, and she looked and saw that Logan was watching her. Coming closer to her. She shifted uncomfortably, and then he sat down next to her on the couch.

"What are you doing?" she asked, keeping her voice low. No one was watching them.

"I'm sitting next to you."

"Why?"

"Because I haven't talked to you all night. And I don't like it."

She blushed. She could feel it. Could feel it flooding her cheeks, making her feel hot. "Yeah, but…"

"It isn't normal for me to not talk to you," he said, his voice full of gravity.

"Yeah, I guess not."

"Have you done all your Christmas shopping yet?"

"No," she said. His bringing up Christmas shopping made her feel hopeful about her plans. "I've been busy."

The corner of his mouth tipped up into a lopsided grin, and it seemed like it lifted her insides right along with it. "With what?"

"My boss has been riding me really hard."

She couldn't resist smiling at her own joke, and he shook his head, his expression grave. "Really?"

"Well, I haven't really had occasion to make a joke like that before."

For a second they were just sitting there, smiling at each other. Then she had a feeling that if anyone were to look over now, they weren't doing the most convincing job of seeming…normal. Her breath caught, and he shifted, brushing against her slightly. Her heart started to beat harder. Even in a room full of her family, being near him like this turned her on. It was a marvel to her that she hadn't realized before how beautiful he was.

That she hadn't been obsessed with his looks every moment of every day since they'd first met. Suddenly, she couldn't even remember how she'd seen him before. It was like another lifetime, that moment when she had felt like the blue in his eyes had changed. Now it was like they'd always been this way. This blue. That sliced through her protective walls and reached the very center of her soul.

That captivated her and held her in place. That compelled her to get closer to him. To press her mouth against his.

"Break it up, you two."

They jerked away from each other and both turned toward the sound of the admonishment. It was Ryder, who was clearly kidding, and was obviously not paying all that much attention to what was really happening between them.

"We were just talking about when we should actually do Christmas presents. Since I think West and Pansy are going to be on their honeymoon on Christmas."

"Why don't we open presents after the wedding?" Pansy asked.

"Won't you be doing your wedding presents and having your reception?"

"Yeah," she said. "But we're the ones getting married on Christmas Eve. And anyway, it's mostly family that's coming."

She felt Logan stiffen just slightly beside her. No one else would notice, but of course she did.

Of course. Family. Family would include West's family.

Logan's family. He didn't do Christmas morning, but he did often come and have Christmas dinner with them, and it would mean a lot of...well, a lot of Daltons around.

"I think it sounds great," Ryder said. "A great big family Christmas get-together."

"Yeah, thankfully Tammy Dalton is helping with the food," Iris said. "It's nice to have another set of hands."

"My sisters-in-law will bring things, too," West said. "My half sister not so much. McKenna doesn't cook. And she was furious at the implication she ought to get involved in that kind of women's work."

She knew no one could see right between herself and Logan. And she found herself moving her hand to touch his. He looked over at her. Her lips twitched. He seemed to understand.

That she was offering comfort. That she was trying to make sure he knew that she cared.

Yeah. The things that Pansy had been worried about seemed pretty valid right now. Because the whole orientation of the room seemed different. She was rooted to Logan's side, and everything that Pansy was talking about in regards to her wedding seemed to matter the very most to her in terms of how they touched the man by her side.

"I'm going to make the wedding cake," Iris said. "And I have huge plans for it." She sounded excited, genuinely excited. And then she saw the light in her sister's eyes get even brighter. "Hey, bachelors," she said.

Colt and Jake looked up. Rose felt somewhat…pleased that Logan didn't.

"Yes?" Jake asked.

"I've been thinking about…things. Like what I want to do with my life."

"Oh, so only small stuff, then," Colt said.

"Right," Iris responded. "Anyway, I want to do something with cooking, and I was wondering how much guys like you might pay for home-cooked meals."

"Well," Jake responded, "I get your home-cooked meals for free."

"But if you didn't?"

"I'd definitely pay for them."

"I thought you were thinking about the bakery?" Rose asked.

"It won't be enough," Iris said, "not at first. But cooking is what I do, so I don't see why I can't find a way to make all my strengths support each other."

And suddenly, things with the world seemed a little bit more right. Because she hadn't helped Iris at all with her meddling. But it looked like Iris was going to help herself.

And it made Rose a little bit sad that yet again, she hadn't been all that helpful, and if anything she had potentially caused harm. But it didn't really matter how Iris found happiness, as long as she did. Maybe she'd been wrong to assume that her sister needed romance to find happiness.

Maybe she just needed…cake.

And what about you?

She looked back over at Logan.

Love.

She genuinely hadn't wanted to fall in love.

But now she had to think about what Pansy had said. Was that what this was? Was that what it had always been?

Chatter had moved on around them, questions being lobbed back and forth about Iris's bakery, and then things shifted to weddings, presents and football.

But things inside of her had not shifted. She was still thinking. About her place in the world. Her place in the family. And love.

Where it came from.

If you had to earn it.

If kisses and sex made it appear. Or if love, in all of its multifaceted states, was just there. Part of who you were. Down in your bones. And what it took was a shift to bring it out. For Pansy, a new person coming into town. For her, the light hitting Logan's eyes a little bit different one afternoon when he came in the door.

And for her family… It was born in them. Then it had shifted and changed when tragedy came. They had cared for each other as they'd needed to.

But maybe it wasn't about earning or doing.

Maybe there was just an inevitability to it all.

And that both cheered and terrified her in equal measure. Because if there was inevitability at play it meant that perhaps that feeling of not being enough, that feeling of being a burden, and needing to earn the affection of her family... Maybe that was wrong.

But on the other hand that might also mean that whatever was happening with Logan... Whatever it was now... She was never going to be able to control what it became.

Which seemed to be an annoying life lesson. That these kinds of truths could be blindingly freeing as revelations went, and utterly terrifying.

She separated from Logan and went over to Iris. "I'm really happy to hear that you want to open a bakery, and that you're going to actually take steps to do it."

"Thanks," Iris said. "You know, I was mad at you. About the whole thing with Elliott. But the thing is... The problem is... Things like that are dependent on other people. There's plenty in my power that I can do to change my life. And I've been happy. I haven't wanted to change it until now."

"You haven't felt stuck?"

"No," Iris said. "Why would I feel stuck?"

"You never even, like...went to any high school dances or anything. You were always taking care of me. And cooking for all of us."

"I know," Iris said. "And after losing our parents I couldn't think of anything better than to be home surrounded by family. It didn't make me sad."

"Oh," Rose said.

"I promise it didn't," Iris said. "Look at Pansy—she left, moved away from the ranch and got a job. Jake and Colt left. The three of us stayed. And Sammy. And Logan. We stayed because we chose to. And I imagine that when you're ready to move on you'll move on."

Terror gripped Rose. Because she didn't want to move

on. She wanted to stay here and work this ranch. She wanted to work this ranch with Logan for the rest of her life.

She blinked.

Well. That was clarifying.

She had always wondered if there was something wrong with her because she hadn't thought much about the future. Because she didn't do a whole lot of dreaming. Because she might have felt compelled to set her sister up with someone, but she hadn't wanted to do the same for herself.

It was because she was where she wanted to be. Next to the man she wanted to be beside.

She swallowed hard. "Good," she said. "Good."

"Are you okay?"

"Yeah. I'm just… I'm sorting some things out. I'm really sorry that I dragged you into me sorting things out."

"You made a mistake. It's not that big of a deal. You don't have to keep punishing yourself for it."

"Thank you," she said. "And I meant what I said before. Whatever grunt work you need… For the bakery or for the wedding. I promise I'll help."

"Good."

"I'm going to head out," Logan said, moving over to where she was.

"I'll walk you out," she replied.

She thought that maybe her family would think it was strange, but they didn't. Because only she and Logan were aware of the shift between them.

And anyway… She was starting to think she didn't care. Because it all just felt…like it had always been there.

Inevitable.

She grabbed her coat and a hat, and Logan layered up too, and she walked outside with him.

"I'm glad you came," he said. "Because I was going to find a way to get you to sneak out anyway."

"Really?"

"Because I have your present. And I wanted to give it to you privately."

"Oh," she said, the breath escaping her body in one intense burst.

Logan didn't give presents. Ever. He didn't do any official Christmas things. And she hadn't expected this at all.

He cleared his throat and reached into his jacket. The gift he pulled out was wrapped. "Did you do that yourself?"

"I did," he said.

He'd wrapped a gift. For her. This man who didn't do Christmas. It felt so much bigger than the beautiful little box in her hand.

She smiled. "What is it?"

"Come on. Don't ask me that. That's cliché. Open it."

She did. And inside the wrapping paper was a slim white box. She opened it, and then frowned. Inside the box was a delicate gold chain. And on the chain was a charm.

She looked closely at it, examining it as best she could in the dim light. It was a cameo. White and light blue. She had never owned anything remotely like this. Nothing half so feminine or delicate or pretty.

"What is this?"

"It was… It was my mom's," he said. "And it's just been sitting in a jewelry box for the last seventeen years with no one wearing it. I just… I was looking at it the other night, and I thought it would look good on you."

She touched it, carefully, reverently. "It was your mom's?"

And she knew then what she had to get him for Christmas. She'd considered it earlier, and she knew she had to do it now. Her throat went tight, her eyes filling with tears. She swallowed. "It's beautiful," she said. "And no one's ever given me anything like this before."

"I've never given anyone anything like it before. I…"

She loved him. She really did. She hadn't even realized it, for all this time. All this time, when she had woken up in the morning, gone outside and worked next to the man she loved. All this time, when she had been in the place that made her happiest in the world, she had been with the person who seemed to be the person who made her happiest.

She had been living her dream.

And it was only now that it had shifted into place. That it had become everything. It was like she'd been looking at a view through a dirty window all of her life, thinking it was the whole view. Thinking she had seen so clearly. But now she did. Now she did.

Now she saw it all. And she couldn't believe that she hadn't realized all that she'd been missing before.

Like that girl who didn't know what it looked like when a man wanted her was from another life. From another time.

Now she was a woman who knew.

A woman who wanted that man right back. And who knew what it was to have him.

Except… Did she?

She loved him. But she didn't know what he wanted out of all this. Except that she knew that he didn't seem to think he was a man who wanted commitment or anything like that.

She hadn't even really started thinking of it in those terms.

But she supposed that was what it meant when you loved somebody. That you wanted to marry them.

Make a family with them.

Except, Logan already was family, so what did that mean?

He had given her this necklace, and she didn't know what that meant, either.

"Let me put it on you."

He lifted it out of the box and fastened it around her neck, the cameo sitting heavily between her breasts. "Thank you." She wrapped her arm around his neck, cradled the back of his head and brought it down for a kiss. They were right outside, and she supposed anyone could walk out and see them making out underneath that clear sky, silver stars scattered against the black velvet like glitter.

She didn't really care. Not right now.

Right now, she felt ready to accept any consequence. Any and all.

She felt ready to stand and defend what they were. Because it wasn't… It wasn't new. It was just a shift. Which didn't make it less. No. It was a miracle.

A shift that made her see everything in her life differently. That made her see herself differently.

So she kissed him. Like it didn't matter if anyone knew. And part of her hoped…wished that they would get caught. Because if it was out in the open, then they would have to decide. To fight for it. To keep it. Call it something. To make it something.

But no one caught them, and the kiss ended. "I should go back inside," she said. "You know. For a while."

"Sure," he said.

"Logan…" She flung her arms around his neck and kissed him again, deeper, harder. And he scooped her up, lifted her feet up off the ground, returning the kiss with as much ferocity as she gave. "Your present will come soon," she whispered.

He hesitated for a moment. "I hope that means you're coming to my house tonight."

"You can count on it."

Then she released her hold on him and ran back to the house, her heart thundering hard, and when she went inside, she was thankful for the cold, because her cheeks would be pink from the weather. At least, that was what her family would assume.

She knew that she was flushed from his kisses. From her desire for him.

From the overwhelming…everything that was rolling around inside of her.

She saw Pansy's laser focus go to the necklace around her neck. Rose touched it and nodded slightly.

A smile curved Pansy's lips, wistful, but accepting.

Though, she hoped that Pansy didn't think it meant that Logan… That he felt the same way. But what if he did? He said that he'd wanted her all this time. What if it was more than wanting?

She felt like she had to sit with that for a while. Because she didn't know what to do with it. Not completely.

For now, she figured she would just enjoy what she was certain of. Her family. Sammy beckoned her to where the girls were sitting and pulled her into their conversation. And she tried to pay attention. But her mind and her heart were with Logan.

It was different. But it didn't really make her sad.

It was just part of life. Changing, moving on. Everything at Hope Springs Ranch was changing. But in the years since their tragedy, they had only added people into the fold. They hadn't lost any.

And in the face of the tragedy that had come before, Rose found that to be incredibly cheering.

Whatever happened between herself and Logan. Whatever happened in the future…

Her life felt full right now.

She was going to cling to that as her Christmas miracle.

And then tomorrow, she was going to have to go hunting through the barn that had all of their parents' things for a recipe. Then she was going to have to practice her cookie baking.

CHAPTER SIXTEEN

IT HAD TAKEN two hours of relentless digging in the barn where they stored all of their things for Rose to emerge triumphant with the recipe.

She remembered Jane Heath's oatmeal chocolate chip cookies well, and she knew exactly how they were supposed to taste. The problem was, she didn't actually know how to bake. Which could present a bit of an issue. The other problem was, she knew that there was a certain amount of trial and error that she had put into the recipe, and that what was written down wasn't precisely what she had done in the end to produce the cookies that they were used to.

And Rose had been just a kid the last time she'd had them, so whether or not her memory of them was exactly accurate, she didn't know.

Iris and Sammy found her frustrated and surrounded by piles of cookies three hours later.

"What are you...doing?" Iris asked.

"I'm baking," Rose said, furious.

"You're baking?" Sammy asked. "You. You, the master of bringing soda to potlucks?"

"Me," Rose growled. "Yes, me."

"Why?"

"I'm trying to make Logan's mother's cookies."

She knew that saying that was going to be... Well, maybe it was revealing, maybe it wasn't. She was having difficulty sorting through what was just a normal thing to do for your friend, and what was the thing you did for a man you were in love with, who you got naked with.

She supposed the fact that she had never made cookies for him prior to getting naked with him was evidence enough that it was a little bit suspicious.

"Okay," Iris said. "What's going wrong?"

"I don't know? I just know that they don't taste like they should. And I really want them to. I want them to be right. Otherwise I'm just giving him random chocolate chip cookies, and there's no real meaning behind it. And that's kind of a stupid Christmas present."

She looked imploringly at Iris and Sammy. "Can you help me?"

"Sure."

"Of course," they said at the same time.

They washed their hands, and both of them began to examine the recipe. Cutting and talking between each other.

"What are you doing?" Rose asked.

"Game plan," Iris said.

"Wow. I didn't know baking was so serious."

"Baking is deadly serious," Iris said.

After that, they tasted every single cookie that Rose had produced. Sammy had never had the original cookies, so she couldn't taste them in that way, but Iris had, and did remember them.

"I think... I think your problem is the amount of vanilla. And, I don't think these are the right chocolate chips. I remember her using a really specific brand. You need to make sure that the chocolate chips are semisweet."

That resulted in a quick trip to the store, followed by the most successful batch of cookie dough she had produced so far.

"So, if this is it make sure to write down all your tweaks," Iris said. "And you can give him that, too."

She smiled slightly, and she could feel heat blooming in her cheeks. "Right. I could do that, too."

"It's very sweet of you," Iris said slowly. "To give that to him."

"He's been talking about her lately," Rose said. "About his mom."

She did not touch the necklace that was hanging from her neck. Nobody had commented on it, nothing beyond the look that Pansy had given her when she had come into the house wearing it. So, if anyone had noticed that she was suddenly wearing jewelry, she had no idea.

"I just… I thought it was really sad. He said it was one of those things that he just had to miss. That he could never have her back, so he could never have her cookies, either. And… I don't want him to miss that. He'll always miss his mom. I know I do. Our mom and dad. His mom. Our aunt and uncle."

Sammy smiled faintly and touched her stomach. "It makes me feel good to hear that you miss them. Not because I'm glad that you do… That's not what I meant. It's just… I don't know what it's like to miss my parents. I miss the idea that I could've had functional parents. That I could've had something. A life that I didn't get. But that's not the same as missing actual real people that you loved. Since I'm going to be a mother… It makes me feel good to know that kids love you that way. I'm going to get to be loved that way. Of course, the way that Ryder loves me has been pretty great and amazing."

"I'm happy for you both," Iris said. "We've missed enough love. It's nice to have it."

Iris sounded slightly wistful. "Of course, baking feels a lot like love."

"Hopefully cookies do," Rose said softly.

She saw Iris and Sammy exchange a glance. But neither of them said anything to her. And she wondered if she should. She decided not to. Because her feelings for Logan were not something she wanted to share with somebody before she shared them with him. Not that she was embarrassed about it. Not because she wanted to keep them a secret. She didn't particularly. She was getting to the point where she felt like they couldn't keep it a secret anymore, frankly. She just didn't want to have a whole discussion about feelings for him without him involved. She would tell them all when the time came. And she would know when it was time.

Anyway. It was clear they were suspicious.

So, they could just go on being suspicious. It wasn't like they were going to be blindsided by it.

"You know," Sammy said slowly, when they were taking the cookies out of the oven and waiting for them to cool. "He cares about you."

She looked at Sammy, and she wondered very much what her sister-in-law knew.

"Yeah," Rose said. "I know."

"Good," Sammy said. "I'm glad you know. I think you're really special to him."

Sammy might have an idea that Rose had some feelings for Logan, but what she suspected was that she didn't know that things had progressed between them. That things had become...naked between them. And again, that was something she wasn't going to talk about just yet.

"Well, hopefully he cares about these cookies. And likes them."

Iris got a spatula and slipped them beneath three cookies at once, plopping them onto a plate. She did the same to the rest, and the three of them picked them up.

"We need milk," Iris said. "Remember, we would always dip them in milk?"

They got the milk out and poured three glasses. Then the three of them dipped their cookies and took a bite.

"This is it," Iris said, triumphant.

"It is," Rose said in wonder, memory flooding through her.

Of all of them in the kitchen. Logan's mom having just baked cookies with her mother. Of all the kids, happy, chatting.

Her eyes filled with tears. "It's so hard for me to remember them sometimes," she said. "This makes me remember. The way it was."

"Yeah," Iris said. "Cooking always makes me remember. It's why I love it so much. It's how you bring moments, and people, right to the table with you. How you take them out of the past."

She looked at her sister, remembering what she had said to her the other night. About how taking care of Rose had helped with her grief. How it had helped make her feel close to their mother.

"I love you," Rose said. "You took such good care of me."

"I love you," Iris said. "Just you being there took care of me. Trust me."

She wrapped her arm around her shoulders and gave her a squeeze. And Sammy wrapped her arms around both of them, her big pregnant belly bumping up against Rose's side. "And I love you both. Thank you for adding me to your kitchen. And making me part of your house." She squeezed them. "I know Logan is grateful for it, too."

It all made sense to her then, why their table felt best when it was crowded. Because that was how it had been before. It was why they added people to Hope Springs with such ease. Because happiness had been best experienced there when they'd shared it around.

Her parents had never been rich people. But they'd been a tight-knit family, with her aunt and uncle, her mom and dad, and Logan's mother there all the time. Dinner had been a constantly changing affair, with different combinations of them all present at any given time. And sometimes, of course the boys would bring friends, and sometimes there would be more people, sometimes less.

It had all been family.

It was easy, sometimes, to think of herself as someone who had lost a lot.

But right then she felt like someone who had an awful lot, and who had a lot still. Someone whose roots and foundation were so rich and sturdy, that she was lucky. No matter what in her life had hurt.

Maybe it was just because she was still riding high on the realization that she was living her dream. That happiness had been right in front of her the whole time, and all she had to do was take a little step out in faith.

Be a little bit brave.

Quit trying so hard, and just start enjoying what she had. That had been the key.

To stop trying to earn what she had already, and just look at all the blessings that came with it.

"We have a good life," Rose said softly.

"Yeah," Iris responded. "We do."

"I used to wonder why Ryder kept the name of the ranch

the same," Rose said softly. "Why he kept it Hope Springs when it felt like hope died along with our parents. But it didn't. They left us hope. And hope is what kept us going. They left us cookie recipes and Christmas traditions, and joy taken in big family dinners. They left us each other."

"Hope is what keeps you going," Sammy said. "That's what Hope Springs was for me. A beacon in the darkness. The first place I thought I might be able to escape my abusive father. It's why I came here. Because you all look so happy. And I could see… I could see a way to have a better life here. With you. With your family. Hope is the one thing everyone needs. Without that… Without that, I guess you think nothing could change. That the darkness might be permanent."

Rose nodded slowly. And she wondered… She wondered if that's what Logan felt like. She wondered if Logan saw the hope here.

She looked at the plate of cookies. And remembered what he'd said. That he could never have them again because his mother was gone.

And she wondered if he was so determined to remember the loss, that he couldn't let himself look at any of the things he still had. That he couldn't let himself accept that while their parents were gone, they lived on in their hearts. In the way Iris cared for them and baked them food, the way that Ryder worked the land and kept the ranch going. The way that Pansy was determined to keep the town of Gold Valley safe, like their father had before her.

In the brash boldness of Colt and Jake and their rodeo dreams. And in the steady, constant care that Logan gave to everything, even at personal cost, just like his mother had done.

They hadn't just been shaped by the losses of their parents, but by their lives. She wondered if he let himself feel that at all.

"When are you going to give him the cookies?" Iris asked.

"I'm not going to give him the cookies, I'm going to go over with the cookie dough and I'm going to bake them at his house. After the wedding." That really did earn her some none-too-subtle stares. "Do you have a question?"

"None," Iris said.

"No. None," Sammy said.

"We have to hide these cookies."

"Well," Sammy said, laughing, "I have a pretty fair idea where we can hide them. Considering your brother loves cookies. And I imagine Colt and Jake would accept a peace offering in the bunkhouse."

"Probably."

"I can pester them about their favorite foods, too. I'm thinking keeping some prepared meals at the bakery wouldn't be a bad idea. And I need to do something to help with the overhead. Lord knows renting on Main Street isn't cheap. I'm going to need money before I get started."

Iris was suddenly so keen and determined, and different from the way Rose had always seen her. Now that Iris had found what she wanted, she was jumping in with both feet.

It was a lesson to Rose. About assuming she knew everything there was to know about what was in someone else's heart.

She felt like she had discovered the world had a whole different dimension to it. It was weird, slightly confronting. But overall, something she was glad she was contending with.

She was growing. Changing. Sometimes it made her feel a little bit smaller. Sometimes it made her afraid. But mostly, it made her excited for what might come next. Because life was deeper and richer and love was a lot more than she thought it was only a month ago. It made her giddy to imagine what she might know in another month. Or two. In a year.

All the things she might have discovered by then.

Who knew that sex and baking cookies could be quite so informative?

CHAPTER SEVENTEEN

IT WAS WEDDING TIME. And Pansy had insisted that the men wear tuxedos. Logan was honored to be part of the wedding, as she had insisted that her family be groomsmen. Of course, she didn't know that he was also the groom's family. Yeah, he was honored, but things were a little bit more complicated than Pansy realized.

Also, he didn't particularly enjoy being in a suit.

They were all hanging out in the house, and he knew that the Dalton contingent and West's half brothers were in the barn already. So many people were in the wedding, he wondered if anybody was going to be sitting in the audience.

He and Ryder were sitting down in the living room, drinking beer. Colt and Jake were seeing to last-minute setup details. And the women were all upstairs, fussing with bridesmaid dresses, hair and makeup. He was sure that Sammy had said something about false eyelashes, but he couldn't be certain.

He lifted a beer. "Congratulations. You get to give one away."

"Yeah," Ryder said, taking a drink of beer. "I guess I really did make it." He laughed. "Of course, then in a few months I'm about to have a baby."

"No empty nest for you, I guess," Logan said.

"Wouldn't know what to do with one anyway," Ryder said.

"You did a damn fine job," Logan said. "You had to raise all of us."

"Oh, you were mostly raised. Maybe I had to do a bit with the girls. But you guys helped a lot. Iris helped more than she should have had to. And then there was Sammy."

"I get the feeling we all supported each other pretty well."

"Yeah, I think we did." Ryder looked at him hard, and Logan felt suddenly uncomfortable.

"You going to do all this?" he asked.

"Me?" His stomach tightened. "Not. Not for me."

"Why is that?"

"Just isn't."

"And there's no other reason why? Because you're not exactly going out on the town prowling around, and so I don't think it's because you don't have it in you to settle down. In fact, you don't really seem deficient in any way."

"Well, neither did you. You didn't figure you'd get married."

"Right," Ryder said. "I didn't. Just takes the right woman, though, sometimes."

"Sometimes the woman can be right as anything, but it still doesn't make you the right man," Logan said.

Because when he pictured Rose, all he could think was that she was right in every way.

He was the one that wasn't quite.

"That's when you figure out how to become the right man, Logan. When she's worth it."

He didn't say anything. But the fact of the matter was, sometimes the woman was so worth it you had to be man enough to give her the space to find a man who was just as worth it. Sometimes that was the better part of virtue. He knew that Ryder and Sammy were halves of the same whole. And it might have taken them a while to realize that, but Logan had seen it from the beginning. He understood why Ryder had imagined he couldn't have those things, and didn't want them.

Even when he downplayed it, it couldn't be denied, that Ryder had raised them all. That he had seen them off into life. That he had sacrificed his dreams and everything that he was for them.

Logan was happy being a rancher. He had never wanted anything more. Ryder's father and uncle had been his father figures. Ranchers, and their dad had been a cop, too. Those had been his dreams. To be the kind of steady that they'd been.

Yeah, he hadn't given anything up.

Ryder had imagined marriage and kids would be more of the same sacrificing. More of the same work.

It wasn't the same for him.

Not at all.

"Well. Either way. You did it."

"Yep. Probably the happiest a guy whose sister is marrying an ex-convict could possibly be."

They both laughed at that. Then a few minutes later, he heard the rustling of fabric, and footsteps on the landing. He turned, and the procession coming down the stairs made his heart go still, then slam hard against his chest.

Pansy in a wedding gown made even him feel sentimental. And he could tell by the look on Ryder's face, that his friend wasn't faring much better. She was like a pocket-sized angel in the flowing fabric, her dark hair loose and falling around her shoulders in waves.

But then he saw Rose. And after that he couldn't see anything else. The Christmas-green bridesmaid dress she had on hugged her curves in a way that made him ache. She was just so damned pretty.

He could hardly stand it. Having restraint around her was damn tough now. He had done it for five years years. Five long years. And then… Then, he'd spent the past month glorying in every fantasy he'd ever had about her. And all he wanted to do now was get up off the couch, pull her into his arms and kiss her. Kiss her because she was there. Because she was his. And he couldn't do that. So he sat there, drinking his beer, not moving.

And he could swear he felt Ryder's gaze boring a hole through the side of his face.

"Don't you two clean up nice," Sammy said, looking them both over openly.

"We tried," Ryder said. "For Pansy's sake."

"You didn't wear a suit for me," she said.

"You didn't want me to."

"True," she said, laughing.

The girls came closer, and he and Ryder both stood, because it seemed wrong to stay seated in the face of so much beauty. Pansy ran to hug Ryder, who pulled her into his arms and held her tight. But Sammy, he noticed, was staring at him. Rose was too, and he felt damned flattered over the way she was looking at him. But it was difficult to enjoy when he felt essentially pinned to the wall by his friend's wife.

"You look great," Rose said softly.

"So do you," he said.

"You do look good," Sammy said. "You know, I was down in the barn earlier. And saw all the guys in their suits there. They look a lot like you."

No one else heard what Sammy said, except for Rose, who rounded quickly and faced her. "Don't," Rose said.

"Let Pansy and West have their wedding. Dig into things later."

Rose's defense of him was unexpected, but welcome.

"That's fair," Sammy said, looking between the two of them. "I'm beginning to think there's a few things that aren't being talked about right now that maybe should be."

"Nothing needs to be talked about between the whole room," Logan said. "Like Rose said. Especially now."

"I'll behave myself," she said. "Promise."

A promise of good behavior from Sammy wasn't worth the paper it was printed on, but he would take it. Honestly, if it weren't for the fact that he cared about Pansy so much, he wouldn't really mind. He didn't have anything to say about any of this. Nothing at all.

And Sammy could pry all she wanted. He might even tell her. It was just that there wouldn't be a resolution to it. Not the one she was after.

"We have to all hold on to Pansy's dress," Iris said. "It's going to get dirty."

Iris, for her part, looked pretty. She didn't have the more obvious beauty of Rose, who was curvy and impish and always looked a bit like she was up to no good, which put a man in the mind to get up to no good with her. Granted, that could be the chemistry they had. Pansy, also, was more obviously cute. Petite and springy. Feisty.

Iris had always been smoother. Taller, and with a more willowy frame. To him, she had always been a bit nondescript.

Then, she definitely played into that, and in the green bridesmaid dress he could see that there was more green in her eyes than he'd ever noticed before. She would probably be a pretty girl, if she didn't almost intentionally blend in with the wallpaper.

But none of them could hold a candle to Rose. Not in his opinion anyway.

Biased though he was.

They all gathered pieces of Pansy's skirt and headed for the door. Then they walked her to the barn, where she took her place. Hidden from any of the guests. Hidden from her groom.

West was waiting at the front of the barn, along with the pastor. And he knew, having seen it already, that everything inside was decorated in a grand fashion, fit for a Hope Springs wedding. They had frosted fat red cranberries with sugar and strung them around evergreen garlands, and there were Christmas trees all situated throughout the room, lit up with bright white lights, and strung with more of the berries. They'd made popcorn strings too, and he'd enjoyed doing some of those on the floor of his cabin with Rose, who had continually taken bites out of his, resulting in him taking a bite out of her neck, and that had ended in them making love on the floor.

Yeah, that was a good memory. And not one he particularly ought to have right now.

They weren't doing a formal walk down the aisle paired off. There were more men than women, since West was including his half brothers.

His and Logan's half brothers.

Ryder was walking Pansy down, and then there was his half sister, McKenna, and Sammy, Iris and Rose. When they were all gathered at the back of the barn, a strange tightness overwhelmed Logan's chest. He thought that it would be fine. That it would feel just…like nothing. Why should it feel like anything? He'd seen Gabe, Jacob and Caleb at school many times over the years. He never met McKenna Dodge, but what did it matter that they shared

DNA? It shouldn't. They didn't have a connection. But they were right there.

And there was something strange about it. There was also a certain sameness to their features that it was easy to miss when he was standing next to West, but with all of them there, the collection of blue eyes and build was a bit much to ignore. He didn't have the same nose as West, but his was similar to Gabe's, his chin a lot like Caleb's. And they all had those eyes. The same blue.

It was McKenna, petite and without some of the physical similarities the rest of them shared, who looked at him sharply. "I don't think we've met," she said.

"No," he responded.

Sammy was watching the interaction closely, and he saw Rose break away from where she was standing by her sister. She moved beside him.

"Hi," she said. "I'm Rose Daniels. I'm Pansy's sister."

"McKenna Dodge. West's half sister."

"I'm Logan Heath," he said. Because not introducing himself would cause more questions to be raised than not.

"Nice to meet you, Logan," she said. She looked like she wanted to say more, but he supposed even in their particular situation it wasn't the done thing to just ask: who's your daddy?

McKenna paired off with Gabe and Jacob for her walk down the aisle. Caleb took Sammy's arm. Iris linked arms with Colt and Jake. Which left Rose and Logan, and he had to wonder if that was a bit by design. He was starting to think their secret wasn't all that well-kept.

West's brother was already standing next to him, and when they made their way down the aisle and took their places, the first person whose eyes he landed on in the front row was Hank Dalton.

Yeah, he really hadn't thought this through. Or thought at all about how impossible it was going to be to ignore the Dalton contingent. They were everywhere.

They were… They were West's family. Somehow.

They'd never been his. But somehow, they were.

You never spoke to any of them. You could have. You didn't.

He was not having this breakdown right now. There would be ample time. They'd been living across town from each other for years. There was no reason for it to all come to a head here. Hell, sometimes they were all in the same damn grocery store. It was just, they weren't usually wearing matching suits. Which did make the whole thing a little bit harder to ignore.

Then Pansy and Ryder started to walk down the aisle, and he determinedly put his focus on them. Decided that he wasn't going to think about his own shit anymore. There was no time for that. Not here. Pansy was getting married. But still, he found himself looking at Rose, and he felt… something. His whole family was here. And so was Rose. And all of it just seemed…

His family.

He had never thought of them that way before.

They were the Daltons.

He'd had a family.

His mom had been his family. She had… She had sacrificed for him. Had given up her dreams for him.

And then she had died. She had never gotten to be in that space where it was any easier. She had never found love. She had never gotten to be free of the millstone around her neck that was…this kid that she'd been saddled with because Hank hadn't taken responsibility for his actions.

No, they weren't his family.

His mother had been his family. And that was it. There was nothing more to say.

There never would be. He would not allow Sammy and her big, dewy eyes to make him feel guilty about anything. He didn't have to give answers to the questions in McKenna's gaze. He just didn't. He didn't know the woman. He didn't owe her a damn thing.

He didn't owe any of them anything.

He gritted his teeth against all the emotion that was rising up inside of him. Things he didn't have a name for. Things he didn't like at all.

And he focused on West and Pansy. On the miracle that was the two of them saying their vows. Looking at each other like two people who had never lost. Who had never been hurt. He knew that wasn't the case. Not for either of them.

It was a hell of a thing.

And the day was about them. He was determined to let that be true.

When the wedding was finished, when they had kissed and been pronounced husband-and-wife, the island tables were cleared, and everything for the reception was set up.

There was a band, and Colt picked up his guitar and started to play country music, like he did at family gatherings. Colt wasn't necessarily big on performing music, but the guy didn't have a shy or modest bone in his body. And Logan had a feeling it was all the same to him, riding a bull in front of a crowded stadium of people, a ride that might be televised on national TV, playing a guitar for family at a barbecue, or playing it now in a hall full of people.

The song was fast and fun, and couples went out onto the dance floor in droves. Including McKenna and her husband, Grant Dodge, Gabe and his fiancée, Jamie. Jacob, his wife, Vanessa, and their baby.

His nephew.

That hit him uncomfortably.

Then there was his half brother Caleb, who was dancing with his stepdaughter Amelia, who he supposed was his niece. Caleb's wife, Ellie, looked on with a sweet smile on her face. Logan turned away from the scene.

And there was Rose.

"Dance with me," he said.

"Sure, cowboy," she said.

She didn't seem embarrassed at all, and she went into his arms with ease. It was a quick dance, so it didn't require him to hold her too close. A blessing, because if he had to do that, he might've embarrassed them both.

"I hope Sammy didn't bother you too much earlier."

"Look, she's not an idiot. Sammy knows more about me than a lot of people do. And, she's pretty insightful at that. I guess I shouldn't be surprised that she picked up on it."

"I think McKenna might have, too."

"Yeah, it's that thing of having us all in the same room. But look. This isn't about me. It's about West and Pansy."

"I know," she said softly. "Are you okay?"

"I'm fine. Look, my blood isn't exactly news to me. I understand that it's a point of interest for the rest of you. But I made my decisions about what I was going to do with the Daltons a long time ago. I'm sticking to it."

"All right," she said.

"I want to dance, not talk," he said.

What he really wanted to do was lead her out of the barn, and find someplace quiet. Kiss her. Strip her naked. Yeah, that was what he wanted. What he wanted to do was bury himself and all of his problems in her beautiful body, and find his release.

And when the song changed to something slow, he thought about suggesting it. He wrapped his arms around her waist and drew her fully against him.

"Logan," she whispered.

"I don't care," he responded.

But then, he caught movement out of the corner of his eye, and when he turned, it was to see Hank Dalton coming toward him.

He froze.

Because he might have been around his half brothers quite a lot during the course of his life, but he'd never seen Hank Dalton anywhere but at a distance. And the man had certainly never looked at him. Certainly never crossed a room to speak to him.

"I'm sorry," he said. And he stared at Logan with eyes that matched his exactly. "But I have to ask. Who are you, and who's your mother?"

Logan just stood there, stunned.

"I don't think this is the time," Rose whispered.

But it was that, that soft denial, that said more than his answer ever could have.

"Who is she?"

"It doesn't matter," Logan said. "She's dead."

"You're Jane Heath's son," he said. "You're *my* son, aren't you?"

And that was when he realized that everyone on the dance floor had stopped. Everyone was staring.

All this had come home to roost and in public no less.

Well, wasn't this a shit show.

"This is West and Pansy's wedding," Logan said. "Not

a family reunion. So maybe we save the conversation for another day."

"I'm your father," Hank said. "I'm sure of it. I remember her. And I was really sorry to hear that she died. I didn't know she had a son that could've been mine, though."

"You know what, Hank," Logan said. "It's real interesting to meet you right about now. But this isn't news to me. I gather that it is to you. I'm not sure how."

His gut twisted with the knowledge. That Hank hadn't known he was his. He was sure that he would have. How could he not have? How could he not have known? Given that his mother had been offered that payoff.

None of it made sense, and he didn't want to sort it out now, but he couldn't deny the fact that Hank looked shocked. That he looked like he hadn't known. Hadn't expected this.

"I didn't know," Hank repeated. "I didn't know about you." He shook his head. "Where did you grow up? Who took care of you?"

Rose stepped in front of him. "We did. We took care of him. And it's not…"

"What the hell?" That came from West, who had crossed the space between them and was now standing directly in front of Logan. "You knew? You knew all this time? You knew that I had come back here looking for family, and we… We've been having dinner together. You knew and you didn't tell me."

"Because I haven't told anyone," Logan said. "And I haven't admitted a damn thing. Look, you had to come here and make your own decisions about what you wanted to do with the Daltons. I grew up here. I made my decisions a long damned time ago. And I made my family. I don't know why anybody wants to have it out here and now."

"How could you just keep it a secret like that?" Pansy asked. "I brought your half brother home to you, and you just kept it a secret."

"Yeah," Logan said. "It was my secret to keep. I don't owe any of you anything. And I don't owe you any damned explanations for my behavior. It's not up to you what I do or how I handle this. But hey, here you go. Here's your wedding gift. I'm a damn half brother."

"Were you just never going to tell me?"

"West," Logan said. "You marrying Pansy brought you about as close to me as anything could have. I didn't figure it mattered."

"It matters," West said. "I…I threw everything aside for Emmett, because he's my blood. I came back here to Oregon looking for family, because the Daltons are my blood, imperfect or not. You knew that. You knew all that, and you didn't confide in me."

"Have your wedding," Logan said. "Have your wedding, and enjoy yourself. Don't make it about me. We'll talk when you get back from your honeymoon."

"You expect me to just go on like this didn't happen?"

"It doesn't change anything. I went to high school with them," he said, pointing at Gabe, Jacob and Caleb, who were staring. "It wasn't like we had some supernatural connection. We didn't even ever talk."

"This is my fault." It was Tammy Dalton who stepped forward then, a petite blonde with Dolly Parton's sense of style. "I'm the one who talked to your mother. I didn't know who she was, and I didn't want to. I gave her money and I sent her on her way. Hank didn't know."

Her words hit Logan like a punch to the gut.

"He didn't know," he echoed.

It didn't change anything, though. Didn't change his

mother's pain. It didn't bring her back, didn't make any of this better.

It didn't matter.

It couldn't.

"No," Tammy said. "He never knew. And it's something that we've been dealing with, the two of us, because we hurt each other in a lot of ways, but we hurt other people with it. And I'm sorry, I'm so very sorry." She choked up. "Now it's ruining West's wedding…"

"My wedding isn't ruined," West said.

"I…I don't know what to say to this," Logan said. "And it's not the right time to be saying anything. This wasn't supposed to happen today." He looked at West and Pansy when he said that.

"And I'm sorry," Hank said. "Because everything I did more than thirty years ago just keeps coming up and up again. Just keeps coming back to bite… Well, everyone else in the ass. All these things that I did. And no matter how many times I say I'm sorry, I just still…keep having to look at how I hurt people. And I don't mean to say that to make you sorry for me. It's just… I can't seem to be sorry enough. And you're right, you don't owe me a thing. But I suspect I owe you an awful lot. So if you'll let me… If you'll let me, I'd like you to be part of this family. We are not perfect. We're still finding out how not perfect we are. But we're trying. We're trying to be a family."

Logan pulled away from Rose, and he turned and walked away from all of it. Out of the barn. Outside.

He heard footsteps behind him, and he expected it to be Rose. But when he turned, it was McKenna.

"What?" He sounded mean. He didn't care.

"I just wanted to say, that… I didn't have anyone, either. I mean nobody. I came here to get money off Hank. I didn't come here to find a family. I didn't give a shit about my brothers. I didn't care at all about Hank Dalton. I grew up in foster care. My mom's not dead, she just didn't want me. And I...I didn't expect anything. I didn't want it. I came here, I started working for the Dodge family, and I met Grant. I got a whole lot more than I bargained for there. And then... And then I met Hank. And he told me to leave. He offered me money. And I was... I was devastated. Because it turned out that part of me really did just want a family. I thought that I was independent and strong, and that I didn't need anyone. And then it turned out I needed a whole lot of someone's. So maybe you do, too. I don't know. But speaking as someone who never had anyone, who came into the Dalton family... I think you should give them a chance."

"You don't understand," he said, his voice hoarse. "I had someone. I had a family. I had my mother. She loved me. And she died. Hank hurt her, McKenna. I'll never forgive him for that. I don't expect I should have to."

And this time, when he walked away, nobody came after him. And he did his best not to feel disappointed by that.

LOGAN WAS GONE, Pansy was livid, and West was fit to be tied. Rose felt like she was split in half. Because part of her desperately wanted to go after him, and another part of her figured she needed to stay at her sister's wedding reception and deal with the intense amount of drama that was happening.

"You knew," Pansy said. "You knew that he was West's brother."

She understood. Her sister could only feel defensive of the man she loved. The man she was afraid might be hurt by this.

But Rose felt the same.

Logan had protected his mother with everything he had. Logan had felt rejected by the Daltons. He owed them nothing.

"He didn't want to make today about him," she said. "And he didn't. Hank's the one who did that. Logan doesn't deserve your anger."

The Daltons were having a heated discussion among themselves, which Rose had the sense was common in that group.

"She's right," West said. "Look, I handled it how I did but he doesn't owe us or me anything. He had a different life. That's the thing. We all had different lives."

"Whatever Logan wants to do is up to him," Ryder said. "Let's get back to the wedding."

And they did, to the best of their ability. Rose felt torn because it was her sister's wedding, but knowing Logan was in pain made it impossible for her to enjoy herself.

It took another two hours for the guests to disperse and then for the Daltons to go home. It had been decided that today was not the day for anyone to try and enforce a family reunion.

"I should go talk to him," West said.

"No," Rose said firmly. "You go on your honeymoon. He'll be here when you get back. I'll talk to them."

She knew that the way she had taken the lead on this issue said a lot. But still, it wasn't anything her family seemed willing to call her on at the moment. And she was going to go ahead and take that. If there were hard conversations to have, and there were, they could wait until after the dust settled. They could wait until after the wedding was over. Until after Pansy and West returned from their honeymoon.

Yes. It could wait. It could all wait.

For now, it was a wedding. And it was Christmas Eve.

And there was a big stack of presents with Logan's name on it, and she was going to make sure he got them.

They saw the bride and groom off with great fanfare, and then Rose began to fill a plate with leftover dinner from the buffet table.

"Hungry?" Ryder asked.

"No," she said, stubborn. "I'm taking some food to Logan and I'm going to see how he's doing."

The glare she gave everyone came with a warning.

"You're going to go talk to him?" Jake asked.

"Yep," she said, daring him to comment.

The girls, for their part, were looking in other directions because they suspected Rose's deeper connection to Logan, and obviously weren't going to be the ones to confirm anything.

"Maybe I should go," Ryder said. "He's my friend."

"He's my friend," Rose said. "I work with him all day every day. I… He's my friend."

That seemed to shut her brother up, and set him back a little bit. He didn't say anything, though. Not as she took a plate of food and beers and loaded them up into the truck.

She drove across the property and picked up all the ingredients for the cookies, concealing them in a tote bag, then hauled it all to Logan's cabin. Gathering her items, she tromped up the porch with her arms full, banging on the door with her foot.

The door jerked open, and there was Logan, his suit jacket gone, the tie gone as well, his shirt unbuttoned halfway down and untucked from the black slacks.

This was a whole different kind of hot.

Him all angry and disheveled. She had never particularly thought about the way that suits looked on men. But today had been quite educational, and this was yet another moment of pure fascination. "What are you doing here?"

"I brought you dinner."

"You didn't have to do that."

"It's Christmas," she said softly.

"You know I don't like Christmas," he said, his voice rough.

And what a mess of a Christmas it had been. Everything had gone wrong. Everything. And this pain he'd hidden for so many years had been dragged out in the open with a full audience.

"I'm so sorry," she said, tears filling her eyes. "I know you didn't want that to happen. I just… Let me try to make it better?"

"You can't."

"Then can I make you feel better for a while?" She shifted. "My hands are full and I'm freezing. This dress is pretty, but it's not doing anything to keep me warm. Can I come in?"

"Where does Ryder think you are?"

"Ryder knows where I am."

She let that truth settle between them.

"So anyway. Food."

"I don't know what all this is going to mean. If everyone is pissed at me. West married Pansy. He's part of the family."

"Not the way that you are. Not to me."

"That's awfully sweet of you, Rose. But still…"

"No." She unburdened herself, setting all her items down on a side table. "Logan… You're part of us. You're part of me. I understand why this was all…terrible timing." She fidgeted, looking down at the bag with the ingredients she'd brought. Maybe this was bad timing, too. "I have something for you…"

"The only present I want to unwrap is you," he whispered. "As long as you'll have me, Rose Daniels. You're the only Christmas present I really want. And ever since I saw you for the first time, in that beautiful bridesmaid dress, I was imagining taking it off you."

"Were you really?" she asked, her voice hushed.

"Yes. Oh, you have no idea. Honey, when I first started fantasizing about you I thought there was something broken inside of me." He laughed, a jagged, painful sound. "Well, forget that. I had always known there was something broken inside of me, but when I first started looking at you like that I thought maybe that was it. All the evidence of it that I could ever need. It tormented me."

"It did?"

"Yeah. You were…you know, barely nineteen. Pretty as hell. You were around all the time and then…then it just changed and I couldn't change it back."

"When?"

It suddenly seemed imperative to know. When things had changed for him. For her it had been in stages. There had been that change when she had suddenly realized, not that he was a man, but that she was a woman, and that meant that him being a man didn't put him off-limits. There was the wanting him. And then there was the slow realization that the feelings that lived inside of her were love. That they always had been, but when they were mixed together with desire, naked bodies, and laughing beneath the covers, it created alchemy that spun connection into love.

Being *in* love.

Not just the kind of love you had for a family.

And suddenly she wanted to know. Where the changes had happened for him. And what they had turned into now.

"You smiled at me." He shook his head. "We had just delivered a calf. You were covered in blood and other things. We were tired, it had been a long night, and when we walked out of the barn, the sun was rising. You turned and looked at me, and the sunlight caught your hair. You smiled. I felt it right here." He pressed his hand against his stomach. "And after that, it just wouldn't let go. And I did everything I could to turn away from it. To let go of it and you. But it only got worse. It got to the point where I couldn't just go find another woman to take the edge off."

She gritted her teeth against that portion of the admission. She didn't like to think about him with other women. She never wanted him to be with another woman again. She wanted him. And she wanted him to be with only her.

"And I told myself that I couldn't do anything about it out of respect for Ryder. And then I realized, that he had nothing to do with anything. Our relationship is ours. You don't need his permission. Any more than I do."

"I never really thought about whether or not I was pretty. I never really worried about it. I'm really glad that I was to you."

"I think you'd be pretty to the whole world." He pulled her into his arms and brushed her hair out of her face. "But then, I'm biased. Because I know how pretty you look without your clothes on."

"You're the only one who does," she said fiercely.

It was a promise. That he would be the only one ever who did.

She had never given that much thought, either. She had assumed that she would have to date a few people, when she was ready to start. Had never given a lot of thought to forever or marriage. And it wasn't marriage that she thought of primarily now. It was just... They were bonded. Deeper than skin. Deeper than paperwork. There was no question about dating a few people. There was no question of there being anyone but him.

And that was when his intensity seemed to reach the boiling point. He hauled her against his chest and kissed her. This was no sweet, tentative meeting. Nothing like the sweetness they'd shared after he'd given her the necklace. This was something else entirely. It was fearsome and frightening. Wonderful.

Electric and explosive.

She was all right with it being too much. All right with that sense of being overwhelmed. Because she wanted it. Wanted to be overwhelmed by him. Wanted to be consumed by him.

She wanted to pour all of the feelings that she had into him. Because she wanted to add that layer that he left out. That shift that had occurred inside of her.

From the discovery of want to the inevitability of love.

This love that was just right there for them to take, for them to claim. She wanted him to claim it, too. She wanted it so very, very badly. She worked the buttons on that shirt that was mostly open, moved her hands over his muscles, his hard torso.

He was a thing of masculine beauty. The most incredible of God's creations in her opinion. Sculpted perfection. He had taught her. He had taught her passion. He had taught her how to move to please herself, to please him. He had taught her to love this part of herself. This wild, unrestrained, passionate creature that only he had unlocked.

He had taught her to recognize these feelings. These moments.

And now, she was unleashing it all on him.

Now, she was holding him at her mercy.

Now, she wanted to show him something.

She wanted to show him her heart. How she felt. That great, driving need that existed inside of her.

She wanted to show him all of that and more.

He undid the zipper on that dress, and it fell down to her hips. She wiggled out of it completely, leaving her only in the strapless bra she had bought just for the wedding, and a pair of seamless underwear that were a bit more brief than she typically wore.

Judging by the fire in his eyes, he approved.

It made her want to get herself a variety of underwear. Different colors. Different shapes. Lace.

Anything to find new ways to tease him.

Suddenly, a whole lot of things made sense to her that hadn't before. But wasn't that the theme of all of this?

That life with Logan took on new dimension, new meaning. As their relationship did.

He made quick work of the bra, his hot mouth finding her nipple unerringly, sucking it in deep. She loved it when he was like this. When he didn't treat her like she was fragile, or younger, or less experienced. When he came to her as an equal. As her lover.

When all the lines between them blurred, and nothing mattered but the moment they were in. Nothing mattered but the way they could touch each other, taste each other, make each other feel.

She loved it when nothing mattered but this.

When their bodies and desires melded into one.

She arched against him, rolling her hips, bringing the center of her need into contact with the evidence of his arousal.

And he was very, very aroused.

She broke their kiss so that she could give her focus to his belt, to getting his pants off, and when she did, she saw his face. There was something there that went past sexual desperation.

He was raw. And he was hurting.

And he was looking to her to heal him.

She had bandaged him a few times in his life.

He needed it from her again. But this was more than just putting a Band-Aid on cuts. More than kissing a bruise.

She couldn't hold back. She had to give him everything.

And that meant that she couldn't be safe.

But for him it was worth it. For him it would always be worth it. He held on to her tightly, and went down onto the couch, bringing her so that she was straddling his lap. Which brought her breasts right to the same level as his mouth. He teased her, suckled her, tormented her. And she loved it.

She surrendered to it.

He was a man who seemed intent on devouring her, and she was happy to let him.

She rocked against him, trying to ease the ache that was centered between her thighs. But there was nothing that would work except for him. Him inside of her. That was what she needed.

"I need you," she moaned, pressing her hand to his rock-hard arousal. She curved her fingers around him through the fabric and squeezed.

He dragged the fabric of her panties to the side and began to stroke her, pushing two fingers inside of her, teasing her that way while she rocked against him. She opened his pants, and settled herself over him, placing the head of him right where she needed him and sinking down.

His head fell back, his breath hissing between his teeth. He grabbed her hips, and seated her more firmly on him with one harsh movement. She gasped.

If she had thought to take control this way, he wasn't going to allow it. He established an intense, harsh movement, his hips bucking upward, his hands bringing her down hard over him. She rolled her hips like she was taking a rough ride on a horse, sank into the rhythm and gave herself over to it.

Pleasure built inside of her until she could barely see. Until words ceased to exist in her mind and everything became feeling. Pleasure blooming in her stomach and lower, emotion expanding in her chest. When her orgasm took hold, she gripped his shoulders tight, freezing as she found her pleasure. Glorious. Intense. Everything. She saw stars. Brilliant and bright, like that clear sky above them when they had kissed in the open. That promise of something more. Something deeper. His climax followed hers, a growl that echoed in his chest. He gripped her hips so hard she thought it might leave bruises. Wanted it to, even. When it was over, she collapsed against him, spent and wrung out.

He lifted her, cradling her against his chest like she was something precious. She had spent her life being cared for by others. But she had never felt quite so cared for and protected as she did in this moment. The same man who pushed her, who challenged her, also offered the greatest protection. It was like a miracle.

Feelings like they had between themselves was like a miracle.

With his pants still halfway around his hips, he carried her to his room, and deposited her on the bed. He shucked his clothes the rest of the way as she wiggled out of her panties. Then they crawled beneath the covers, and he held her.

There had been a time when she'd ached for the Christmases of her childhood. Her early childhood. When she had longed for those gatherings when everyone had been there. They had been wonderful. And that time was over.

They had made a new kind of Christmas magic tonight.

It was wonderful to know that you didn't have to leave magic behind in childhood. But that you could find it in the simplicity of a clear December night, held in the arms of the man you loved.

Right then, she couldn't remember if she'd ever been quite so happy before.

And for once, she just decided to rest in it.

CHAPTER EIGHTEEN

WHEN HE WOKE UP the next morning, it was Christmas, and Rose wasn't in bed with him. He groaned, pressing his hands over his eyes. He would rather just sleep through the day. It was too much of a whole thing. He would rather that Rose were here with him. But of course, she had to get back to the main house, to spend Christmas doing regular things. And she couldn't exactly have stayed with him overnight without it being noticed.

Then he heard clattering coming from outside of his room, and he sat up.

Could she have come back already?

He got out of bed and pulled a pair of jeans out of his dresser, yanking them on and buttoning and zipping them before heading out to the living room. She wasn't there, and he went into the kitchen, and there she was.

Wearing one of his T-shirts, and that was it. She was fussing around with the oven and a mixing bowl. And she looked like... Well, she looked like Christmas morning. Like the very best present a man could ever ask for.

"What are you doing?"

"Oh," she said, starting slightly. "I'm... It's your Christmas present."

"My what?"

"Your Christmas present." She shrugged. "I was going to make it for you last night, but things got a little bit... Well.

And so, I figured there was nothing wrong with having it on Christmas morning."

"Don't you need to be back at the house?"

"They did the gifts and everything last night."

"Still. Don't you think you're going to be missed?"

"Maybe."

"What is my Christmas present?" He decided to ask that instead, because it was clear she wasn't going to concede his point on the fact that she should have maybe gone back to her brother's house as would be expected.

She was playing it fast and loose with his physical safety, as far as he was concerned.

You're playing it fast and loose with your own, and you know it.

"Chocolate chip cookies," she said. "Oatmeal chocolate chip cookies, to be exact. I found your mom's recipe."

He stiffened. "You did?"

"Yes," she said. "I found the recipe, and I…I wanted to give it to you. Because I wanted you to… I want you to know… I want you to understand that even though we lost something amazing, something really important when we lost our parents…we didn't lose everything. And there are some things that we bring with us. Some things that we are meant to carry on. I really believe that."

"Rose…"

His chest went cold, his stomach going tight.

After everything that had happened yesterday this just felt like… It was too much. It was just too damned much.

"Don't. Don't argue with me. Look, I understand that this is all really hard for you. And I don't pretend to understand all the ways that it is. I understand that it is, and that's enough."

"You didn't have to do this," he said.

"I did," she said. She sighed heavily. "I wanted to give you something. Like, really something. I wish… I wish that…"

She closed her eyes for a long moment. "Logan," she said. "I just want us to be healed. To be fixed. I spent a long time protecting myself. Ignoring all of my feelings. Because I just didn't know how to have them. I'm so grateful for everything that everyone did for me, but it doesn't change the fact that I'm missing something from my life. I'm missing my mom and dad. And…it hurts."

There was something about those words that hit him right in the chest. Echoed in him. He'd always thought Rose was strong and brave. Always. But right now she was the bravest he'd ever seen. Admitting she hurt. Which was something Logan couldn't quite bring himself to do. "I never wanted to think about that. That I was still wounded. That there were just things I would always feel the lack of. I didn't want to think about my own loneliness. I wanted to fix Iris up and not myself, because I didn't want to look at the things that held me back. My fear of needing someone. The fact that I actually desperately want to be coddled a little bit, but I feel like I have to be tough. Yeah. I didn't want to look at any of that stuff. It all scared me. Terrified me. But slowly, really slowly, over the course of our time together, I realized some things."

She looked down at her hands for a moment. "One of the biggest ones is that we can always keep changing and learning and growing. And it's this kind of magic gift. Recipes don't have to stay buried. Necklaces don't have to stay in boxes. And our hearts don't have to stay… They don't have to stay so guarded. Everything we've lost… Everyone we've lost… They might not be here with us in the way that we want them to be, but they're still here. They're part of us. If we'll let them be."

He looked at her, and for the life of him, he couldn't figure out how he was supposed to respond to that. She was standing there imploring him like she was so desperate for him to understand, and he didn't know what the hell he was supposed to do with that. Didn't know how the hell he was supposed to say anything right now.

Because she was standing there, looking like the embodiment of a future that he had never believed he could have. A woman, wearing his T-shirt, baking his mother's cookies. A woman who could...

His stomach pitched.

He hadn't used a condom last night.

And there it was. Hank Dalton, coming home to roost. Or maybe it wasn't even Hank. The man hadn't raised him. He wasn't dumb enough to believe that blood might make a man do something quite so stupid as not protect the woman that he was sleeping with.

No. It was just him. Not facing up to the reality of things.

It was him, imagining that things could be different when he damn well knew they couldn't be. He had imagined a life where he would wake up every morning alone. No one would be in his kitchen bustling around making him anything.

But here she was. Radiant as sunshine, and looking something like hope.

"Logan," she said. "You know, I wondered, why I never wanted anything more than what I had. And I thought maybe some of that was about my self-protection. I was starting to ask myself... What were my dreams? Because you know, Iris is going to open that bakery. And Pansy is the chief of police. And Ryder is coaching the high school football team. Sammy's jewelry business is going amazingly well. Colt and Jake are out riding rodeo. And here we are. We are here. I was asking myself... Why don't I have dreams?"

"You can do whatever you want," he said, his throat dry, tight. "You could be whatever you want."

"That's just the thing. I am what I want to be. I love this ranch. With all my heart. This land is in my blood. It fuels my soul. I don't remember my parents as well as everyone else. I was only six when they died, after all. Working the same ground my uncle did. Investing my sweat in the soil the same as my father did. Being in the same house where my mother raised us... This place built me. The loss of them built me. And keeping Hope Springs alive sustained me. Working with you sustained me. You wanted to be a rancher, right?"

"I don't know. I don't know what I would've been if things would've been different."

"What, would you choose to do anything else now?"

"No," he said. "I could have. A long time ago. But this is what I love."

"It's the same for me. And then I got thinking. Why hadn't I dated? And yeah, maybe some of it was all that self-protection that I told you about before. But I think it was more. Logan, you always felt like another part of me. When you're angry I can feel it. When I annoy you it makes my teeth itch. Like I can feel how yours are set on edge. And when we make love, I can feel all that pleasure echoing around inside of me. And I know it's different. Not just me feeling good. I know I feel you, too. I think you feel the same about me. I don't know if it's soul mates or what. But I felt that from the beginning. Like my connection with you was something inevitable. Real. Like we made it working this land. So the roots are deep. Something happened. It all shifted. And that was when I realized, I'm in the place I love the most, with the man I love the most."

"Rose," he said, using the word to try and deflect what she just said. To keep it from sinking down deep beneath his skin like a bullet. But he wasn't sure he could. He wasn't sure anything could. Because she'd said it. She'd said it, dammit. And he couldn't unknow it. That Rose had said she loved him.

Love.

"I can't," he said.

"You can. We are. There's nothing more... It fits. We fit. In all the crazy ways that we shouldn't, we do. It's so silly, isn't it? Because I'm twenty-three, and you're thirty-three. Because I was a virgin, and you've been with... No, I don't want to know how many women. Because of those things people think we'd be too different. But we've lost. And we've lived. And we work the same piece of ground with all the passion we have to give. And when we come together at the end of a long day it's like magic. The only thing close to magic I've ever known in this world. I'm not a dreamer. I never schemed for myself. But I've been a scared little girl all my life that the people around me might get tired of me and leave me. And when I accepted that I didn't have anything to earn, I could finally enjoy these things I was given. This is our life, Logan. It's the one that we have. Yeah, our parents died. And it's awful. No one should have to deal with that at the age that we did. The magnitude of our tragedy was... It was awful. But why does it get to have the say in who we are? Why is it everything?"

"Because some things scar you," he said. "Some things change what you are, and you can't un-change it."

"Of course not. Of course we were changed by all of

this. Of course we were. But we don't *stop* changing. That's been my lesson. These last weeks. I learned more about life since all of this began with you than I had in years. I thought that I was grown, and I was done figuring it all out, but I'm not. And now I realize how little I know, and I'm happy about it. Because it means... It means there's no end to the wonderful things that could happen. To the wonderful things I could know."

"There's no end to the shit that could happen, either."

"Logan. There's shit in life. There's nothing we can do about that. But why can't we have something good?"

Desperation flooded his chest. And he couldn't quite put words to why. It was just a feeling. Deep and enduring, and it felt like it was threatening to change the very makeup of all that he was.

"That's the thing," he said. "You are young. And you were a virgin. So I get that you think that this thing between us is love. But it's not. It's... It's not."

Saying that burned. It tasted like a lie. But looking at her, with all her great and glorious optimism, this idea that the world and all that she could be in it was ever-expanding...

He could never give her that sense of wonder. Not forever. He couldn't be what she needed. There was just no way. She deserved more. She deserved a hell of a lot more.

A hell of a lot more than a man who wrecked her sister's wedding by standing there in a tux looking identical to the people he was blood related to. People he lived across town from for years, and hadn't shared any words with.

Yeah. She deserved a hell of a lot more than that.

More than what he'd been to his mother. A drain on her resources and her emotions. His one gift sending her on the trip that ended her life.

He was toxic. And it was unavoidable.

"Logan," she said, "you accused me of not having any clue when a man wanted me. And you were right. You were right, I didn't know. But you don't know when the people around you love you. You wouldn't recognize it if a woman stood in front of you and told you. And that's on you. That's some kind of dumb."

"Rose…"

"I love you. I love you, and I know that you feel it. I know it. Because you know me better than anyone else. You know me. And I know you. You know I'm not making this up, or dramatizing, or anything like that. Don't you dare dismiss me, Logan. Because you've never done that. You've never treated me like I was a stupid kid. Don't you dare start now. Don't you dare act like you don't know me now. Like I don't know you. Don't be scared."

Those words hit him with all the force of a bullet.

"I'm not scared," he said. "I could say yes to you. I could be with you. I could take all the best years of your life, Rose. I could keep you in my bed, in my house, and I could give you every damn thing I'm capable of giving. But you know what? That is not enough. It's not that limitless wonder that you're talking about. I don't know how to love somebody. Not really."

"Why do you think that? You held on to your mother's necklace all this time, and you think that."

"I did love my mother. So much. And she loved me. That's the important piece of that, Rose. She loved me. She lived poorer than she would have, if it weren't for me. She was single for a long time, because of me. Because she didn't want to bring a stepfather in my life who might not treat me right. Because she didn't want to be distracted by dating while she was supposed to be raising me."

"No offense, Logan, and I'm sure that she thought she

needed to do that. But it was a choice. It was her choice. Nobody made her do that, and she didn't have to."

"What she did. For me. And Hank Dalton cut her open, Rose. He hurt her. He couldn't be everything that she needed him to be, and he devastated her. Left her on her own with me. And I was a pretty piss-poor substitute. She gave me so much, and I wanted to do something good for her. So when your parents started talking about going on that trip to Alaska… She really wanted to go. But she knew that she wouldn't be able to spare the extra money out of the budget. So I started saving. I did odd jobs around the ranch for your dad. I saved and saved. And I gave her the money to go. To pay for her part of that chartered plane that went down on its way there. To pay for a hotel room she never even used. Yet. That was my gift to my mother. The last Christmas gift I ever gave anyone. Before you." His chest burned.

"Logan," she said, looking utterly stricken. Devastated.

"Why do you think I don't like Christmas?"

"Logan… It's…it wasn't your fault."

"I know it," he said. "I'm not an idiot. It would've happened whether she went or not. And maybe… Maybe your parents would've paid for her to go even. In the end. But I can't let it go. Because that trip was the deciding factor about whether she was here for all of my life or not. That was what happened when I tried to show that I cared. You don't get that stuff out of your head, Rose. You just don't. It stays with you. What you do today. You take that road or the other road? Do you go on the trip or do you not? Do you get on the horse today, or do you stay in bed? Because those decisions matter. They make the choice as to whether you live or die, whether someone you love lives or dies."

"But you make choices. We all do. We make them every

day. And there's nothing anyone can do about what happens. We can't control the universe, Logan. We can't control if other people decide to do us harm. We can't control any of that. All we can do is try to do the best we can with what we've got."

"It's not good enough for me. It's not good enough for you."

"Don't you dare tell me what's good enough for me. You say this is because you're not scared. And you say you're not blaming yourself. But you are. You're frozen. And you figure if you just…keep things the same that you won't have to deal with the consequences."

"No. No. I had a family. I destroyed my family. I took it from myself. I took her from the world. My gift took her life. I don't get to have another family. I don't get to do it again."

"We didn't use a condom last night," she said, honing right in on his earlier realization. He should have known she'd realized it, too.

"They make a pill for that," he said.

"No," she said.

He sighed heavily, the weight of the room pressing down on his shoulders.

"No," he agreed. "I know. It's just… It won't be anything. It'll be fine."

"Logan, I wasn't even going to demand anything of you. Nothing except for love. I never gave a moment's thought to getting married or having kids. You make me think that might be the future I want. But it has nothing to do with why I want you. I'm not one of those people who dreamed about a wedding, or romance. I didn't want it until I had you. I just… I love you. Not the idea of you. Not some romanticized version of a family or life. We can call it a family or not, I don't care. I just want to be together."

"Already you're settling for less. Less than you should."

"Is a soul mate less than someone should settle for? There's no settling about it. I get out of bed every morning in part so I can see you, you big idiot. It's half of why I look forward to my job."

"It's just new relationship stuff. And someday it will be old relationship stuff. And you'll get over it. You'll barely remember that this happened between us."

"I'm not going to forget."

"That's the thing, Rose. You will. Because this was nothing. It sure as hell wasn't love."

CHAPTER NINETEEN

ROSE COULD FEEL the pain and the fury rising up inside of her. Part of her had known. She had known that he would fight this. And she had also known that it was time to have the fight.

She hadn't realized he would fight quite so hard. That he would fight quite this way.

And she realized that he was expecting things to go back to normal, because when they had been talking in terms of him teaching her about sex, they had both agreed that would happen.

But things had changed. They'd changed.

"You think you're just going to go back to the way things were? That you're going to work with me every day on this ranch in spite of the fact that you broke my heart?"

"We talked about this."

"Yeah. But things change. Feelings change. People change. I did. You should have the balls to change too, Logan Heath. But you don't. You just hide. You hide in plain sight. You act like everything's great, everything's fine, but you're a big mess of fear. Hiding from your family. Hiding from me. Make all the excuses you want, but that's what it is. I know, because I recognize it. It's easy to stay safe when you don't think about anything. When you don't think about your feelings. When you don't let yourself want anything after you had something you loved taken away. Just keep it all in a box."

"Isn't that what you're doing still? You're telling yourself that you're living some kind of dream? But isn't that just you keeping to the status quo?"

"You know, I might agree with you. Except me keeping the status quo demands that I stand here in a damn T-shirt, with a bowl of cookie dough from a recipe that I dug out of a mouse-infested barn. It demands that I humiliate myself. That I bare my soul to you. What does your hiding let you do? Lets you pretend that your damn father doesn't live within walking distance of you. That your brothers weren't in class down the hall from you all through high school. You know what, I think you do blame yourself for your mother dying. And I think you find it a great comfort. Because as long as you can find a reason to blame yourself, you can find a reason that you can't be happy. And that's the real thing you're afraid of. You're afraid to be happy, because then you'll have something you might be able to lose again. I'm not going to be afraid of being happy. Not anymore. Not ever again. I refused to believe that a tragedy we suffered seventeen years ago means we have to live broken."

"I don't want you to live broken. That's why I want you to want something other than me."

"Then you're gonna have to find somewhere else to go," she said. "You're not using Hope Springs to heal you anyway. You're using it to hide. To keep you hurt. Well, I love you enough to not allow that anymore. And I love me enough to not put myself through seeing you every day after this."

She didn't really have the power to send him away. And he owned part of the ranch. She knew that. She knew that she was being bitter and angry. That no part of her was being a friend or family the way she had demanded every-body who was angry at him during the wedding be.

But she loved him. Big and bright. And her hurt was just as big and bright now. And it demanded some kind of compensation.

A muscle in his jaw jumped. "Fine. If that's what you want."

"It is."

She stomped into the living room and picked up her green dress, shimmying it up to her hips underneath the T-shirt. She grabbed her high heels, and she walked out the front door, making her way barefoot to the truck.

"You cannot leave like that," he said.

"I can leave in whatever the hell manner I wish. I'm not going to tone my heartbreak down to make you feel better. But don't worry. You can go back to hiding really soon. And I know how much you like to hide."

She got in the truck, and didn't spare him a backward glance as she drove away. It was a good thing that she knew the road back to the main house by heart. Because she was crying so hard she couldn't see anything through her tears.

CHAPTER TWENTY

HE'D SPENT THE rest of Christmas Day drunk. He hadn't had that much to drink since high school, and had learned his lesson in the years since. But the whole point of drinking had been to dull the pain, and when it hadn't worked, he had just continued. And continued, and continued. When he woke up that morning, his headache had been the stuff of legend, and somehow that had seemed fitting in and of itself.

He deserved to have a splitting headache. He just did.

It was about the only thing that matched the ache in his heart. About the only thing that made all of this make sense.

Pain. That was all he deserved. It was all he had.

Two things repeated in his mind, over and over again.

That she loved him.

And that she wanted him to leave.

He owned part of the ranch. She couldn't make him go. But he...

Well, he had to talk to Ryder. Dammit. Had confessions to make. Because Ryder would buy him out. He was sure of that.

And that was about what needed to happen now.

There was no getting around it.

So, completely hung over, and with no pride whatsoever, he got in his truck and drove over to the main house.

He knew there was a chance that he might run into Rose.

And she was right. Just the idea of that…

Just the idea.

No. It couldn't happen. They couldn't work together every day.

He was miserable as hell. But what could he offer her? Just a broken, bound-up asshole who couldn't seem to figure out how to open himself up.

You're afraid.

Her words echoed inside of him.

That he did blame himself for his mother's death. And that he found some comfort in that blame.

Because without someone to blame… Wasn't it all just random?

He slammed his truck into Park, turned the engine off and headed to the house.

He walked up to the door and knocked. It only took a moment for it to jerk open. And there was Ryder. He didn't know whether he was relieved or not that it was his friend who answered the door. "Damn," Ryder said. "You look rough."

"I feel rough." He met his friend's eyes, and it felt like… like he might just know. "We need to talk."

Ryder shrugged, and tilted his head back toward the house.

"Not in there. Outside."

"All right," Ryder said.

"I need you to hear me out," Logan said when his friend had stepped out onto the porch and closed the door behind him.

"I wasn't planning on not."

"Yeah, but you might not want to hear what I have to say." He took a long, harsh breath. "You need to buy me out."

"Okay." Ryder said nothing more after that.

"That's it?"

"You just told me to hear you out. Don't be obnoxious."

"You need to buy me out," he repeated. "Because... Look, I have to tell you... Something happened with Rose."

"Is this the part where you confess to me that you're sleeping with my sister?"

Logan took a step back. "Did she tell you?"

"No," Ryder said. "But I'm not an idiot. And you two are about as subtle as a rockslide."

Logan felt like he'd been whacked upside the head. "Why the hell didn't you stop me?"

"Was I supposed to? Was I supposed to grab you by the dick and lead you into town, shaming you on Main Street? Put you in a chastity belt? You're grown-ass people. What you do is not my responsibility, nor is it my business. Rose knows her mind. As much as it pains me. And it's been pretty obvious to me that she's had a thing for you for... Well, a long while."

"She didn't," Logan said. "But I've had one for her. Probably a hell of a lot longer than is okay."

Hard look. "Did you touch her then?"

"No."

"Then it's not a problem, is it? You didn't touch her before it was legal. You didn't touch her before she wanted you to."

"Well, it's over. That's the thing."

Then Ryder's face turned to stone. "Did you break my sister's heart?"

And that question was asked with such gravity, such intensity, that Logan knew whatever lack of response he had gotten out of the admission that he had slept with Rose, he was about to get it here.

"Yes."

"There we have a problem," Ryder said. "Because you're right. I can't let you just hang around here if you broke her heart. And I have some choice words for you on that score."

"Which are?"

"Stop being a *raging fucking idiot*."

"I'm not being a dumbass. It just is what it is…"

"Right. Just like it was what it was with me and Sammy, right? Except you were full of all kinds of advice then. But you know what, I don't know that I would have taken that advice if I'd realized you couldn't take it. And the Daltons were right there…"

"My mom died," he said through gritted teeth. "I just did my best to make a life out of that."

"Except what if your mom was wrong, and what Tammy Dalton said is true and Hank didn't know? What if he didn't reject you or her?"

"What does it matter? She and I were all I needed. And I wanted to protect her reputation. I…"

"That's noble, and no less than I expect out of you, Logan. But it's an awful lot of baggage to carry that just doesn't need to be carried anymore. And if it's for nothing, then maybe you breaking my sister's heart is for nothing."

"It's not. You want her to have better than me, believe me."

"Better than a decent man who works the land and treats her with respect? Why the hell would I want better for her than that? Better for her than a man who cares about the same land I care about and won't take her somewhere far away? You're my best friend. You're one of the best men I've ever known. You're…about the only asshole I'd ever think was good enough for her."

"Because I… Look, I paid for my mom to go on that trip.

The Christmas before. It was my gift to her. I wrapped it up and put it under the tree and it might as well have been a loaded gun. Maybe if I hadn't done that none of our parents would've gone."

"Is that supposed to shock me? I'm sorry that you're wandering around feeling that way, but I don't… Maybe the pilot could've gotten sick. Maybe my dad might've decided not to go. Something could've come up at work. One of the kids could've gotten sick, and they could've decided to stay home. Any number of things could've come up to prevent them from going that day, and any number of things could've enabled them to go. But nothing came up. And they did go. And there's just nothing anyone can do about that. There's no amount of what-if that brings anyone back. I've never been able to play the what-if game. It just doesn't work. I've had a lot of problems in life. And you know it was… Well, it took Sammy telling me she was going to go off and have a baby with another man for me to finally do something about the fact that I was in love with a woman that I wouldn't let myself have. But I've never done the what-if game. Because that's the kind of thing that drives a man crazy, Logan, and I can see that you've damn well driven yourself there."

"You were supposed to get angry at me."

"Oh, I'm plenty pissed at you." Ryder paused. "Oh for what? Was I supposed to be pissed at you for sleeping with her? Got it. I was supposed to punch you in the face and tell you to never touch her again. Or, I was supposed to get mad at you and say, *you bastard, you killed our parents, get out of here and never come back*. Is that what you're looking for?"

Logan didn't speak. He just stood there and listened to

his friend as he pulled all these deep dark truths from the bottom of his scarred soul.

"Damn," Ryder said. "All of this must be confronting for you. Because Hank Dalton didn't know about you, so he didn't reject you. So you could just wander over there and have a family if you felt like it. And I'm not going to condemn you, so you could just stay here. I'm not going to tell you to keep your hands off Rose, because if you could love her, if you could really be with her and give her everything that she deserved—and I believe that you could— then I have no issue with her being in a relationship with you. You're my best friend, you idiot. My best friend in the whole damned world. Why wouldn't I think you were good enough for my sister?"

"Aren't you supposed to get all protective and say that I can't have my dirty hands on her or something?"

"I never thought that my sister was going to stay a virgin for her entire life. Frankly, I'd rather her or Iris sleep with *you* than Johnny Khakis."

"Well, that's the damn truth."

"But I'm not going to take the heat off you. And I think that's what you want. I think you want me to tell you to walk away. But I'm not going to. Nobody's telling you that."

"Rose did. She said I couldn't just break her heart and then stay."

"Well, that's her call. And your call if you want to listen."

"I…"

"Nobody's gonna give you what you want, jackass. All I'm going to do is tell you to get your shit together. You were friend enough to tell me that when I needed to hear it.

I feel like I ought to tell you the same thing. But you should quit being in the way of your own happiness."

"You make it sound like it's simple. That it's not just… I spent so long keeping everyone out I don't know how to let them in."

"No, the problem is I think you do. I think you don't want to. Keep Hank and everybody else sectioned off into a part of your life you're never going to go into. What did you tell my sister? That it was going to just be sex?"

"Basically," he said through gritted teeth.

"Right. Like that was ever going to work. You were going to just sleep with my sister, and then go back to working with her like it was nothing? Watch her date other men? Marry another man?"

"That was the plan," he said. "So maybe you want to get rid of me now. Because my plan was to take her virginity and then let her go."

Ryder looked suddenly aggrieved. "I don't know why everybody seems to think I need to know they took my sister's virginity, but, you poor idiot. You got taken down by a virgin. And I don't even feel bad for you. Again, not my problem to solve. This is between the two of you. I'm going to repeat my firm suggestion to you. Sort your shit out. Because if you don't, you're going to make my sister miserable. And the fact of the matter is at twenty-three she was able to sort it out. I think that you should be able to sort it out then, at your advanced age. I was able to sort it out. Sammy got it together. Pansy's just fine. Why can't you figure it out?"

"Because I…"

"Because you're so uniquely broken? Join the damn club. I thought that was the entire point of this ranch. That we were broken, but we weren't by ourselves. We might not have had everything, but we had enough here. And from one closed-off asshole to another, let me just tell you, when a good woman wants to love you, you just get down on your knees and thank God, thank her, and you don't question it."

"Glad that works for you. But I don't think it's going to work for me."

"There been a whole lot about things in our life that we didn't choose. You're choosing this. And there's no absolving yourself from it. So you just know that. You didn't choose to have your mother die. You didn't choose for Hank Dalton to be your daddy. But you're choosing to be alone. You're choosing to let this break you."

"Are you going to buy me out or what?"

"If you want me to. I'm not going beg you to stay." He rocked back on his heels. "Sounds to me like my sister might have already done that. And I don't think you need two Daniels begging you for anything. But when you come back, and I think you will, because I think you're going to realize that what you chose for yourself really sucked... I hope she makes you do some begging of your own."

Then Ryder turned and left him, shutting the door quietly behind him.

And Logan realized that he wished his friend would've just punched him in the face. That he wished he would've ended it with fists.

Because that at least would've been... Well, it would've felt like something he deserved. Would've felt like no less than he had earned. But instead, all had been quiet. There had been no anger to offer Logan justification. There had been no recrimination. There was nothing to rail at except for…himself.

Yeah, he would've preferred a punch in the face over that.

CHAPTER TWENTY-ONE

ROSE DIDN'T KNOW how she managed to get through Christmas without weeping. Nobody had asked her where Logan was, and she hadn't said his name at all. But now she felt wretched, like a pathetic creature, ready to curl up in a ball and wail. She was avoiding her chores, because she didn't want to run into Logan. And she knew she couldn't do that. Not for a serious length of time, because they were a practical reality in ranching.

Cows didn't care if your heart was broken.

When she finally slunk down to breakfast, it was late. And the only one in the kitchen was Iris.

"All right," Iris said, putting her hands on her hips. "It's time for you to tell me what's going on."

Rose looked at her. "You never meddle."

"I am about to meddle hard-core. Because you're upset, and I can tell. And things have changed over the last few weeks, and you were baking cookies for Logan Heath, and I need to know what's going on."

"I…" She found herself helpless to find the words, and the more she searched for them, the more it all hurt. Her eyes began to fill with tears, much to her horror, and then one escaped. "I… I think my heart is broken," she said. "I'm so… I didn't want this. I didn't want any of this. I wanted to do something for you. I wanted to set you up with somebody, and I ruined that, I hurt you. And somehow… Somehow it made everything go wrong between me and Logan. There was just supposed to be a blacksmithing demonstration, and then he got mad at me, and he backed me against the wall. And then… And then we kissed." She closed her eyes. "He was mad at me. Because Elliott wanted me and I didn't know. And he warned me. He did. He told me I didn't know what it looked like when a man wanted me." She shook her head. "I didn't. I wish I could go back to not knowing. I was so thrilled with myself. So thrilled that I had uncovered the mysteries of the universe."

"The mysteries of the universe?" Iris asked.

"Well. Predominantly what men look like naked in person. I just thought… That I was in some kind of golden age of discovery. I guess I am. I guess I'm discovering. What it's like when you find someone. What it's like when you lose them. It's not fair. We lost Mom and Dad—why do I have to lose him, too?"

Iris sat down heavily at the table. "Are you telling me that you slept with Logan?"

"Yes. A lot of times. Like, a lot of times in the last month. A very lot of them."

"Oh." The look of absolute distress on Iris's face would have almost been funny if Rose didn't feel devastated down to the very bottom of her soul.

"I thought I knew what I was getting into," Rose continued. "But I didn't. I thought that because I wasn't really all that romantic and I didn't have a lot of fantasies about finding the right guy and settling down and getting married that I would be safe. That I could just… Well, he's really hot."

"Very hot. Yeah."

"It's all fun and games until you fall in love. Or realize you've been in love forever, or on the verge of it. I don't really know. Do you believe in soul mates?"

Iris blinked. "I thought you weren't a romantic."

"I wasn't. And now I am. Do you believe in them?"

"Well," Iris said, her words short and clipped, "I am a romantic. So yes. I've always believed in that. And I guess I have always believed that…that there could be magic between two people. And you might be able to just find the one. And have there only be the one. I…I would really like to be someone's…one." She cleared her throat and looked away. "And I've never really believed in hooking up just for the sake of it."

"Well, I thought I could. But I think I found my soul mate instead. But he doesn't want to be my soul mate. And what are you supposed to do with that?"

"I don't know, Rose," Iris said. "I really don't."

Her sister took a deep breath, and it was as if she had conducted a miniature rally inside of herself. "But here's what I know about you. You're strong. You were strong for me. And you'll be strong through this. I can't tell you how you'll survive. I just know that you will."

And right then, she felt the lack of their mother more than she had in a very long time. She knew they both did. Because right about now they could both use a word from someone who knew more than they did. Someone who had wisdom and experience.

Well, they didn't have that.

But between them they had a whole lot of love. That was what they'd always had here at Hope Springs.

Love enough to cover the shortcomings.

Except, she didn't seem to be able to cover this thing with Logan.

He has to fix it himself.

She didn't know where that voice came from, so certain. But it was there, resonating in her heart.

She could only take it so far. And the rest was going to have to be his choice. She'd made a lot of choices over the past month. She'd let go of a lot of her past pain. Or at least, figured out how to allow it to exist alongside the feelings of love that she had for him.

She reached across the table and squeezed her sister's hand. "Thank you for loving me. Even when I'm a pain in the butt."

"Rose, I love you especially when you're a pain in the butt. Because it makes me feel… I love who you are. I love that you're so brave."

"I really don't feel all that brave right now. I feel kind of bruised."

"Yeah. Well." Her sister's face looked thoughtful. "Sometimes I think you have to be bruised to get really brave. And I'm sure that you can do that. I'm sure that you can take this and turn yourself into the best Rose yet. Whether or not he'll do the same…"

"That's up to him," Rose said. "But I kicked him out of the ranch."

Iris actually laughed. "You what?"

"I kicked him out," she said fiercely. "Because he's an asshole. And I'm not going to work with him anymore if he's going to be such an asshole."

"Wow. Well, you do know that he owns part of the ranch, right? You can't actually kick him out."

"But I did," she said. "I threw him out. And I'm sure that Ryder will support me."

"Oh. I'm sure he will. But… Like all wounds, I suspect this one might just need a little bit of time."

She did not call her sister a virgin. Because that would be mean. And she did not say that Iris didn't understand.

But in this case, she felt like her sister didn't understand.

She might be making her best effort toward understanding. But she had never been through anything quite like this. But Rose knew that she supported her.

She didn't need the exact perfect advice to feel supported.

As for the rest. She was going to have to figure out how she lived her dream when half of it was gone.

Well, she didn't know what she could do about her dream. But she had some thoughts about being stuck and what she was going to allow her life to look like in the future. What she was going to allow from herself. Because she damn well knew that pain could make a person mean. And the only solution to that was to find a way to not let it infect you.

She had worried a few weeks ago about becoming Barbara Niedermayer.

And that was why she found herself driving into town with a plate of leftover cookies, and a thermos of spiced cider.

When she knocked on Barbara's door, the older woman opened it. She looked shocked.

"Have you come to yell at me some more?" she asked, her tone prickly.

"No," Rose said. "Actually thought you might like some cookies. And an apology. And maybe… Maybe a visitor."

Maybe she couldn't fix Logan. She couldn't fix anyone who didn't want to be fixed. And right now, there was no fixing her heart.

But she could mend some fences.

And all things considered, that mattered.

CHAPTER TWENTY-TWO

HE HAD LOOKED for answers on his best friend's front porch. He had looked for them in the bottom of a whiskey bottle.

But he was miserable.

He was out of places to look for answers. There was only one other place he could think of. One place where he might be able to find what he was looking for. He didn't want to go there. Especially not this time of year. When the ground was frozen and everything was dead.

Guilt choked him. He never went there.

And he was the only one who would. Because he was the only one who cared about Jane Heath. But he had never been able to bring himself to go and stare at a cold, dead stone that was supposed to stand monument to everything his mother had been. Alive. Warm and beautiful. How could a rock over a hole in the ground ever be her resting place?

She wasn't contained there. He knew it. Her soul was out somewhere else, being bright and brilliant because he could never believe that death was just the end.

And because he carried in his heart that idea that she was somewhere else, he had never made pilgrimage to her grave. Not since the funeral.

But he was miserable, and he was on the verge of having to leave the only place he really cared about. The only woman he'd ever really loved, and that was bringing him

..o a point where he had to ask questions. Because Ryder was right. He wanted to be told he had no choice.

He wanted to be sent away. He wanted them to condemn him, to confirm that he was the villain in the story. Because that was the safety of guilt.

That guilt that he carried over the gift he had given to his mother. It kept him safe.

It kept him separate.

Made sure he carried all the responsibilities that he had given to himself during her life. So that he never had to take a risk with the Daltons. So that he never had to take a risk with anything.

He parked his truck at the gate to the old graveyard, and slowly, a bouquet of flowers clutched in his hand, he made his way up the path. He might not have been back here for seventeen years. But he knew exactly where the gravestone was.

He stood frozen, staring down at the spot. Staring down at his mother's name.

And he knew the real reason he didn't come here.

Because it hurt. Because it all hurt so damn bad. And time didn't do anything to take it away. It was just there were some days when he didn't think of it. Some days when he woke up, and the first thing on his mind wasn't her loss.

But when it was there… It was as fresh as the day, and it all came flooding back here and now.

Jane Heath.

Beloved mother.

Not daughter. Because her parents had disowned her when she had become pregnant on her own. Not wife, because Hank Dalton hadn't loved her that way.

Mother. His mother. It was all she had been in the end, and he had felt so… He felt so much like carrying on her memory and honoring her hurt was the best thing he could do.

That carrying the guilt over what had happened kept her memory alive. Because God knew it actually hurt less than just carrying around the love of her.

It gave him something to do.

A grudge felt pretty active. Even if that grudge was against himself. Making talismans and putting holidays off-limits. Not celebrating Christmas because he had decided he didn't deserve it. Not giving gifts. Not getting them.

Not allowing himself to love the one woman that he truly wanted.

"Mom," he said, his throat tight. "I'm so sorry that I haven't… That I haven't visited. I miss you." He swallowed down the rock that was climbing up his throat. "I haven't been too busy. I'm just a coward. It hurts to stand here. To have to face the fact that you're gone. Which is dumb, because I know you're gone."

He knelt down, his knee connecting with the cold, hard ground, the ice that covered the top of it melting and leaving a wet spot on the denim. He pressed his palm to the earth. "I feel that you're gone every day. But there's something… Well, when I'm here I just want to talk to you. I haven't had the words to say I'm sorry. I'm so sorry that I failed you. And I know that you would say I didn't. That it wasn't my fault. But I haven't been ready to hear that."

He closed his eyes. "I didn't want to be forgiven. I didn't want Ryder's forgiveness. Or Rose's. Or anyone's. And I know I just would've had yours. Because you loved me. Because you loved me in ways that I'm afraid I grew up to not deserve. And I can't ask you, because you're not here."

He felt choked with his grief, and he fought hard to take a breath.

"I haven't been living how you'd want. But the way you'd want me to live means letting go. Making peace with some things that I've been using as walls. Hank Dalton didn't know about me. His wife lied to him. She lied to you. And now I wonder... I wonder if I'm allowed to make a family with them. It won't be the same." He swallowed hard, and he let himself remember. Really remember.

Not just the ways his mother had been hurt. Not just the ways he protected her. But the way she'd smiled, and the way she'd laughed. The story she'd told him when she tucked him into bed. The way she'd bandaged him when he'd fallen down.

Rose was the only other person who'd ever done it.

"No one will ever replace you. Because you shaped me into who I am. Because you taught me what I should care about. Because you chased away the monsters that were under my bed. No one will replace you."

And with that, he gave voice to his deepest fear. That somehow, by getting to know any of the Daltons, even just the half siblings, that he would somehow erase the importance of his mother in his life. Diminish that loss. But nothing ever would. Because no one could ever replace all that she'd been. And just as no one could take away the sting of the loss, no one could take away the joy of the sixteen years of life he'd spent with the best mother in the world.

He lowered his head, a smile curving his lips. "You were the best. You didn't really need me to pity you, did you? I spent all this time focusing on the way you were hurt. Not the way that you loved. And the way you love, that was the important thing, wasn't it? That's what you want me to remember. It's what you want me to carry on." He chuckled. "I'm in love with Rose Daniels. Bet you didn't see that coming. I know I didn't. And she's… She's the bravest. You would like the way she turned out."

And just like she had spoken into the air around him, he also knew his mother would have been fit to be tied that he had broken Rose Daniels's heart.

"You're not any madder at me than I am at myself. She puts me to shame."

And like a whisper had come through the wind, he heard words inside his head.

Let go.

He opened his fist and released his hold on the bouquet. He let the flowers drop in front of the gravestone.

Let go.

Not of his mother. Not even of his grief.

Because grief was an echo of love that didn't have a person you could give it to anymore. And it wasn't always bad. It just was.

It was the guilt.

It was the guilt that stood in front of everything. His protection from his pain, and the wall between him and the love he wanted to give Rose.

And yeah, it would mean getting rid of his protection. Because he couldn't love with all he was and protect his heart.

But a life without Rose wasn't life.

And it wasn't a grudge his mother would want as his monument to her. It was his happiness. Everything she had done had been for his happiness. For his protection.

And he had built an idol to the wrong thing. Because he had wanted to worship at the safer altar.

Love was terrifying. Love was wild, and it wasn't safe.

Love was like Rose. Bright-eyed and relentless, and nothing he could control.

"I love you," he said. "Nothing will ever change that."

Nothing. Whether he decided to make some family connections with the Daltons or not. Whether he went and found some happiness of his own.

For the first time in seventeen years, he felt peace. The oddest sense of peace as he stood there looking at those flowers on his mother's grave. Because there was nothing left to do for his mom but love her. He didn't have to hate himself, he didn't have to hate other people.

He just had to live.

And he knew exactly what he wanted.

Because all these years, his mother had been gone, and his tribute had been self-imposed exile.

But he realized now. He could love. As freely, as big as he wanted. And all these years he'd chosen not to. He had shrunk himself down and made his life small. His mother deserved a better tribute than that.

His life deserved a better tribute than that. He'd survived, but he hadn't been living.

It was the most humbling damn thing. To realize that he was the one who hadn't known all this time. That he was the ignorant one. All those times he'd accused Rose of not understanding, of not seeing what was right in front of her, but he was the idiot.

And Rose was right. He hadn't been able to recognize love when he saw it. But more than that, he hadn't been able to recognize what made life worth living.

You could live with low stakes. You could live without fear or pain, you could live with guilt just fine. As long as you didn't love anything.

But that was gray. A dull existence with no Christmas decorations. When the alternative was a brightly lit tree and cookies from his childhood, a woman who had been putting bandages on his wounds for almost two decades. A woman whose love would be strong enough to heal all that burned inside of him now.

He had to find her. He had to find her and he had to tell her. He had to pray that it wasn't too late.

Christmas might be over, but he needed a miracle.

He had stopped praying a long time ago. Because he had felt like God must not like him a whole lot. Must not really want to listen to him. But he prayed now. Because he needed hope. A hell of a lot of it. It was amazing how hope could change things. Amazing how love could.

And he was desperate now, for both.

He looked down at those flowers, sitting on the grave. That was like love. Love in the middle of a world that was filled with hurt. Filled with uncertainty.

Love.

He had never expected to go into a graveyard and come out more sure of love and life than he ever had been before.

And it occurred to him then that perhaps his mother wasn't as gone as he'd been thinking.

Because she had still managed to teach him something, even now.

"Thank you," he whispered into the air.

And when he walked back through the gates of the cemetery, he felt lighter than he had in years.

ROSE WAS BUCKING hay, but sadly. She hadn't known it was possible to do that job with such low energy. But she was learning it was true. Here she was, trying to live her dream. Trying to find the same sort of magic in Hope Springs that she had always seen in it.

It wasn't there, not now. And she was beginning to come to the conclusion that while you might be able to survive a broken heart, it was just going to hurt for a while. She wanted to be strong. She wanted to bounce back. She had always been that way. And some of it had been out of a desire to avoid being a burden to her family. But some of it was just that she didn't like to feel bad.

Her conversation with Barbara had been weird and rewarding. The woman was lonely. And Rose was beginning to understand lonely was a very sad place to live. Finding a connection with someone she'd disliked before made her feel...well, better for a minute. But not for long.

She was just living in a particularly sad moment in time, and she had to accept that.

That her work would feel a little bit heavier for a bit. That the joy would be gone from her day-to-day. Until she found a way to make new joy.

And she was fresh out right about now.

Logan was her other half. She felt like she was wandering around, missing a crucial part of herself.

Asshole.

Her movements became a little bit angrier after that.

Anger wasn't a whole lot more fun than sadness, but at least it had a bit more energy.

She heard heavy footsteps crossing the barn and she turned. Her anger ignited. "I thought I told you that you had to leave?"

"You did," Logan said, his perfect, beautiful mouth set into a grim line. She wanted to kiss that mouth. And she wanted to punch it.

"Well, then, why are you here? You have some nerve, showing up and standing there, and just being...there."

"I'm here to beg for your forgiveness, if that helps."

"I don't want your pity. I don't want your apology."

"What about if I told you I loved you?"

She stopped, and she dropped the shovel, the thick wooden handle making a heavy sound as it hit the ground. "Go on."

"I'm a coward. You're right. And I went to your brother, and I basically dared him to punch me in the face. For him to tell me that I needed to leave you alone, that I wasn't welcome. Something to let me off the hook. But he wouldn't. I wanted Ryder to punch me in the face and say that debauching you was the worst thing I could've ever done."

"Please tell me you did not tell my brother you...debauched me."

"I did. I figured he would hit me. Good and hard. But he didn't. He said that we'd be good together. Provided that I can give you what you deserve. And he believes that I can if I quit being a coward. He did exactly what you did. He made me accountable for my choices. I hated that. I had to get down to what really bothered me. And what you said... What you said kept ringing in my ears, Rose. That it suited me to blame myself for my mother's death. And you're right, it did. For a thousand reasons. Because if there was someone to blame, it felt like there was a reason. Like maybe I could keep other bad things from happening. That by not loving you I might be able to keep you safe. That I might be able to keep myself safe. If I made it so I didn't deserve any of this that I might not have to face the fact that I was just afraid. Afraid to love you, because losing you would devastate me. But I can't live like that anymore. I can't be death's bitch. I can't let my grief decide who I'm going to be."

"Logan..."

"I love you," he said. "I think I have for the last five years. Since that moment you smiled at me. Since... You're part of my heart, Rose. Part of the healing that this place brought to me, and I was too much of a damned coward. You are right. It was all here in Hope Springs. But I didn't want to heal, because healing meant taking chances again. And it's so much easier to just not take chances."

"I know," she said. "I've been there. Fearful and just a wreck. Not able to enjoy the life I had, the love that I had because I was living scared. But I wasn't too afraid to love you. I was brave. I took a chance. And you… You devastated me."

"I know," he said. "And I'm sorry. And it's a piss-poor excuse, Rose, I know it is, but I have to tell you… The feeling that I had when I came out of my room and saw you standing there in the kitchen, wearing my T-shirt, baking the cookies… It reminded me of when I saved up enough money to send my mom on that trip. The look on her face when I gave her that cash. I was so proud. And I was so… happy. With where I was in life. And it was so soon after that that it was all taken away from me. That feeling, that hope, that happiness, it goes with that kind of devastation for me. It's a whole process of unlearning it. Of being brave enough to trust that moment. I'm sorry I wasn't before. I'm sorry that I hurt you."

Her heart crumpled. And she felt her face crumple, too. She couldn't stay mad. Not in the face of that. Not in the face of that vulnerability. That honesty. She could imagine him too well. That proud teenage boy who had worked so hard to give his mom that break. And to have that moment destroyed the way that it had been… She hurt for him. And she couldn't hold herself back. Not anymore. She closed the space between them and pulled him into her arms. "I forgive you," she said. "We've already lived with enough hurt. We can just… We can just love each other now."

"I'd like that," he said, his throat tight, his words coming out hoarse. "I really would."

"Are we going to get married and stuff?"

"I expect we should," he said.

"I'd really like that. I never wanted to be a wife, Logan. But I'd really like to be yours."

"Well, that suits me," he said. "Because I never particularly wanted to be a husband. But I would like to be your husband, Rose Daniels. Because you're my other half. You're right. We're soul mates. And I found out the hard way that I don't function very well without half my soul."

"Yeah. Me neither."

"I've always thought life was pretty mean. But it brought me you. It brought us together. I prayed for this. For us. Here we are. Might change the whole way I think about things."

"Logan." She stretched up on her toes and kissed his mouth. She kissed him with everything she was. Everything she had been. Everything she would be.

"I love you," he whispered.

Rose Daniels was happy with her life. And she hadn't realized quite how full it was, until the man who worked by her side had become the man who held her in his arms.

This man who was, and always had been her horizon line, guiding her. Loving her. It was miraculous. And after everything they'd been through, she was happy to accept a miracle.

LOGAN WAS SURPRISED how well the family took it. But then, it was pretty obvious that they'd all figured it out at that point. So when he and Rose showed up later that evening at the main house, hand in hand, no one seemed particularly shocked, though Ryder took him to task and asked his intentions. Logan asked for Ryder's permission to marry her, then said he intended to do it with or without his permission.

"It's not his permission you need," Rose said. "It's mine. And I already gave it."

Ryder gave it to them anyway. Logan was half convinced he'd done it just to make Rose angry, because Ryder found Rose's anger amusing.

The only person who seemed somewhat muted was Iris. Though she pulled her sister in for a hug, and gave her a kiss on the cheek.

They had missed Christmas together, and it was nice to be sitting around the Christmas tree now, even though they'd missed the day. It felt right. It felt like home.

But better.

So much better.

"You know," Rose said later, when they were lying in bed back in his cabin, "it occurs to me that I'm actually a really great matchmaker."

"What makes you say that? You're actually the worst matchmaker in the entire world."

"No. I might have been wrong about Elliott. But it was Elliott who ultimately brought us together. And I'm going to go ahead and take credit for that."

"If you're going to think of it that way, then it was Elliott, blacksmithing and Barbara Niedermayer."

"All right, all right," Rose said, snuggling against him. "Maybe it was everything."

Warmth spread through his chest, love so bright and heavy it was painful. "Yeah," he said. "I think it might've been everything."

Everything. All the pain, all the uncertainty, the doubt, the fear, had brought them here to this moment.

And he knew that whatever happened from this po
on, they would be together.

And that was the happiest thing that he could possibly
imagine.

EPILOGUE

IT WAS LOGAN's first Christmas as a husband. And more notably, the first Christmas he had truly celebrated since he was sixteen years old.

He bought presents for everybody. Maybe too many. Especially when it came to Rose, who he had been lavishing for the last eleven days. She had called him unbearably cheesy. But she had also accepted her presents cheerfully.

Tomorrow morning, they would all open presents together around the tree. And it would be the first time for him since he let it all become grief and misery. And somehow it felt like magic. That here he was, on Christmas Eve, beneath swirling snow falling from the sky, holding on to his wife's hand.

His mom would be really proud of this life. This one that he found himself living now. Full of laughter and healing.

And family.

"Are you ready?" Rose asked. "I hear tell that the Christmas Eve barbecue doesn't last long. Because there are so many Daltons that it all gets consumed quickly."

He had been slow to build a relationship with the Daltons, particularly Hank. West was easy, since he already knew and liked the man. The other brothers and McKenna... It was coming along.

But this was the first time that he'd consented to go to something at their house. Because it had felt right. Because it was Christmas. And he was just ready. Ready to set asi[de] whatever ill will he had felt toward Hank. Any anger he had left inside of him at Tammy.

Because he had discovered something else over this past year. That life could expand and grow in infinite, wonderful ways when you quit putting it in a box. That there could be joy so deep and real you hadn't known it could exist, so long as you quit holding on to anger.

He was ready to test the limits of that joy.

"Well, then, I guess we better go inside," he said.

"Just a second," Rose said, suddenly tugging on his hand and stopping him from walking forward.

"Why? You're the one that said we had to go inside."

"I know. And I wasn't going to say anything to you, not until tomorrow. But…I have to tell you."

"You have to tell me what?"

"I hope you're going to be happy."

"You have to tell me now."

"You're going to be a father."

That word echoed inside of him. *Father.* Something he'd never had, and even now that he was building a relationship with Hank… It still wouldn't ever be the same.

But he was going to be a father.

He was.

"It's a miracle," he whispered. "It really is."

"Are you happy?"

He picked Rose up off the ground and spun her in the snow. When he set her back down, his eye caught the necklace she wore around her neck. The one he had given her last Christmas. The one that had been his mother's.

He reached out and touched it, then touched her face. "Rose Heath, you make me happier than I ever thought I could be."

And he knew that from now on Christmas would forever be this moment.

This moment with his wife, the woman he loved more than anything else. This moment when he had found out he would be a father.

The greatest gift of all, because Rose had taken something dark and full of guilt and shame, and had turned it into the most beautiful moment he could've ever asked for.

She had taken his grief and turned it into joy.

She had taken guilt and turned it into love.

She had taken a broken man and made him whole.

He wrapped her in his arms, and he kissed her. "I will love you forever, Rosie."

She smiled. "Forever is a long time."

"I know," he said. "That's the thing. It's forever."

* * * * *

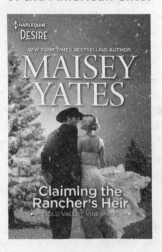

*It's Christmas and rancher Creed Cooper must work with his rival,
Wren Maxfield—and tempers flare! But animosity becomes passion
and, now, Wren is pregnant. Creed wants a marriage in name only.
But as desire takes over, this may be a vow neither can keep...*

Read on for a sneak peek at
Claiming the Rancher's Heir
by New York Times *bestselling author Maisey Yates!*

"Come here," he said, his voice suddenly hard. "I want to show you
something."

There was a big white tent that was still closed, reserved for
an evening hors d'oeuvre session for people who had bought
premium tickets, and he compelled her inside. It was already set
up with tables and tablecloths, everything elegant and dainty, and
exceedingly Maxfield. Though there were bottles of Cowboy Wines
on each table, along with bottles of Maxfield select.

But they were not apparently here to look at the wine, or indeed
anything else that was set up. Which she discovered when he cupped
her chin with firm fingers and looked directly into her eyes.

"I've done nothing but think about you for two weeks. I want
you. Not just something hot and quick against a wall. I need you in
a bed, Wren. We need some time to explore this. To explore each
other."

She blinked. She had not expected that.

He'd been avoiding her and she'd been so sure it was because he
didn't want this.

But he was here in a suit.

And he had a look of intent gleaming in those green eyes.

She realized then she'd gotten it all wrong.

"I…I agree."

She also hadn't expected to agree.

"I want you now," she whispered, and before she could s   herself, she was up on her tiptoes and kissing that infuriating mout.

She wanted to sigh with relief. She had been so angry at him. So angry at the way he had ignored this. Because how dare he? He had never ignored the anger between them. No. He had taken every opportunity to goad and prod her in anger. So why, why had he ignored this?

But he hadn't.

They were devouring each other, and neither of them cared that there were people outside. His large hands palmed her ass, pulling her up against his body so she could feel just how hard he was for her. She arched against him, gasping when the center of her need came into contact with his rampant masculinity.

She didn't understand the feelings she had for this man. Where everything about him that she found so disturbing was also the very thing that drove her into his arms.

Too big. Too rough. Crass. Untamable. He was everything she detested, everything she desired.

All that, and he was distracting her from an event that she had planned. Which was a cardinal sin in her book. And she didn't even care.

He set her away from him suddenly, breaking their kiss. "Not now," he said, his voice rough. "Tonight. All night. You. In my bed."

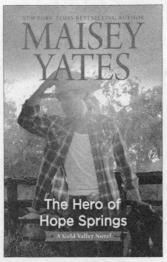

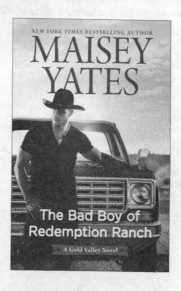